BREAKING THE CYCLE

BREAKING THE CYCLE

EDITED BY ZANE

A

SBI
PUBLICATION

A STREBOR BOOKS INTERNATIONAL LLC PUBLICATION
DISTRIBUTED BY SIMON & SCHUSTER, INC.

Published by

Strebor Books International LLC
P.O. Box 6505
Largo, MD 20792
http://www.streborbooks.com

ISBN-13: 978-1-59309-021-0
ISBN-10:   1-59309-021-8
LCCN 2003112283

Distributed by Simon & Schuster, Inc.
1230 Avenue of the Americas
New York, NY 10020
1-800-223-2336

Cover Design: www.mariondesigns.com

First Printing March 2005
Manufactured and Printed in the United States

1 0   9   8

...Only in retrospect do I find it strange that a beautiful 13-year-old would seek out the company of six-year-olds. Yet, even as I stood there, I knew that something was very wrong—and it wasn't my puerile jealousy anymore. Though Tisha was physically maturing into womanhood, she acted as though she were six. Gone from her play was the imaginative virtuosity of previous afternoons—maybe that virtuosity had never been there and I had only imagined it in my desperation. As I looked on, I realized that her play with the boys seemed rushed, yet calculating— as though she were on some kind of deadline. It all seemed bizarre to me; and then, she asked the little boys the question she had asked me the day before—except that now, instead of it being "Who are you angry with?" it was "Who do you hate?" The little boys rushed up to give their responses. They didn't succumb to the hesitancy that had gripped me the day before. The boys were natural born haters— perhaps we all were. They had people in their lives who mistreated them—and even abused them. The constant trickle of resentment was easy to dam into a reservoir of hatred. Growing up in the ghetto, surrounded by poverty and people who hated their lives, it wasn't difficult to bring forth hate. Learning to hate was essentially about learning to hate one's self—about realizing that one was in a situation that one didn't have the wherewithal to change. Hatred isn't so much about what others have done to us, it is about what we cannot do to them. Oppressors may disdain those they oppress, but the oppressed always hate their oppressors. There is a power relationship there: the realization that no matter what one does, one will never be able to correct the inescapable injustice of one's everyday existence.

From "The Lonely Echoes of My Youth" by D.V. Bernard

TABLE OF CONTENTS

INTRODUCTION

This book is a departure from my typical books. However, in many ways, I consider this my most important contribution to the literary world. Fiction can often serve as an educational source for those who shy away from reading manuals or textbooks. *Breaking the Cycle* is a means to an end. From this book, I hope that you will walk away with a clearer understanding of the importance of compassion for others. Abuse is a major problem in our American society and throughout the world. No one has the right to lay hands on another person; yet it happens every single minute of every single day. People live in fear in their own homes. Instead of worrying about being carjacked, robbed out in the streets, or becoming the random victim of a crime, a crime is committed against them where they live; over and over again.

Domestic violence is a form of oppression. In the words of Stephen Biko, founder and martyr of the Black Consciousness Movement in South Africa: "The greatest weapon the oppressor ever has is the mind of the oppressed." While most people tend to concentrate on the black eyes and bruised ribs, domestic violence does the most damage to one's psyche.

No, I don't think this book will stop domestic violence altogether. It is way too big for that. All I am asking is that you keep your mind open as you read this book. If you are being abused by someone, get help. If you are witnessing someone you love being abused, encourage them to get help. Be their support system. Let them know they are not alone. Convince them that life does not have to be a daily battlefield.

For those of you who equate abuse with love, you are wrong. Contrary to the old adage, "Love means never having to say you're sorry," people should be sorry for using their lover or their children as human punching bags. In fact, it should never happen in the first place. There are tons of people who need anger management classes, stress reduction classes, and drug and alcohol rehabilitation. I name these things specifically because often times certain behavior patterns tend to lead to lashing out.

Domestic abuse is a universal issue but this book is focused on people of color because in our communities we tend to try to sweep a lot of things under the rug. Incest, abuse, mental illness, and all the rest of the issues plaguing society as a whole also affect us.

The contributors to this book were hand-selected by me and I can't begin to thank them enough for stepping up to the task at hand and developing magnificent stories that truly hit home. While I realize escapism is often a reason to read fiction, I implore you to read this book from cover to cover, no matter how painful it may be. It might save a life.

Please wake up and realize that we all must take matters into our own hands and assist those in need if...

...we intend to break the cycle.

ZANE

BREAKING THE CYCLE

ZANE

There are some things in life for which one can never be prepared. You can never be prepared for puberty, sexual intercourse, childbirth, death or abuse. These are all peaks and hardships in life but something beautiful almost always comes from them. All except abuse.

From puberty comes understanding; from sexual intercourse comes satisfaction; from childbirth comes the creation of a soul; from death comes the rest and peace of a soul; but from abuse almost always comes nothing positive. Sometimes, if you are strong and have a great deal of faith, you might be able to rise above abuse. Sometimes, you might be able to go on and lead a normal life. Sometimes.

Daylight. It couldn't come fast enough for me. I had laid awake all night, pondering over every little detail. Had Momma and I thought of everything? As far as I could tell, we had.

By 7 a.m., I couldn't take it anymore. The breeze entering through my open bedroom window was chilly but refreshing. I imagined myself soaring through the sky like an eagle. Having the sense of total freedom. How I longed to be free and, in just a few more hours, I would be.

I jumped up out of bed once I heard my mother's bedroom shoes slapping against the wooden hallway floor. She was on her way to the kitchen to begin her morning routine of brewing coffee, frying bacon and eggs, and fetching the morning paper from the front stoop of our apartment so it would be spread open to the sports section before Josh finished getting dressed for work.

I got down on my knees and retrieved my faded green duffel bag from under the bed. It was crammed with my most treasured belongings. I had to wrestle with it the night before in order to get the zipper closed. There was so much more I wanted to take, but Irene had been adamant about the one bag per person rule. I did manage to fit my small photo album into the bag. It contained pictures from my youth, back when Grandma was still alive and Momma was reasonably happy. Back before she married Josh and turned both of our lives into a living hell.

I was going to miss my friends the most. While we had only been living in Richmond for a few years, I felt extremely close to a couple of people. There was Amanda, fourteen going on thirty, exactly like me, and the only person other than myself who believed in my ability. We spent most of our lunch hours huddled in the corner of the cafeteria discussing plans for our future. We often fantasized about riding motorcycles up and down the California coast once we got our driver's licenses, being beach bums the summer after our senior year of high school, and starting our own jewelry company to sell the bracelets we made out of wire.

Then, there was Mrs. Cowan, our next-door neighbor. She was an elderly woman who always smelled like rose water. I loved sitting out on the balcony during the summer in lawn chairs, drinking her homemade lemonade out of Mason jars, and listening to her reminisce about her adventures growing up in the 1930s. Even though there were more than sixty years between us, I could somehow relate to her more than I could relate to anyone else. In many ways, she reminded me of Grandma and in just as many ways she didn't. Unlike Grandma, she didn't take abuse from men and let them brutalize her until there was nothing left. Unlike Grandma, she didn't let her children grow up watching a man dole out ass beatings on a daily basis.

I never blamed Momma for the predicament she ended up in with Josh. It was all she knew because it was all she had been exposed to as a child. I never blamed Grandma either. The situation was the same for her. My great-grandmother had been victimized by the man that supposedly loved her as well. I wasn't around back then but I am positive it happened. Grandma told me all about it on her deathbed. There she was, lying on the sweat-drenched hospice bed, struggling for every breath, when she admitted it. She made Momma promise it wouldn't happen to her. That she wouldn't allow men to beat on her until the irreparable damage affected her insides and killed her. It was time for Momma to finally live up to that promise and Irene was going to help us. I was going to miss everyone in Richmond terribly, but there were no other options. It had all come down to one simple truth. Escape or perish.

I came out of my room and headed to the bathroom to scrub my face and brush my teeth after Josh vacated, leaving the mirrors steamed up with fog. I could hear him through the thin walls, covered with peeling plaster, singing "Bad to the Bone." He was, indeed, bad down to the very bone. He was pure evil.

He bumped right into me as I exited the bathroom. I immediately pulled the belt on my robe tighter. I hated it when he stared at me like that, with a mixture of lust and anger in his eyes, licking his lips like I was a plate of greasy fried chicken. He needed to shave and the odor emitting from his body made me wonder if he had even picked up a bar of soap in the shower. He winked at me and whispered, "Good morning," before strutting off down the hallway to the kitchen like he was the king of the castle.

Josh thought he was fine but he was really mediocre. His 5'9" frame wasn't big enough to handle the two hundred thirty-plus pounds he was hauling around and he needed serious help from both a dermatologist and a dentist. I never could understand what Momma saw in him in the first place. She's gorgeous, tall, with long, wavy black hair and smooth caramel skin. I must look like my natural father, who has always remained nameless. I'm short, even for a teenage girl. If I ever get to five feet, I'll do somersaults for weeks. I'm a lot lighter than Momma, too. I often wonder if my real father is White. It doesn't really matter. A deadbeat dad is a deadbeat dad.

I went back into my room and threw on my typical Saturday outfit: a pair of sweats, and a baggy T-shirt. Everything had to appear normal. Josh was a lot of things, but stupid wasn't one of them.

When I came into the kitchen, he glanced up from the sports section just long enough to leer at me and then returned to the game scores. I told Momma, "Good morning," but she didn't reply. She kept her back to me and busied herself washing dishes. I got a plate from the cabinet, a spoon from the silverware drawer, and sat down at the table.

"Could you pass the bacon?"

Josh totally ignored me, pulling the paper up closer to his face and flipping the page.

"Josh, can I have the bacon?"

"What do you say?" he replied snidely, exposing a mouth full of half-chewed bacon and eggs. "What's the magic word?"

I sucked in some air through my teeth, holding back an expletive. He had a lot of nerve, correcting my manners when he didn't have any himself. "Please!"

He folded the paper up and tossed it on the table. "That's better." He scooted the plate of bacon toward me and stared while I put three pieces on my plate. "Don't waste any of that. We can't afford to waste any food around here. Not the way I work my behind off to provide for you two trifling bitches."

I heard Momma sigh but didn't bother to look in her direction. She would never stand up to him and he knew it. He made comments like that for the simple reason he knew he could get away with it.

I ate my bacon in silence, opting to leave the eggs alone because they often gave me indigestion. Josh finished off his breakfast, gulped down a tall glass of orange juice in less than ten seconds, and then pushed his seat away from the table. Momma immediately ran over to retrieve his plate and empty the remains into the garbage. I tried to establish eye contact with her, but she paid me no mind.

Josh went into the living room, grabbed his heavy uniform jacket out of the closet in the foyer, and yelled out, "See you two whores tonight!" before slamming the front door shut behind him.

"I hope he rots in hell," I blurted out the second he left. "I hope one of those stores down at the mall gets robbed and he gets shot right in his little rent-a-cop outfit."

"Kandace, you shouldn't say things like that about people." Momma finally opened her mouth. As usual, it was after Elvis had already left the building. She sat down across from me at the table with both hands wrapped around a steaming hot mug of coffee. "God doesn't like it when you talk ugly."

"And God doesn't like it when you sit around and let a man beat on you either," I immediately retorted. Momma rolled her eyes and took another sip of her coffee. "So, you all packed? What time are we leaving?"

"Leaving to go where?" Was she serious? She couldn't be.

"Today's the day, Momma. It's March 30th." She looked puzzled. "We're supposed to meet up with Irene today in D.C. so she can take us to the Safe Haven."

"Oh that," my mother replied with disinterest. "I forgot."

I panicked, slamming my fist down on the table. "How could you forget? This is the single most important day of our lives. This is the day we get away from all of this."

No response.

"It's okay, Momma. I'll help you pack." I came to the conclusion that all she needed was a little push in the right direction and we would be out of there within the hour. "You can only take one bag, but we'll make it a big one and, once we get settled in, we can get some more clothes."

"I'm not going any damn place and neither are you," she stated vehemently. "I suggest you drop this nonsense right now."

"But, but, but we planned this all out, me and you. We met with Irene at the diner and went over everything. Today's the day."

"Today's the day for you to clean up your room and scrub these filthy floors. That's what today is." She rose from the table, poured her remaining coffee down the drain and threw the mug in the sink. "Josh told me last night that he's sick of this apartment being nasty."

"Who cares what Josh says?" I went over to the sink, swung Momma around, and grabbed her by the wrists. "We're leaving this place today. You promised me we would. You promised Grandma."

My mother yanked her hands away. "Don't bring your grandma into this, God rest her soul. She was on the brink of insanity those last few moments and didn't realize what she was saying. I would've told her anything to let her go in peace."

"Grandma was the sanest of us all," I said defensively. "She knew exactly what she was saying and you know it."

"Whatever, Kandace." She headed into the living room and started fluffing the toss pillows on the couch. She picked up the universal remote, hit the power button, and started flipping through channels until she landed on some music videos.

I couldn't believe things were turning out this way. "My bag's already packed."

"Well, goody for you," Momma snickered. "You might as well go back there and unpack it."

"Or I could go back there and pack yours." I sat down on the couch beside her, trying to decide the best course of action. There was no way I was giving up on our plans. "Momma, don't you realize that this all has to end somewhere?"

"What has to end?" She leered at me out the corner of her eye and that's when I noticed it, the slight puffiness of her bottom cheek.

I grabbed her chin and shook it. "This has to end. Josh hit you last night, didn't he? He put his grubby little hands on you like you're his personal punching bag."

Momma slapped my hand and then slapped me clear across the face. "How dare you talk to me like that? I suggest you remember who is the parent and who is the child."

"You're not much of a parent," I mumbled under my breath, clenching my hands into fists but determined not to lash out in anger. My life had been dysfunctional and full of violence long enough. It took years for me to realize that violence is not the solution, but it had finally sunk in.

"What did you just say, you little tramp?" Momma asked, fighting back tears and wiping the corner of her eye with the sleeve of her tattered gray sweater. I could tell it always hurt her inside to hit me. She knew how it felt firsthand. She grew up in the same exact situation.

I garnered some nerve from someplace, raised my voice, and reiterated my last statement. "I said, you're not much of a parent if you make me stay here in this type of environment. Can't you see that this is never going to change? Josh will continue to beat on both of us whenever he feels like it until one of us ends up in the graveyard next to Grandma."

"Don't speak such lies! That's blasphemy!" She jumped up from the couch and started pacing the living room floor. "Josh has never hit you!"

"Momma, please!" I stated sarcastically. "Josh has hit me so many times I lost count. He simply waits until you go to work to do it. That's all." My next statement was going to be cruel but I let the words escape from my lips anyway. "Not that it matters. Even if he did hit me in front of you, you wouldn't do anything. Just watch and wait for your turn to get a beatdown."

Momma's bottom lip started trembling and her eyes watered up even more. We stared at each other in silence, neither one of us backing down from the other; the only sounds in the apartment being the music emitting from the television and the leaky faucet in the kitchen.

Finally, she broke the stare. "I don't have to stand here and take this crap from you." She headed off down the hall to her bedroom. "It's time to get ready for work. Mr. Andrews will dock my pay if I'm even five minutes late."

I followed behind her, went into her room, and plopped down on the bed. The sheets were dank and smelly and I shuddered to think about what had taken place in there the night before. While not an expert on sex, it was clear to me that whatever Josh and Momma did together wasn't normal. Far from it. I could hear them through the walls on a nightly basis when he returned from his security job at the local mall. I wouldn't go so far as to call it rape, but it was definitely borderline. Rape was something he was more than capable of. I knew that firsthand as well.

I watched Momma slip into her maid uniform. She had been working as a housekeeper at the Motel 8 down the street ever since we moved to Richmond and found out that Josh didn't intend to, nor could he keep, all the promises of the good life he had promised us.

"Momma, you're not going to work today," I insisted. "We're going to get in your car and drive to D.C. to meet Irene, just like we planned."

"Oh yeah? With what money, Miss Know-It-All?" She finished buttoning up her uniform and slid her feet into a pair of worn-out black loafers. "Cars run on gas and gas takes money. I'm flat broke."

I clenched my teeth together, holding back the words gathering in my throat, and counted to ten. "How could you not have any money, Momma? I thought we were both going to save up for today?"

She grabbed a bottle of lotion off her dresser and pushed the pump down, letting the cool liquid drizzle into her palm. "First off, Kandace, we don't know a damn thing about that Irene woman. She's some crazy woman you met on the Internet that polluted your mind with a bunch of nonsense."

"Irene is a woman just like you. She's been where you are and her children have been where I am." Momma hissed and rubbed the lotion on her arms and legs. "Besides, you met her and you know she isn't crazy. What she said made a world of sense and that's why we have to make a run for it now."

"Make a run for it?" Momma giggled at my statement. "You make it sound like we're runaway slaves headed for the Underground Railroad to get away from the massa."

"Josh is your massa!" I exclaimed, speaking the truth and nothing but the truth. "When was the last time you stood up to him about anything?"

Momma raised her hand to me and I blocked my face with my forearm. "Girl, consider yourself lucky I don't slap you silly!" She lowered her hand. "Talking to me like that! I'll knock your head off!"

"I realize you're scared." I could see the fear in her eyes. "Sometimes, we just have to turn it over to God. Remember when Grandma used to say that all the time."

Momma flung her arms around me, wrapped me in a bear hug and whispered in my ear, "Turn it over to God."

It was so wonderful to have her arms caressing me lovingly. It had been so long, I almost forgot what her embraces felt like. "Yes, Momma, let's turn this over to God."

One of her tears made a cavalcade down my right cheek. She released me and looked at me through tear-drenched eyes. "I'm scared, just like you said. If we leave here, Josh will find us."

"No, he won't," I stated adamantly. "Irene has assured me that there's no chance."

"This isn't like television and the movies, Kandace. This is real life and he won't stop until he finds us." She went back over to the dresser, picked up a wood-handled brush, and started grooming her long, wavy black hair. "Perfect people with perfect lives in perfect towns only exist on the silver screen."

"No one's life is perfect," I readily admitted. "But we aren't supposed to live like this. We're not supposed to live every day in fear."

I could see Momma grin in the reflection of the mirror. "I have an idea. Why don't you go? I can stay here and then Josh won't have any reason to follow."

I had managed to hold back my own tears up until that point, but that statement slashed through my heart. Would she really make me leave her? "I can't do this without you, Momma. I'm only fourteen. I need you. I need you to be a real mother for a change."

She swung around to glare at me, the smile transforming into a frown. "Are you saying that I've been a bad mother?"

I had no idea how to respond so I told the truth. "I don't blame you, Momma." I really didn't blame her either. "I don't think it's been intentional but, yes, you have been a bad mother. I understand that it's not your fault, though. You're only repeating what you've seen. Abuse is all that you know." The expression on her face was blank; devoid of emotion. I couldn't tell whether she wanted to hit me or kiss me. "I have thirty-seven dollars. I saved it from my baby-sitting money. That's enough gas to get us to D.C. and we can make some sandwiches, in case we get hungry. That way, we don't have to buy any fast food."

"I can't do this, Kandace." Momma shook her head in dismay. "I can't pick up and leave Josh like this. He's my husband. I promised to love and honor him forever. I took vows."

"And he's broken all of them," I quickly pointed out. "He lies, he cheats, he beats on you."

"What do you mean, he cheats?" Momma grabbed me by the shoulders and started shaking me violently. "What the hell do you mean, he cheats?"

I let out a hideous scream and she let me go. "He brings other women here when you're not home, okay? There, I've said it." I paused while the reality of the situation sunk in. "Then, there's me."

"You?" Momma clutched her chest, feigning a heart attack.

"Yes, don't pretend you haven't seen the signs, Momma." I sat down on the bed, scared to death and ashamed, but it was time for everything to come out in the open. Momma was still showing reluctance about leaving Josh. I had to come clean. "He started having sex with me when I was twelve, about a year after you got married. He told me that if I ever told, he would send me away. That he would split us up for good and that there was no way you would ever believe me. It was his word against mine."

"You lie!" Momma whacked me on the arm with a vengeance before I had a chance to protect myself. "Take that back right now! Take it back!"

I rubbed my arm, trying to ease the pain, and stared up at her. "I guess he was right," I whispered. "You don't believe me."

"I don't understand you sometimes, Kandace." She sat down beside me on the bed. I was craving affection, the affection that usually followed immediately behind the hits, but she didn't reach out to me. "The things that come out of your mouth."

"If I'm lying, Momma, how would I know he has a scar inside his left thigh? About the size of a silver dollar? He said he got it climbing over a wire fence when he was five." Shock overcame her face. It was no time to let up, so I continued, "I'm right, aren't I?"

She snickered at me. "Josh could have mentioned that to you at any time. It doesn't mean you've had sex with him."

"You remember that time, about two years ago, when you came home from work and found me in the bed bleeding?"

"Sure! You were starting your periods."

I shook my head. "No, Momma, my periods didn't start until last year." I reached out for her hand and grasped onto it. "That was the first time. That was the first time he hurt me."

"This is absurd!" Momma shouted, peeling my fingers away, grabbing her purse off the door handle, and heading for the hallway. "See what you did? You've fooled around and made me late. I have to get out of here."

I couldn't believe that, after all I had said, she was still planning to stay with Josh. Desperate times called for desperate measures. She was halfway out the front door when I said, "Look at this, Momma. If you look at this and you still want to stay here, then I'll stay, too." She turned around and I came closer so she could see the large bruise on my left side in the sunlight. "I'll stay here until I lose a kidney or something."

Momma let her purse strap fall off her shoulder and the bag tumbled to the floor. She gently fingered my side and struggled for breath. "Josh did this to you?"

"Yes."

"When?"

"Tuesday night, when you were working late." I pulled my shirt up even higher so she could get a better view. "This is what he did to me when I refused him."

"My poor baby!" Momma squealed, continuing to run her fingertips across my side. "How could that animal do this to you?"

I pulled my shirt back down. "Have you seen enough yet?" I asked, praying that she had. "Can we leave now?"

"Yes, yes we can leave now," Momma replied without the slightest hesitation. She ran back down the hall toward the bedroom. "Just give me a minute to throw something in a bag and we're out of here."

I was so relieved. "Let me help you," I called after her. "We really need to hurry, if we're going to meet Irene by noon."

"Look in my bottom left drawer, underneath my bras, and get the money," she called out to me as I entered the room. She was inside the closet yanking clothes off hangers. *Money*, I thought to myself. She claimed she didn't have any. I didn't comment when I found her stash that had to amount to at least five hundred dollars. She had planned on escaping all along. "Let's go, Baby," she said excitedly, brushing past me. "Where's your bag?"

"In my room," I answered, running into my room to get it. I grabbed my baby-sitting money from under my alarm clock.

Less than two minutes later, we were in the car, a raggedy, but still running, powder blue 1989 Pontiac LeMans. Momma revved the engine and we settled into the customary five-minute warm-up time.

"Kandace, are you sure we can pull this off?" Just like every other aspect of our lives, she was looking for guidance from me instead of the other way around.

I held her hand. "Yes, we can pull this off because we're going to turn it over to God. Right here and right now; we're in His hands and He won't let us down."

We sat there in silence. I'm not sure what Momma was doing but I was praying like I had never prayed before. There was still a lot of uncertainty surrounding what we were doing. She was right. I had met Irene on the Internet but I knew that was the way it was supposed to be. Destiny sent her into my life at that exact moment in time.

I was in the school library about six months before, searching the Internet for information on the government of China when I decided to type the words domestic abuse into Yahoo. Thousands of sites resulted but one caught my eye immediately, so I clicked on it and sent an email to the women of the Safe Haven. Irene replied to me that same day and I read her message the next morning. There was a toll-free number for me to call. I waited until Momma and Josh were in their room asleep the following night and dialed the number.

From that moment on, there were a series of late-night phone calls and dozens of emails back and forth. I explained my home situation to Irene and she said the Safe Haven was there to help victims of abuse, but only if they were trying to help themselves. I lied and told her that Momma wanted out; that it was all she ever talked about. Irene insisted that we meet somewhere locally and I was shocked when I finally got up the nerve to broach the subject with Momma and she agreed.

We met Irene at the Tastee Diner and she told us all about the abusive husband she escaped from along with her three kids. One of them, a daughter named Sheila, was about my age. We worked out plans that very night to flee on March 30th. That would allow us enough time to get our affairs in order, not that we had any affairs, and save up a little spending cash. Irene said that we wouldn't need much because the shelter had certain benefactors who believed in the right of women to be free from such despair.

So there we were, about to embark on the first day of the rest of our lives. I glanced over at Momma and she was frozen in time, trembling like a leaf. "Momma, I think the car is warm enough. We can go now." She didn't respond; simply sat there staring into space. "Momma?"

"Okay, Baby," she weakly replied. "Give me a second to get my bearings together."

"It's okay to be scared." I caressed the hand that was gripping the steering wheel. "I'm scared, too, but it has to be like this."

"You're right." She glanced over at me. "It has to be like this. Besides, I did promise Momma."

"Yes, you did, and I'm sure she's looking down from heaven at us right this second cheering us on." I looked at the dashboard clock and saw that is was 9:30. "We have to go now so we won't be late. Irene is waiting."

Momma put the car in reverse and backed slowly out of the parking space. I took one last survey of the building we had inhabited for a few years and bit my bottom lip when I spotted the lawn chairs out in front of Mrs. Cowan's apartment. I was going to miss her so much. I wondered what she would think once she realized we had picked up and left town. I was sure Josh would ask her what she knew about our disappearance. I hoped he wouldn't be too hard on her. I got the feeling she wouldn't take much, if any, of his disrespectful nonsense anyway.

Momma and I barely said a word to each other the hundred or so miles to D.C. Since the radio in the LeMans had been busted for years, I hummed songs like "Amazing Grace" and "His Eye Is on the Sparrow" most of the way. The same songs Grandma used to hum to me.

When we got to the 14th Street Bridge, I reached over the seat to get the piece of paper out of my duffel bag with the directions to Union Station scribbled on it and then proceeded to direct Momma the rest of the way there. We parked in the indoor garage, just like Irene had instructed us, grabbed our bags, locked the car, and caught the escalator down two levels to the terminal.

My eyes had a hard time adjusting to the bright lights as Momma and I searched for Irene. Union Station was packed. I remember thinking I had never seen so many people in one place in my entire life.

"Momma, I don't see Irene. Do you?" I asked in a panic. The huge clock in the center of the terminal said five minutes after twelve. I was hoping she hadn't left because we weren't there exactly on time.

"Isn't that her over there?" Momma pointed toward a tall brunette in a gray trench coat. I thought she was right until the woman turned around and didn't look a day over twenty.

"No, that's not her." We walked hand in hand past hordes of people rushing to catch this train or that train. "She has to be here someplace. She just has to be," I whined.

Then I heard it, a faint but distinct cry. Someone was calling out my name. I swung around in the general direction of the voice and spotted Irene half-running toward us. She had these deep-set gray eyes that were so piercing you could see them a mile away.

Momma let out a heavy sigh. She wasn't the only one relieved. "There she is. Our angel," Momma remarked.

Irene caught up to us and hugged us both simultaneously. "It's so great to see you," she cheerily stated. "I was beginning to be afraid you wouldn't show." Momma and I ogled at each other for a few seconds. If Irene only knew how close she was to hitting the nail on the head. "I see you only have one bag each. That's great! We have to travel light."

"That is what you said, one bag apiece," Momma replied, shifting her weight to her other foot and pulling the thick strap of her bag higher onto her shoulder. "The last thing we're trying to do is impose."

"Nina, it's my pleasure to help you and Kandace out," Irene quickly retorted. "There was a time when someone helped me and I feel it's my duty to continue freeing women from their oppressive situations." She glanced down at her watch. "I hate to rush you, but we better hurry to the gate. The train is already boarding."

The curiosity was killing me. "Where are we going?"

"I'll tell you once we're on board."

"What about my car?" Momma asked.

"The car, the home, even the names are part of your past life." Irene took Momma's hand and held it tight. "The members of the Safe Haven are going to help you start anew." Momma managed a smile, albeit fake. "Let's hurry! We're leaving from Gate 8."

When we got to the gate, Irene flashed three tickets at the uniformed agent who waved us on. Within minutes, we were seated comfortably on the train in two double seats facing each other: Momma and me on one side, Irene on the other. She handed each of us a ticket. "Hang on to these. The conductor will collect them a little later."

I was likely to faint when I read the name on my ticket. "Rhonda?" What kind of name is Rhonda, I thought to myself. I leaned over, trying to see Momma's ticket. "What does yours say?"

"Gladys." She chuckled. "Gladys Stevenson."

"That's right," Irene confirmed, letting out a slight giggle of her own. "From this moment on, you are Gladys and Rhonda Stevenson from San Antonio, Texas."

"Texas?" I fell out laughing at the mere thought of it. "Shouldn't we have accents or something?"

"Not necessarily." Irene started eyeing Momma's purse. She held out her palm. "Hand over your wallet. Any identification that has your old name on it."

Momma hesitated for a brief moment and then complied, taking her driver's license and our insurance cards out and placing them in Irene's hand. "I can keep the pictures, can't I? They're all the memories I have."

"Do they have names written on the back?"

"No. No names."

"Then you can keep them." Irene stood up and headed toward the door of the car, swinging it open and stepping out on the platform separating it from the next car. The platform was surrounded by an air-tight rubber seal. Momma and I both gasped as we watched her fling Momma's things out of a slightly ajar window. She came back inside, sealed the door, and took her seat. "There, it's done. Now off to Maine we go."

I looked down at my ticket again. The destination was Portland, Maine. That seemed fifty million miles away to me. It was a place I had only read about in books. I glanced back up at Irene. "Can I ask you a question?"

"Sure."

I hesitated, not sure whether or not I should mind my own business. "Irene isn't your real name, is it?"

"No, and my kids are really not Sheila, Alice, and Adam either." We all shared a good laugh. "Don't worry. You'll get used to it soon enough. It's kind of like playing a game; except the stakes are higher and all mistakes have serious repercussions. Both of you have to make sure you never mention your real names again."

"Cool!" I exclaimed, treating it like an espionage mission. "This is going to be a blast!"

Momma didn't seem as excited. "What about Kandace's, I mean Rhonda's education?"

"The school records, immunization forms, and everything else have been taken care of," Irene soothingly reassured her. "Just relax and enjoy the train ride. You both must be mentally and physically exhausted."

I had to admit she had a valid point. As if to confirm her suspicions, Momma and I were both asleep within the next fifteen minutes.

After we got to Portland, Irene hailed a cab and shuffled us inside. She explained Safe Haven in more detail on our way there. It was originally started by a group of Catholic nuns in the early 1940s and had been going strong ever since. The only people who knew the exact location were those who stayed there at one point or another. She stressed that we must never reveal the location to anyone, or Safe Haven would become not only unsafe but downright dangerous. All the women and children there were hiding from something or someone, including her, and the protection of the group rested totally upon the shoulders of the residents. No one ever dropped by for visits because no one was ever invited. The length of stay per family depended upon a variety of factors, including but not limited to, gaining steady employment, progress in the therapy sessions because everyone was required to undergo some form of therapy or counseling, and emotional strength to go forward alone.

Momma assured Irene that we would be there two, three months tops. She didn't want to impose on them any longer than that. I couldn't fathom how she came to that time frame, considering she was always so reliant on Josh throughout their marriage, but I kept my two cents to myself.

Safe Haven was breathtaking. It was right on the coast and sat on at least a hundred acres. It looked like something out of a movie. There were huge, thick wooden doors with a silver knocker positioned in the middle of each one, cobblestone floors throughout the entry level, and the biggest fireplace I had ever seen in the living room.

Everyone was so nice, it was incredible. Sheila and I hit it off right away. She was a tall brunette with deep-set gray eyes like her mother. It looked like Irene had literally spit her out. Her younger siblings were adorable and jumped all over my lap until I couldn't feel my legs. I didn't mind. It was refreshing to be around happiness for a change. I hoped some of it would rub off on me.

There were ten families currently residing at Safe Haven, excluding us, and the upstairs was divided into four wings. Irene introduced us to Maddie, who ran the day-to-day operations while Irene was traveling cross-country rescuing troubled souls. She was a heavyset woman with pale skin and salt and pepper hair. She huffed and puffed up the flight of stairs and showed us to our room in the south wing. It had twin beds and a private bath. Momma's face frowned up the second Maddie left.

"Not much space in here, Kandace."

"You mean Rhonda!" I lashed out at her, correcting her mistake. "We have to be extremely careful, Momma. You heard what Irene said."

"Well, it's easier for you," she replied, with an edge of sarcasm in her voice.

"You never call me Nina anyway. You still get to call me Momma. I'm the one that has to adjust."

I sat down beside her on the bed. "We both have to adjust, Gladys." We both chuckled. "I love you, Momma."

"I love you too, Baby." Momma embraced me again and it hit me that she had hugged me more times in the space of one day than she had the entire time she was married. "Are you hungry? Irene said they saved us some dinner."

"No, it's really late." I got up and heaved my duffel bag onto the other bed, unzipping it to search for the large red tee I always slept in. "I think I'm going to hit the sack. Tomorrow's a brand-new day."

"And a brand-new life," Momma added, turning down her own bed. "I'm too tired to even change. That nap on the train helped, but I'm still worn out."

I went into the bathroom to change and brush my teeth. When I returned, Momma was snoring softly. I covered up her legs and got into my own bed. My new bed in my new room in my new home. I wondered what Josh was doing at that very moment. Probably pacing the floor or throwing dishes against the wall or some other immature behavior. Maybe he was actually concerned and had the local police over there filing a report. I was glad Momma didn't leave him a note. He didn't deserve one. He didn't deserve anything.

One Year Later

Momma lasted three weeks. Three lousy weeks before she went crawling back to Josh. Irene had arranged for her to wait tables at a Mom and Pop restaurant in town. She hated it and came home exhausted every night. As far as I was concerned, anything was a step up from scrubbing toilets and changing funky sheets at that motel. I guess she didn't see it that way.

One night, Maddie went into town to pick her up, and the other waitress, Peaches, told her that "Gladys" had asked one of the regular customers, a trucker who went by the handle of Red Dragon, for a ride out of town. I was devastated when I heard the news and didn't eat for four days. Everyone tried to console me, but to no avail. How could Momma do that to me? How could she choose a man over her own flesh and blood?

I tried to convince myself that she hadn't gone back to Josh. I dialed our old number and it was disconnected so I decided to call Mrs. Cowan. She was elated to hear my voice and asked me why I didn't mention that I was moving to Atlanta to stay with relatives. The Atlanta comment threw me for a loop. Mrs. Cowan told me that Momma had personally explained the situation to her when she and Josh were cleaning out the apartment and piling everything into the back of a U-Haul. She said they left no forwarding address and the landlord was pissed because the rent was two months in arrears when they fled like bandits in the night. I promised Mrs. Cowan I would write and tell her the truth. I was too upset to go into it over the phone. She wished me well and told me that she would keep me in her prayers. I told her that she had always been in my prayers and thanked her for being a surrogate grandmother during my stay in Richmond. I could hear her weeping on the other end of the line and I fought back my own tears until we hung up. Then I buried my head in a pillow and cried myself to sleep.

Standing here on the coastline, watching the waves crash against the shore, I have no regrets about leaving. I wish Momma could be here. I wish she could have been stronger and I realize now that I will never see her again. Sure, miracles can happen but I sense a closure to my past life and, in my heart, I know she'll never come looking for me. She made her choice and I made mine.

For the first time, I am on the honor roll at school. I even tutor some of the younger kids here at Safe Haven in math and science. Those have always been my stronger subjects. Sheila and I are going to a school dance tonight. I am so nervous. There's this boy, William, who I'm crazy about. I'm not sure if he's ever noticed me. If he hasn't, if he never does, that's still okay. Someone else will come along, someone capable of loving me for me, and when he does, the way he will touch me will be with love and affection. No man will ever beat on me. Not ever again.

Grandma, wherever you are, I want you to know that I've turned my life over to God. I even attend church every Sunday now and sing in the youth choir. Pastor Geoff is always telling the congregation what a beautiful voice I have and it makes me feel proud. I'm singing the Easter solo next Sunday.

I wish you could be here to hear me. I wish Momma could be here, too.

I can't promise that I'll grow up to be a surgeon or a lawyer or a famous singer. I can promise that, no matter what I grow up to be, I'll be happy. I'll be happy because I know, at least for this family, that the cycle of violence has finally been broken.

Zane is the New York Times *Bestselling author of ten books* (Afterburn, Addicted with a Twist, Skyscraper, Nervous, The Sisters of APF, Gettin' Buck Wild: The Sex Chronicles 2, The Heat Seekers, Shame on it All, Addicted, *and* The Sex Chronicles: Shattering the Myth) *and the editor or contributor of several anthologies including the upcoming* Love is Never Painless *and the Publisher of Strebor Books International. She resides in the Washington, D.C. Metropolitan Area.*

GOD DOES
ANSWER
PRAYERS

J.L. WOODSON

The beeping noise hummed under the sound of frantic voices. Consistent, like a dripping faucet, it wore on Steven's nerves.

What is that noise? Steven opened his eyes. People in green, blood-covered hospital suits stood over him with surgical tools, preparing to do something to his body, but he didn't know what. He could hear them faintly, and their faces were covered with bright white masks so he couldn't tell male from female, or doctor from nurse.

All he could really hear was that consistent beeping noise from the heart monitor. And then it happened. The beeps became slower, slower, sloooooower. His twelve-year-old heart was slowing by the second.

Steven still hadn't realized that, somehow, he could see everything perched from his spot right above the operating table. How did he get there?

"What are they doing?"

It looked like they were trying to save his life or something, but he wondered how that could be when he felt fine. "He's bleeding out. Get the clamps," one of the nurses yelled.

He scanned the room—green tiled walls, bright white lights, and extra surgical equipment stood near the bed where his body lay on the white sheets. A flutter of activity took place near the upper part of his body as nurses passed tools, followed quick commands, and overall moved in synchronization as though this entire act were a dance.

For some strange reason, they were still trying to save his life, but they actually walked straight past the "real" him. A glance to his left found his mother and father both crying behind a large plate-glass window. His father's face radiated shame, while his mother kept on banging on the glass, mouthing the words, "Save…him…please."

Who was she talking about? She couldn't have been talking about him. He was sitting up, feeling fine, and watching everything. Steven's face wrinkled in confusion, until one of the doctors lowered the window shade, blocking out the view of his parents. Steven slowly glanced behind him, and shock exploded from every corner of his mind. His own reflection glared back at him. He looked exactly like the Steven he remembered and, at the same time, looked nothing like the Steven he had been for twelve years.

Jumping further away from the table, he soon hovered in the upper corner of the room as questions whirled in his mind. How could that be me? I'm standing right here. It was painful to see himself lying on an emergency room table as doctors feverishly worked on his body, trying to get his heart back to a normal speed. Now he knew the reason for his parents' tears. But how did he get like this? How did Steven end up on that table? Steven wasn't in a gang, so that couldn't have been it. There were no accidental shootings at school that day, so that was out of the question.

Steven was startled by the loud beeping sound, which suddenly switched from a beep to a flat, solid tone.

"He's flat lining. Get the paddles."

A nurse disappeared and a few seconds later, a loud bursting noise came from behind him. He turned around and quickly moved out of the way as a nurse rolled in the cart with electric shock paddles. The nurse splattered liquid on the paddles and placed them on his chest. "Clear." She paused, then added, "No pulse, Doctor."

"I need more. Give me three cc's of—"

Steven hovered there, witnessing how fast everything was flashing before his eyes. "Ouch, what the—" Although Steven wasn't connected to his body anymore, he could still feel the shock every time the jolt of electricity passed through his body. He also felt weak, as though he were fading, drifting away.

"Clear."

Steven lowered to the ground.

"We're losing him…" one of the nurses screamed.

What happened to me?

"Clear!"

"Run!"

That one word would keep Steven up all night.

"If he somehow gets into the house tonight," his mother said softly while stroking his head, "I want you to run. Run as fast as you can, as far as you can. Just get away this time."

She had said those words some thirty minutes before he brushed his teeth, slipped on his green and blue plaid pajamas, and went to bed. Her full lips trailed a tender kiss on his forehead, leaving a thin print of burgundy lipstick as a reminder of a goodnight. The goodnight that happened right before he saw the flowered robe covering her full figure disappear from his bedroom into the dimly lit hallway. Right before the fear in her tear-filled, dark brown eyes could strike worry in Steven's heart. She didn't have to say who "he" was. In Steven's mind, "he" was synonymous with evil. And evil, at least in their house, was synonymous with "Dad."

But Steven hadn't listened to his mother. He lay in bed, wide-awake, eyes shifting swiftly in each direction, waiting for something to jump out. In his heart, Steven realized that he couldn't leave anymore than she could; anymore than she had ever tried. Who would protect her if he left her alone?

Steven was stronger now, almost as tall as his dad. He'd even taken karate classes and definitely knew how to take a man down. So why hadn't he lifted a finger when Hector came bursting through the door? Why was he trembling in the corner of the living room like the last leaf on a snow-frosted tree, watching an instant replay of another world champion Southside of Chicago fight? Why? He'd stepped in front of his mother once before and it didn't matter. It would only happen again tomorrow. Or the next day. Or the next. Watching didn't matter. Watching was normal. Steven had heard the second verse of the same song so many times. And by now, he could definitely sing it from memory.

Angry blows rained down on his mother's body, purple bruises welling up where smooth, dark brown skin should be. As the living room became another battleground of curses and screams, Steven now understood exactly what his Aunt Vinah meant when she said, "When the shit hits the fan, you don't want to be standing downwind." Steven, at twelve years old, could tell anyone that upwind wasn't all that great either.

As his parents fought, every bitter word, every single blow, was like they were aimed directly at him, hurting him worse than any whippings his mother had every given him. It was always about money. Always about responsibility. Always about the fact that drugs were more important to Hector than his family. If Steven had never been born, maybe…things would've been different? At least, he wouldn't be around to see whether or not that was the truth. He couldn't stand to see this happen to them. Mainly, it was painful for him to watch bad things happen to his mother. But, staying in a bedroom listening wasn't much better.

Steven sunk down even further into the corner, under the painting of Lake Michigan and the portrait of silver-haired Grandma Mildred, hoping that she was able to see and hear from her place in heaven, the torturing words slicing and stabbing the soul of a twelve-year-old boy. He always picked the corner of a room to keep safe. And so far it had worked. He had learned from experience that flying objects didn't land in corners. No way! They whipped in and out like a boomerang and either landed on the floor near his feet, or sailed back into reach of one of his parents. Watching his parents fight was as unreal as a video game or an action movie. Only this was one episode he couldn't turn off and didn't want to watch. And, oh, how he wished he could simply change the channel. How he prayed that he could.

Did God listen to anyone anymore? Maybe all along, the answer to "Please God, keep me and my mother safe and help my father to leave the drugs alone," was a big fat, "No!" While Steven couldn't understand that, he did understand that God helps those who help themselves. The only thing he could see was that his dad—angry, high, or drunk—helped himself to giving out an order of ass-whipping. And his mother helped herself to an order of take one, take two, why not take three. Steven could only help himself to a ringside seat in his favorite corner, and there is where the family togetherness ended. Another blow made Steven wince. Tears welled up in his eyes, blurring his vision. At one time, he had loved his dad. At one time, he had felt his mother was the strongest woman on the planet. Each fight proved him wrong and with each fight he felt more alone.

Fear kept Steven's behind planted on the plush carpet. A carpet that barely hid the blood stains from the previous fights. A living room that had been almost spotless two hours ago, now looked like the before pictures in a home makeover series. Drugs had taken over what was left of his dad's mind. But deep down Steven knew that drugs weren't the real cause of his father's anger. The one night when he yelled at the top of his lungs, "I gave up my hopes and dreams to support this family!" was closer to the truth. Hopelessness. Dreamlessness. They wouldn't even have a family, if Steven weren't there. Steven knew then that the fighting was his fault, but what could he do about it now. He was already there.

What was Mom's excuse for staying? Of course it couldn't be because Dad was so good to her or that he took care of their family. Well, to let Aunt Vinah tell it, at one time he was good to her. But as far as Steven could remember, that hadn't been the case. Maybe someone had fast-forwarded through that scene before he could catch a glimpse. But God made other men, good men. Like his karate instructor. And his gym teacher! Good men. Kind men. Didn't God give mothers a second chance when the first husband broke down like a used car in the middle of rush-hour traffic? Couldn't they be traded in like cars? Or toys? Or refrigerators? Mom took that Kenmore back and got a new one—a better one with an icemaker, too. Didn't that say something?

Mom was superwoman. Mom could make a week's worth of groceries last a month. She could juggle bills like a pro. Mom could somehow pay for Steven to attend private school on a salary that said public school would do just fine. Mom could put a smile on even the meanest police officer's face by making small talk. And Steven had seen that many times as she drove away without a ticket. Even he had known that speeding down Lake Shore Drive like an Indy 500 driver was against the law. He never complained because he enjoyed it. Yes, Mom could do all that and more. Well, except one thing. Leave! Yes, just one thing—leave and take him with her. Why did she stay with Dad when all he could do was hurt her? She was strong. Everyone knew that. Superwoman was always strong, right? She was superwoman. But how could she rescue Steven if she couldn't even rescue herself?

The front door wasn't made of kryptonite. It didn't even have bars or a screen door. A few simple steps forward and both of them could run. Hide. Live. Smile. Dream. That's all it would take, right? Just the two of them. Yes, that would be an answer to a prayer. But deep down, he loved his dad, too. Didn't they have places for him to get well? Yes, rehab or detox, or something like that. But by looking at the rage in his father's eyes, as sick as it sounded, it looked like he enjoyed fighting. There was no help for that; not even counseling. Steven could also see hatred. Not just hatred for his family, but hatred for life in its entirety, like life had done him wrong. If anything, Hector wasn't getting it any worse than anyone else. He was learning life's lesson, but he chose to learn the hard way. Even though Steven's mother was his superwoman, he had been waiting on his father to become Superman. Steven could bet that it wouldn't happen anytime soon, though.

The sudden stillness in the room made Steven hold his breath. Something had changed. The fighting had ended, but not the normal way—with doors slamming and sobs and swiping alcohol over blood-crusted bruises.

No, they were still standing. Facing each other. Oh yes, this time was different. Dad had changed the game. He held a small silver gun in his hands. Mom's hands had yanked upward like a criminal when the police say, "Put 'em up."

"Where's the money, Bitch?" That voice, although spilling from his dad's lips, did not belong to the man Steven once knew. And who was he calling a bitch?

Steven could barely recognize his mother's voice, which came out as a frightened whisper, "It's gone. I had to pay bills. We have to eat. We have to . . . live!"

Sweat and blood poured from Dad's forehead as though a faucet had been installed at the hairline. "You're lying. I want that money. You got paid today."

What money? Her money? Mom was the only one who worked. Dad never had any money. Dad didn't have a job anymore—thanks to his best friends—cocaine and crack. Now this scene was new—the gun and Dad hitting Mom up for cash? Or was it an old thing, and Steven didn't know about it? If Steven had any respect left for his dad, he would've lost it at that moment. But Dad had a head start on that a year ago, and had done nothing to gain it back. Steven wasn't sure the man even cared.

"You're lying, Bitch. You always take care of that brat. You've got some money."

Brat? When did Steven become a brat? And who gave his dad a gun? Who in their right, or even their terrible mind, would trust his dad with a gun?

"Hector, put the gun down and leave. Or just leave. I don't have anything. You've been through my purse; you've been through all my hiding places. You've seen there's nothing there."

The gun lifted until he connected with the frightened woman's temple.

Fear was instantly swept aside as Steven scrambled to his feet, leaving the safety of the corner. "Here, Dad," Steven said, stuffing a trembling hand into his jeans' pocket. "This is my allowance. You can have it. I—"

The sudden movement caused his father, and the gun, to swing in his direction.

Powwwwwwwwwwwwww!!!!!!

White heat flooded Steven's body. Pain spread from his chest to his toes and bounced back up to start all over again. Standing became impossible. Against his wishes, Steven lowered to his knees, barely seeing the stunned expression on his father's face. But he could see that his mother had reached out for him, trying to catch him before he landed totally on the floor. She was too late.

"Oh God. Oh God. Oh God," he faintly heard his dad say over and over again as he hit his fists on the side of his head. See? He said God! The man did actually know Him!

"Steven. Ohhhhhh, my baby." Mom's sobs made her body tremble as she pulled Steven's head into the soft curve of her breasts. Soft. Comfort. The living room swam in and out of focus. The world was fading. Slowly. Slowly. Who knew that at twelve years of age, Steven would lay there in his mother's arms wanting more time to live, but not sure whether time was on his side or not.

He remembered his mother telling him, "Before we are born and come onto Earth we choose our parents, our life, and our death." Steven didn't believe it then, but he understood now.

She reached out, yanked the phone from the cradle, frantically dialing for help. His dad sank down to the floor by his side. Both of them looked down on him. The fight was forgotten and something else was more important than money, or pain. Steven. Finally, they saw him. Finally, they had stopped fighting enough to see him. See, God does answer prayers. God does listen to children's prayers.

Know ye not that ye are Gods? He'd read that in the Bible. And if that were true, if Steven was God, he would give anything, everything, to see his parents as they were right now. Hands by their sides, his father concerned with someone other than himself, his next hit, his next high—they were together in at least this one thing.

"I love you, Mom," Steven said softly to the woman whose hands trailed a painful path near his wound. Then he turned to the man whose pale skin, thin lips, and wavy hair were a perfect reminder of his Mexican heritage. Steven struggled for breath, but did the one thing that God would want him to do. "I forgive you, Dad. And . . . if you love me . . . you'll get some help. Get some—"

A single nod from his dad, followed by another, then another, needed no words to explain. With that, Steven Santos closed his eyes and prayed. The soft hum of his mother's voice echoed in his heart and mind as he drifted into a peaceful sleep, hoping to awake and see that his dad's promises were kept and his mother had become Superwoman again.

Steven opened his eyes halfway, then fully. The operating room had disappeared. He was asleep in a comfortable green chair, but noticed "the other Steven" still lying on a hospital bed in a coma. His reflection was on life support—several different machines kept tabs on how close he was to death.

Though he remembered how it all happened, the question now was how could it be reversed? And why was he hanging around like a shadow, a ghost, or something.

His attention was drawn away from his body to his parents talking just inside the entrance. For the first time in a long time, it looked like a civil conversation. No yelling, flying objects, or people getting hurt. He was surprised that they couldn't see him; he wasn't gone but he wasn't necessarily "there" either. Somehow, someone would have to explain that to him and fast.

"How could I have been so stupid?" Steven's mother said as he listened in. "I should've left when I had the chance. This is all my fault."

"Where would you go?" Steven's father said angrily, trying to keep his voice down as though he knew that the "other" Steven could hear. "You don't have any family."

"Any place would've been better than staying with you," his mother shot back. "Especially, if I would've known you were going to shoot my son."

"It was an accident!" Hector said, his brow furrowed in frustration. He glanced over to the hospital bed. "He's my son, too."

"You sure have a wonderful way of showing that he's your son," Mom said through clenched teeth.

Hector got up and walked over to the window, looking out at the gray sky.

Mom, sporting a dark blue overcoat and clutching a worn handbag, followed him, saying, "Ever since you got hooked on those drugs, you've paid attention to nothing else. Not your son, and not me. I guess family doesn't really mean anything to you anymore." She grabbed him, whirling him to face her. "The only family you think about are those people that got you hooked on that stuff."

"I don't need to deal with this right now," Hector said, brushing past her, trying to walk out of the room.

Sprinting, Mom made it to the door and blocked his path. "Yes, you do, Hector. If you don't deal with this now, I know for a fact that you won't deal with it later." Dark brown eyes watered with tears that splattered onto her coat. "When are you going to stop running away from your problems and confront them?"

"I am confronting them," he said, running a pale hand through his straight, jet-black hair. "I'm going to get help for my drug problem."

There was an uncomfortable pause in the room. Both of them knew it was a lie—a lie he told often, and a lie she had believed far too many times to count.

"You almost killed your son," she said softly, her gaze landing on the machines standing guard next to Steven. "Your own flesh and blood, your seed, and there's no telling whether he will survive." She faced Hector, glaring at him. "You don't think there's a problem? I know there's a problem. The fact that you pulled a gun on me—a gun for Christ's sake!—says there's a problem. The fact that we're here says there's a problem. You should be praying and asking for forgiveness."

"Heather, didn't you hear him? Steven already forgave me for that," Hector said, lacing his hands on top of his head, as though trying to block out one memory or another.

She glared angrily at him and her voice became icy. "I'm talking about God—forgiveness from God."

Hector grimaced, inching away from Heather's anger. "God can't do anything for me," he growled. "He didn't do anything for me when I was Steven's age and He sure as hell hasn't done much for me lately."

Dad began pacing the room.

"Hector," Mom began softly, placing a single hand on his shoulder. "I know that your mother was abused by your father, but you—"

"Don't even say it." Hector shrugged, removing her hand from his body. "I already know what you're going to say."

"What?"

Hector turned to look at her. "I'm going to have to forgive him. But why should I, after all that he did to my family?"

Steven's mother looked up at Hector. "For the same reason Steven forgave you...it's the right thing to do. When will this vicious cycle end? It should've ended with you!" She stepped out, covering the distance between them. "You swore that you would be a better man than your father. A better husband. A better father. But you've tried so hard not to be like him, you've become worse than he ever was."

Hector whirled to face her, parting his mouth to speak.

She held up a single hand to silence him. "I've taken a lot from you, things that will take time for me to forgive, but I didn't want Steven to experience this. I don't want him to grow up and continue this thing. If he lives." At that moment, Mom broke down in tears. "No, I mean—when, when he wakes up."

But the words were out. If. If Steven lived. Was this the price he had to pay for his mom's inability to leave a bad situation? Was this the price for Dad's love of drugs—things that took him away from reality and into a land that had nothing to do with responsibility? Why did Steven have to pay the price? He'd been the innocent one in all this.

Hector crossed the room, touching the face of the Steven lying on the bed. "How are we going to be able to say that we have a family? More than likely, I'll be in jail."

"I really don't know how that will work out, but you should try to work things out while you can. This is something you're going to have to do on your own. The only reason I'm talking to you now is because I know Steven would want that. Otherwise, I would've had you shipped out of here the moment we came through the hospital doors, so you wouldn't be able to have any contact with me or my son."

Hector's gaze fell to the white tiled floor. Mom was right; Dad was going to have to do it on his own. Could he? Would he?

Small delicate fingers curled around the lifeless one with an IV sticking out of the back side. The sound of a chair scraping across the tile took over all other sounds in the room for a moment. Hector placed the wide, tan leather chair right behind Mom. She sat down, still keeping Steven's hand in hers. Watching for signs of life—any life—any movement. She bowed her head, and Steven knew at once that she was praying.

"Pssssst. Hey, Kid."

Steven looked to the left of his space in the upper corner of the room. Another kid, about his age, with dark brown skin and a low-cut fade perched next to him. He wore a red and white striped shirt, jeans, and Air Force One sneakers. Steven wasn't frightened. Somehow Steven knew that this "kid" was just like him—in between living and dying.

"What's up?" Steven asked.

"Those your parents?"

"Yep. If you could call them that." Steven forced a laugh of disappointment. "What are you doing here?"

"I'm supposed to keep you company," the boy said, punching Steven in the arm playfully.

"Company? I'm not alone; my parents are here." Steven directed his focus back to his parents.

"No, your parents are there. They can't even see you."

"Am I fully dead?" Steven asked, confused by that one statement.

"Nope, you're just like you thought—in between."

"Whew—cool. So why else are you here?"

"I'm just like you. My parents were domvies, too."

"Dummies?"

"No, domvies—domestic violence parents."

"So you're in a coma, too?"

"Nope, I wasn't so lucky," he said, sadly walking to the window, waiting for Steven to follow. "I'm all the way dead."

"Your dad?"

The boy shook his head slowly. "Mom's aim was a little off with the knife. It slipped past Dad and landed right here," he said, pointing to his chest. "She was trying to protect herself from him."

"Wow, my dad had a gun tonight. It was an accident also."

"Yeah, I know all about it. There are a lot of us floating around here." Michael frowned. "My mama had an order of protection and everything, but that was just a piece of paper. We should've gone to one of those shelters or something."

"Was your dad on drugs?"

"Naw, he was just…mean," the boy said, hesitating, trying to find a polite way to put it.

"Well, at least my dad had an excuse," Steven said proudly. "He was on drugs."

The boy chuckled, his hazel eyes twinkling. "Doesn't make you any less half-dead now, does it?"

Steven winced, realizing the boy had a point. "What's your name?"

"Michael," he said, extending his hand. "Michael Roberts."

"I'm Steven Santos," he said, shaking it. "So, how long do I hang around up here?"

"Depends on you. Just like your parents are making choices, you're supposed to make some also. You can stay here for a while or you can go back when you're called."

Actually, the more he thought about it, Steven didn't want to go back—in between was safe.

"How many are there like you?"

Michael frowned, his mind winding with confusion. "Like me?"

"You know, kids that were killed in domestic violence accidents."

"Oh, domvie kids?"

"Yeah. That's what they're called."

"Lots of us, Man. Used to be diseases and gangs took us out. Now it's parents, or when we simply happen to be in the wrong place at the wrong time." Michael shrugged at the thought. "Just like you tonight. It's happening a lot more now than before," Michael said in a somber tone, reaching to grab two Sprites out of the cabinet behind him, handing Steven one.

"I thought we couldn't taste things here," Steven said, wondering whether he should waste time opening the pop.

"You have a lot to learn." Michael took a long sip of pop.

"Do you…get to see your parents?"

"I check on my mama sometimes." An awful stillness came over the room. "She's not doing so good. Killing me really sent her over the edge. Now they've got her on drugs—the legal kind—but she's no better than some street drug addicts I've seen. I think I'll be running into her pretty soon on this side."

"Will I be able to—"

"We all can. Some do, some don't. It depends," Michael said, gazing over at Steven's parents. "Some of the guys just can't go back, because they feel that they'll make matters worse."

"Aren't you supposed to have, you know, like wings or something?" Steven asked with uneasy sarcasm.

Michael laughed, slapping Steven on the back. "That's a myth—we don't need wings to travel—we just go from place to place. Now you see us." Michael slowly faded from view, leaving only the Sprite can behind. "Now you don't."

"Hey! Come back here," Steven said, realizing he was, in fact, a lot less lonely with Michael around to explain things.

Michael reappeared, a smile on his thick lips.

"Do you think my dad will get help?" Steven walked over to Hector, waving a hand in front of his face. Of course, he didn't notice.

"If I were you, I'd be more worried about your mama," Michael said, directing his attention toward the woman crying into her hands.

"Why?"

"Mamas have it hard. Guilt can kill 'em."

Steven's gaze landed on his mother; a small pain flashed over his heart. "Yeah, she's blaming herself right now."

"They all do." A disappointed frown spread across Michael's face. "But women have to be real smart."

Steven's attention was directed toward the nurse wearing a white uniform; her brunette hair was tied back into a ponytail. She checked his vital signs. "What do you mean?" he asked, turning to Michael.

"When they leave, they have to really leave. They can't just say it and stick around hoping things will get better. Sometimes it never gets better without outside help, and that might not always work," Michael replied, staring at both Steven's mother and father. "Sometimes that means they can't tell their families where they're going, or it means leaving the state. Sometimes, it means pressing charges and putting the man in jail." Steven stared at Michael as though he wasn't quite sure he'd heard right. "My mama had a chance to do that and didn't. And here I am." Michael's hands spread out as though presenting himself for an Army inspection.

"Yes," Steven said slowly, feeling the pain in his heart increase as he watched his mom's tears fall. "Here we are."

Steven was trying to take all of this in at once. He also tried to understand things that he didn't know before about his father. Hector had followed in his father's abusive footsteps, but hopefully, it would stop now.

A tall, black woman, with dark, wavy hair, wearing a blue and gold Dashiki entered his hospital room. Her bright smile and flashing brown eyes showed she was obviously in high spirits. Steven had never seen someone who looked so peaceful. "Good morning, Mr. and Mrs. Santos," she said, extending a hand to his mother. "I'm Kristen Willis, one of the family counselors for Michael Reese Hospital."

Mom absently shook the hand the woman offered, but Hector just stared at her.

Ms. Willis took a quick glance at Steven's body, then looked back at them. "He's a very strong young man."

"How may we help you, Ma'am?" Hector asked somewhat impolitely, as if she were interrupting something, which was far from the truth.

"I was asked to come up here by Mrs. Santos."

Hector took one look at Steven and then back at Ms. Willis. "We don't need a marriage counselor."

"I'm not here for your marriage; I'm here for all three of you," she quickly replied. "Now there's no doubt in my mind that you are having marital issues also, based on your wife's bruises." For the first time, Hector couldn't and didn't say anything to defend himself. "Why don't we take this to my office?" Ms. Willis said smoothly. "People in a coma can hear things and there are some things that might be said that you don't want Steven to hear."

Mom stood and walked to the door behind Ms. Willis. Hector hung back near Steven's bed. Steven watched, hoping that his father would, for once, remember that he promised to get help and would take the first step. Finally, Hector trudged to the door as though the weight of the world rested on his shoulders.

Steven turned to Michael and said, "I sure hate that I'm going to miss the conversation."

"You don't have to."

"How can I leave?"

Michael drained the last of the pop. "Picture your mom and dad in your mind."

Steven closed his eyes. Soon the sound of the machines and monitors became a faint hum. Steven jolted, feeling a strong urge to throw up before he opened his eyes. Michael was still sitting on his left, but the hospital room had now become a slate-blue painted office, with certificates on the wall, two chairs on opposite sides of a cherrywood desk with maroon carpet underneath, and slivers of sunlight peeking through the blinds.

Steven turned to Michael. "You could've warned me."

Michael shrugged. "You'll get used to it." Then he looked down at the scene below.

Ms. Willis pulled out a file and notepad. "Okay, Mr. Santos, what seems to be the problem?"

"I don't know what you're talking about," Hector said defensively.

"I'd like to know what you think is going on with your family," she said, glancing up from her notes. "Based on what I see, you should be in prison right now," Kristen said, pointing to the bruises on Mom's jaws and arms.

Steven was rooting for his dad to open up and let some things out. "Better out than in," his Grandma had always said. Even though she meant it for passing gas, it had to mean other things also.

The silence in the room was cold and hard as the two women waited for him to answer.

Michael elbowed Steven. "Stubborn, isn't he?"

"Shhhhhh!"

Hector glanced at Mom, then to the woman behind the desk. "I have—I have a drug addiction. I feel that's what's tearing my family apart. I need to work on that."

"How long have you had this drug addiction?" she asked.

"Two years; going on three." He felt so ashamed to say even the little that he had admitted, because it was painful for him to admit that he was wrong.

"What caused this addiction to form, and made you turn on your own family?" Ms. Willis asked, analyzing his every move, his every word.

"I was stressed out about not having a job and not being able to support my family." Hector allowed his thoughts to stir and marinate in his mind. "Heather had to go back to work, and I still couldn't find a job. I couldn't take it anymore, so I started smoking weed to take the edge off. Then weed couldn't do it—so I tried cocaine, then something stronger. And now I owe people for not paying."

Mom gasped; her eyes widened in horror. Hector's gaze fell to the window, though he couldn't see a thing with the blinds closed.

Ms. Willis gave Mom's hand a little pat, hoping to keep her quiet.

"My family seemed like they needed more and more from me and I still couldn't find a job. Now what's even more unbearable is that my son's on life support and it's all my fault."

"How is it your fault?" Ms. Willis asked, looking over Steven's chart, as though this information was news to her.

"Last night, I was high and I came to get some money from Heather because I knew she'd just gotten paid." Tears caught in his throat. "I wanted it so much and I was afraid that the drug dealers would kill me this time. She wouldn't give me the money. I lost it and started beating her."

Steven turned to Michael. "Yeah, that's something that I saw happen almost every other day."

This time Michael said, "Shhhhhhh!"

"Steven tried to give me his allowance, but he scared me by getting up so fast. I didn't know he was in the room. Next thing I know, the gun went off and Steven was on the ground." Hector lowered his head in his hands. "I shot my own son."

Heather got up and ran out of the room, covering her face with tears. Hector had forgotten she was even there.

"How do you think Steven felt, watching you two fight all the time; especially watching you beating on his mother over money?" Ms. Willis asked.

43

Hector let his head drop, staring at the carpet. "I know it couldn't have been good at all. I didn't feel good when my dad beat on my mother."

"So, if you didn't enjoy it as a child, why would you do it to your wife and in front of your own son?" she asked for clarification.

"I—I don't know. I guess I felt in control of something, although it was wrong, and I don't think I was in my right mind." Hector rubbed his face, showing that he was tired. "If anything, I should've never put my hands on her, but I needed that money; even if I had to go through her to get it."

The paging system announced the need for a doctor in ER as they continued talking. Steven, for the first time, saw his father pour his heart out. It had been a long while since his father's eyes weren't glazed with a new high. After a moment, Hector's own words penetrated through his thick skull as tears flowed down his cheeks. He realized that the way he handled things in his household was the way his dad had handled his household, except his dad was a drunk. Same old song, different verse—drugs instead of liquor. "I treated them so wrong. The last thing my son said to me was that he forgave me and that if I really loved him, I would get some help."

Ms. Willis could see that his son's words were eating him alive. "At least he forgave you. Many children don't get the opportunity to forgive anyone who treats their mother the way you did, and many of them are still living." She got up from the chair and walked over to Hector. "Come on. Let's go see Steven."

Steven grabbed Michael's hand, closed his eyes, and pictured the hospital room. They made it there before Ms. Willis and his dad, but not before his mom, who sat in the chair next to the bed, rocking back and forth like a child.

The woman placed her hand gently on Steven's head. Steven could feel the warmth from Ms. Willis as he sat next to Michael.

"He has such a good heart," Ms. Willis said softly, "and he's such a good kid; especially since he knows how to forgive. Not everyone knows how to forgive. I'm going to recommend a therapist for your family. You need to get help for the drugs, too, and try to talk to your wife."

Hector stood up, walking over to the bed. "But what can I do? He's in a coma, and I'm afraid to talk to my wife, especially after all I put her through."

"It's going to take some time for her to deal with you, if she still wants this marriage to work."

For the first time since they had entered the room, Mom spoke. "You need to get yourself right with God and right with yourself."

Hector nodded.

"I can make suggestions and offer advice," Ms. Willis continued, "but you're the one who needs to be committed to following through on your son's wish for you to get some help. So far, talking with me today is a good start. But don't worry. I still believe your son is watching over you."

Michael nudged Steven, who for some reason felt the urge to cry. "You'll watch over him, right?"

Ms. Willis glanced at her watch, then reached into her pocket. "Here's my card. You can call me or come downstairs to my office."

"Thank you, Ms. Willis," he said, shaking her hand.

"You're welcome." She touched Hector's shoulder before walking to the door. "Although Steven has forgiven you, Mr. Santos, you need to forgive yourself, follow through with therapy, and break this terrible cycle. Things will only get worse if you don't."

"Yes, Ma'am. As easy as it sounds, I know it's going to take some hard work to get right again." He placed a hand on Heather's shoulder. "I want to work things out with you, but after tonight, I figure our marriage is over."

"Hector," she said in a low voice. "our marriage has been over since the first time you hit me. We've been living a lie and we both know it. I wasn't strong enough to leave, and now I'm paying for that. But more than this marriage, get help for yourself. Keep your promise to Steven."

Hector recollected all of those words that he said about Steven. Saying that he had given up his life for his family, as though it was their fault. That's something that no child should ever hear. Hector paced the room, knowing what to do but not knowing where to start.

"Go on home, Heather. I'll stay with Steven."

Hector's hands trembled with the need for another fix. Sweat poured down his face as though the temperature in the room had turned to one hundred. The drugs were calling him. Somehow, this time Steven didn't think his father would answer.

Hector fell asleep as Michael and Steven talked about their parents.

A young, Asian woman entering the room startled Hector from his nap. He sat up. "Sorry, I thought you were my wife."

"No, I'm just coming to check on Steven's vitals."

Another nurse came into the room, helping to adjust Steven's tubes while the Asian woman wrote notes in the chart.

"Hello, Mr. Santos. How are you this morning?" the nurse asked, retying her brunette hair in a ponytail.

"I'm hanging in. Thanks," he replied, walking back to the window. Even Steven could tell his father was far from okay.

"You don't look so well. Do you need to see a doctor, or anything?" she asked, walking toward him ready to check his vitals.

He stretched his arms before letting out a yawn. "I'm fine. It's just stress and I'm tired."

"Then I think you need to get some rest." She reached into her pocket for a pen and scribbled something on her pad. "The doctor can give you something to help you relax."

"No thanks," he said in a strong, sure voice. "I'm done with pills." Instead, he took a sip of the cold coffee from the cup Heather had left behind. The nurse got him a blanket from the bottom of the closet as he sat down in one of the green chairs. She held it out; he took it, covered himself, and slowly drifted off to sleep.

Michael's lips pursed as though he were about to say something but changed his mind.

"What?" Steven asked.

"You can say something to him."

"My dad?"

"Yeah. When they're in between waking and sleep, we can reach them."

"What about my mom?"

"Right now, your dad needs you more."

Steven hesitated, watching the man stretched out in the chair like he'd be there for a while.

"Dad."

Nothing.

"Dad."

Hector's eyes shot open, but he didn't move a muscle. He didn't remember being in a bright white room, with no window and no hospital bed. Hector looked around the endless space and saw nothing and no one, until he heard a voice behind him call out, "Dad!"

He turned around slowly. Steven stood in front of him, a smile plastered on his face.

"Dad."

Hector's dark brown eyes glistened as he could feel more tears on his face. Hector reached up and touched Steven's face to see if it were real. Although he could sense that he was dreaming, it didn't matter. It was as good as the real thing. Hector pulled Steven into his arms, letting his head drop onto Steven's shoulder. It was as though Steven was the father and now Hector was the child.

Hector's face lifted. "I'm sorry, I'm sorry, so sorry," he repeated with his head shaking in disbelief, all excuses forgotten; everything else forgotten. The only thing that mattered right now was his son.

"It's okay. Remember, I forgave you," Steven said, wiping his father's tears with the back of a trembling hand. "But, Dad, I'm going to need you to forgive yourself. You may have disappointed me, but I've learned that I can't hold onto things either, letting them eat at me, stressing me out."

"Yes, Son. But I'm not sure if things will go back to being the same."

"Remember how you felt about Mom when you first met her? After a while you fell in love with her. You found love between each other, and nothing can top that. I'm not saying that things will go back to normal, because I'm not sure how much more Mom can take. The drugs turned you into a totally different person, and we weren't sure whether you could change back. I know I had my doubts."

Hector hugged him again. "You won't ever have to doubt me again, Son."

"I know that, but Mom needs to know that. She was the one much more hurt by you than me. I'm just a messenger. Don't go back to the way you were, even before you got into drugs. A part of you was hurting even then. Losing your job didn't make you turn to drugs."

"I know I must change, but it's hard. I'm not sure talking will help." Hector's face twisted with confusion.

"Prayer; therapy; Ms. Willis. Do something, because you don't have much time. Before you know it, we'll be gone and the time for healing will pass."

Steven turned away and walked back toward Michael. Hector reached out for him, stopping him. "Where are you going?"

"It's time for you to wake up, Dad. You have a lot of work to do, and only you can do it." Hector pursed his lips to say something else, but Steven was gone.

"Steven…Steven…Steven!!" Hector waited for his son to come back.

"Wake up, Hector." That's what he heard repeatedly until he woke up and found Heather standing in front of him.

"What happened?" Hector looked around frantically. "Where's Steven?"

"He's still in the bed," she said, pointing at Steven lying peacefully, the machines still monitoring his progress.

"I had the weirdest dream. I saw Steven and we were talking like he was fine," Hector explained excitedly, but his enthusiasm vanished when he noticed the tears forming in the corners of her eyes, flowing down her brown cheeks. "Baby, I'm sorry… I'm sorry for everything that I've done to this family. If it were up to me, I'd change everything. I want to make it right and get cleaned up, not just for my family but for me."

She moved out of his reach. "I hear what you're saying, but how can we go back to the way things were? Of course, you know that this will take some time. It's not an overnight thing," she said, running her hands up and down her thigh nervously.

"I know. That's why I want to do counseling. Family counseling, anything

I need to get my life together. I'll be a hero and better father to my son, and a better husband to you," Hector expressed, feeling revived, and willing to do anything to get his family back.

"Give me your hands and close your eyes," Heather requested. Hector obeyed. "Now, I want you to pray."

Hector sighed, hoping he was ready for the beginning of a new life. "Father, I come to You today to ask for forgiveness. Forgive me for every wrong that I have committed. I lay my life down to You because I'm lost. I need You to guide me along the way, to follow the path of righteousness. I would give anything to be with my family and to have my son back. Heal me; heal my son; heal my wife. I have done her wrong also. I pray that she forgives me, too. Help me to keep my promise to Steven. I don't want to fail him again, or my wife. Help me to be a better man in Your word. A better father and husband. In Your name, I pray. Amen."

"Amen," Heather said, opening her eyes, hearing a noise.

Steven held out his hand to Michael, shook it firmly, and walked away. Heather and Hector both turned, facing Steven. They got up and went over to his bed. Steven's eyes fluttered until they opened and he took in a deep breath. Steven's mom had nearly fainted, but Hector caught her, encouraging him to return. Their son was awake. Whether Hector new it or not as he smiled at his son, he had saved Steven, by breaking the cycle.

J.L. Woodson is an eighteen-year-old native Chicagoan, and a freshman at Fisk University majoring in English and Theater. The Things I Could Tell You!, *his first novel, was penned for an English assignment and published when he was only sixteen years old. A keynote speaker for several venues across the country and co-author of* How to Win the Publishing Game, *he has hosted writing seminars and workshops at Borders Books & Café, colleges, high schools and elementary schools. He is the winner of the State Farm, Coca-Cola and McDonald's Youth Leadership Award; top winner of the Chicago Urban League's Business Plan Competition and Stock Market Competition. J.L. currently resides on campus in Nashville, Tennessee where he is completing his next novel,* Superwoman's Child: Son of a Single Mother, *a tribute to the "superhuman" efforts of women from all walks of life.*

THE BREAK OF DAWN

COLLEN DIXON

Standing at the kitchen counter, Dawn heard the sound of water splashing in the bathroom. A warm smile crossed her full, honey-brown face. Her daughter, Asia, was in the claw-footed tub, and the thought of her playing with the soapy bubbles warmed Dawn's soul. "Asia. Stop playing in there," she said, barely able to keep the amusement from her voice. "I'll be in there in a second to get you. And I hope you haven't splashed bubbles all over the place." It was always such a struggle for Dawn to balance her motherly control with the delight she always received from Asia's antics.

With loving care, Dawn stirred the confectioner's sugar and white powder into the chocolate sauce in a bowl. Fresh from the microwave, she tested it with her pinky, to make sure it wasn't too hot. She added a dash more confectioner's sugar and stirred until the fine white lumps disappeared into the gooey chocolate. She poured the topping over two healthy dips of frozen vanilla yogurt, and topped it off with a handful of colorful sprinkles. Grabbing the bowl, she called out over her shoulder. "Asia? Are you ready? Mommy's coming."

"Hush, little baby, don't say a word. Mama's gonna buy you a mockingbird," Dawn hummed on her way to the bathroom.

After she dried the talkative little Asia, Dawn lovingly rubbed her daughter's soft body with sweet-smelling lotion and sprinkled her bottom with baby powder. Dawn exhaled quietly as she prepared herself for the remainder of her evening ritual, amidst a flurry of questions from Asia's probing little mind, like "Can I have a pony?" or "Where do flowers come from?" Dawn sat down with Asia in her lap, in a creaky old rocking chair that was beside Asia's bed.

The room was neat and orderly, with a pretty, white princess canopy bed that had a matching nightstand and dresser. Dawn recalled the joy she had picking out the bedroom set at Huffman Koos, one of the best furniture retailers in New Jersey. She had outfitted the room with Little Mermaid accessories, down to the Ariel-shaped lamps. A fragrant mist sprayed from Asia's humidifier, and Dawn dimmed the lights on the colorful Disney lamp.

Dawn Boyer softly hummed the age-old lullaby as she held her healthy four-year-old daughter Asia, and spoon-fed her frozen yogurt with colorful sprinkles on top. Dawn finished the chorus, and winced as she rubbed her baby's nose with the index finger on her right hand. Dawn's arm was in a sling, from a dislocated shoulder, and even a slight movement such as wiggling her fingers was painful. She fought through it, and bent over and kissed Asia's soft face.

"You know, little girl, I've been doing this to you ever since you were just a dot in Mommy's stomach." Dawn took a long finger and carefully outlined Asia's face. When Dawn discovered she was pregnant, she began forming the bond between her and her developing fetus by stroking her abdomen and reading aloud daily to it while she treated herself to a healthy portion of some fruit-enriched yogurt. This lasted for eight months, until Asia came prematurely screaming into the world. Every evening, Dawn would visit the pre-natal I.C.U., where she'd talk to her little one, until she was able to bring her home. Dawn performed this ritual as Asia breastfed, when she took her first bottle, with Asia's first spoonful of Dawn's home-made baby food, right up until today. Normally, Dawn would give Asia a small portion of yogurt with granola sprinkles, and for a special treat, she would give her frozen yogurt, with nuts and sprinkles. Every evening, as the sun went down and the moon filled the sky, Dawn would read Asia a bedtime story, and it was truly their special thing. A mother-daughter moment that was the foundation of a bond that held them tightly together.

Dawn took a spoonful of yogurt and placed it to Asia's lips, but the little girl just yawned.

"I'm sleepy, Mommy," Asia said, with a long stretch.

"Okay, Baby. No more for you tonight." Dawn took the spoon, licked it, and gently placed it back inside Asia's bowl, which was still about half full of soupy frozen yogurt, swirls of chocolate sauce, and a few melted sprinkles. Dawn made sure she gave her little girl most of the sprinkles. Asia loved those colorful little candy bits.

"I love you, Asia. Mommy really, really loves you. More than anything," Dawn whispered, even though she was alone. Her husband, Todd, was out on one of his weekly "hang out with the fellas" forays. "You look so much like me. But you're even more beautiful than I am. You have my eyes, my cheekbones, and your grandmother's pointy nose." Dawn playfully plucked Asia's nose. "You have a little bit of your daddy right there on your lips. But you act just like me. You have my mannerisms. You remind me so much of myself." In Asia's spirited little nature, Dawn saw herself almost reincarnate. And until today, she was thrilled by her little "mini-me." Shards of a repressed memory shattered Dawn's peaceful existence, to the point that she found herself gasping for air. Her knees had buckled, and her world faded to black as she felt herself retreating into a distant universe.

"You gonna tell me a story, Mommy?" the little girl asked, as she struggled to keep her eyes open.

Dawn held Asia tightly, and the little girl sighed and nestled in her arms. "Yes, I am. I'm going to tell you a story tonight, Baby," Dawn said, as Asia lifted her heavy eyelids. Her deep brown, almond-shaped eyes were full, and Asia again yawned softly. Dawn continued. "One I've never told you before. It's about me, a little princess who grew up to meet a wonderful prince. I was young, just 23 years old when I met your daddy, and we both worked for the *Newark Star-Ledger*. I was a copy editor when Mr. Todd Saunders stepped into my life. Yes, Mr. Saunders was something else. He was the hotshot reporter who had been spirited away from our rival paper, *The Newark Gazette*, and he was taking the newsroom by storm. Your daddy was suave, confident, and although he wasn't what we call 'fine,' he definitely had it going on. He had quite an air about him. His attitude made him extremely attractive. Immediately, every woman set her mark on him.

After all, he was a B.M.W. Black man working," Dawn said with a little snort, and tried not to wince from the pain in her arm. She reached into her pocket, pulled out two bottles, and placed them on the nightstand beside Asia's bowl. One was Tylenol 3, and the other one, Dalmane, was to help her sleep. The emergency doctor had given her a 30-day prescription for both, and had looked at her with a very unsettling gleam in his eye.

"Are you sure you dislocated your shoulder by tripping on your stairs?" the doctor asked. He was a fairly handsome, medium tall, brown-skinned man, who appeared a little young. And a little too inquisitive. "I didn't see a lot of bruising that would be consistent with this type of fall. Is there something else you'd like to share, Ms. Jones?"

Dawn had laughed nervously. She had made sure to use a fake name and had gone to another hospital. It was across town from the one down the street from her apartment, and she had made all of this effort just so she wouldn't have to be questioned by or run into an emergency room doctor she had seen before. The level of the handsome doctor's interest kind of unnerved her.

"I tried to break my fall. As I started falling down the stairs, I, uh, grabbed the railing and jerked my arm out of place. I was just trying to prevent myself from falling," Dawn said. She had become a consummate liar. Something she had to become just to maintain her and Todd's existence. She had to protect Todd. She couldn't give up on him like everyone else in his life had. She had to stick by him. That was the least that she could do.

She understood him. He grew up in Queens, and was exposed to a number of things as a child; things even adults should not have been subjected to. Drugs, crime, murder, and prostitution. He truly came from the stereotypical difficult background. He never knew his father, and his mother worked several jobs to keep a roof over his and his three siblings' heads. Unfortunately, she had died before he turned 16, and Todd was forced into several foster homes, none of which helped to nurture or improve his mentality. Todd managed to graduate from high school and went to Rutgers University in New Brunswick, New Jersey, on a dual wrestling and academic scholarship. He excelled there, and became a very high-strung and extremely driven young man. He majored in journalism, where he found his niche. He was exceptionally resourceful at researching and investigating, and wrote a number of award-winning articles for the local newspaper. Todd wanted to succeed, and made that clear to anyone whom he met. Helping him was the least Dawn could do to support him. He didn't need her bringing him down, too.

She liked his virility, and his take-charge manner. His strength and disposition kind of reminded her of her father.

Todd was a short, medium-framed, light brown-skinned man, who always dressed well. His closet was filled with expensive, tailor-made shirts and suits. Italian, soft-leather shoes. He was almost obsessive about his appearance, and went to the barbershop twice a week for a shape-up and hot lather, straight razor shave. But he wasn't a handsome man. He had small dark eyes, and didn't have many outstanding features. He had large hands and even bigger feet. But he had the typical "Napoleon Complex." The short man's syndrome. He was confident, borderline conceited.

"He didn't notice me from a can of paint. Not until the time I saved one of his articles from getting into the wrong hands. It was full of errors. He eventually confided in me that he suffered from dyslexia. He had a girlfriend who had always proofed his work, but they had broken up, so, that's how the article slipped through. Todd had never learned to type, and wrote everything out in longhand. He would've been too through if anyone ever found out," Dawn said. "Your daddy doesn't like to be embarrassed. He's a very proud man. Yeah, he's really proud."

Dawn had caught frightful glimpses of Todd's arrogance on the job. Whenever something didn't happen the way Todd thought it should, he would explode. He'd throw a tantrum and sometimes wreck his office in a fit of rage. He often said that the other reporters were "jealous of him," or that his editor was "playing favorites," or just plain "out to get him." Whatever the case was, Dawn found herself sympathizing with him, and eventually falling for him.

"I liked that he needed me and trusted me enough to share his vulnerabilities with me. We eventually grew very close."

They shared everything. Dawn worked long hours to help Todd, and proof his work. Eventually, Todd's thankfulness turned to love. Over Chinese food in Todd's cramped little office, once Dawn placed the last key stroke on the third revision of Todd's overdue article, he hugged her, and she heard his heart beating. The bear hug melted into passionate, urgent gropes and kisses.

With reckless regard, he shoved the contents of his crammed desk to the floor, and swung her on top of the desk. Papers, pens, and half-filled coffee mugs scattered across the crowded floor, and Todd tore at her clothes with his oversized hands.

"Wait, wait," Dawn said, and reached for the lever to close the Venetian blinds. "You need to lock the door, too, Todd."

"It's locked," he grunted, his words thick and hurried, as he nuzzled his face into her chest. Never had Dawn been taken so strongly. He yanked her argyle sweater over her head, and released her full breasts from her under-wire bra.

His big hands ravaged her body, and even though Dawn had dated men much larger than Todd, the force in which he consumed her took her by surprise. He pinched her nipples and crammed her breasts into his mouth, sucking voraciously as he pinned her arms behind her back. He bent her head over the edge of the desk and ripped a hole in her expensive pantyhose.

Dawn felt captive and helpless. Swept away with Todd's passion, she wasn't sure if she was experiencing agony or ecstasy. She formed her lips to say no, but Todd covered them with his hand. He entered her and screwed her mercilessly, and she nearly gagged as his fingers slipped in and out of her mouth. Dawn moaned and wanted to scream, but eventually her body relented to his forceful will. Todd was a loud, aggressive lover, who grunted and nearly howled when he came. He collapsed in a sweaty heap on top of her, struggling to catch his breath.

"Damn, Girl. You are something else," he said, and finally released his thick fingers from her mouth. He looked at her, with a curious expression on his face. "You really turned me on, Dawn."

Dawn was almost too afraid to move. When Todd finally slid off her, she slowly sat up, unsure of what to say. "I don't know what to say, Todd. I don't want you to think I do this with every man I see, because I don't." She slowly collected herself, smoothed her clothes down, and thought about what a mess she must be.

Todd stood, and shook himself off, and Dawn caught a glimpse of his package. For a small guy, he was pretty well-endowed. "I got that feeling, Dawn. But damn, with what you got, I kind of don't want to think of you with anyone else," he said with a wink.

Dawn still didn't know what to think or say. "What are you saying, Todd?"

"I'm saying, we obviously work well together. You know what I mean? Let's just see where this goes."

They started to spend more and more time together, and before long, Dawn and Todd were seeing each other exclusively. They had a near perfect routine. He would stay with her during the week at her apartment in Montclair, and they spent lazy weekends down at Dawn's family house in Cape May. On Monday mornings, they'd rush back to town, commuting like suburban newlyweds. They had great conversations, and wonderful debates and discussions, and Dawn liked the way Todd's mind worked. She loved his intelligence and bravado, and felt safe and secure when she was in his company. Their lovemaking was always too intense, borderline a little rough, but she eventually learned to like it. It was just his way, she had convinced herself.

She enjoyed working with Todd, and being with him, even though he was getting a little more uptight at work. It became more and more evident the one evening she and Todd were working late, and he found out that one of his fellow reporters had gotten a promotion. Todd went off.

"God-damned flunky. I swear that motherfucker must be sucking the old man's dick," Todd said as he stormed into his tiny office, where Dawn sat editing one of his articles. He was on a tight deadline for it, and it was full of errors. Dawn was straining her eyes to decipher Todd's sloppy handwriting.

"Did you hear me, Dawn?"

"Huh? I'm sorry, Todd. What did you say?"

"I said, that sorry ass motherfucker got a promotion," he said.

"Who?" Dawn asked, her eyes still scanning his rumpled pages.

"Aren't you listening to me? Bob, that 'bobbing his head' Hodges. That ass-kissing son of a bitch."

"Oh, really?" Dawn rubbed her tired eyes. "Don't worry about it, Baby. I'm sure that things will work out for you, too."

"What the fuck do you mean by that, Dawn? What the fuck you mean?" Todd's eyes turned dark and his left eye began to twitch.

"I'm just saying, things will be okay. You're a good reporter, Todd. An excellent one, at that. You'll get your promotion soon. I just know it." Dawn peered at Todd, but quickly went back to the article.

Todd kicked the door shut and stared at Dawn, a look of disbelief on his face. "What kind of shit is that? Don't talk to me like I'm some fuckin' kid."

Dawn picked up her half-empty can of Pepsi, and placed it to her lips. "I'm not, Todd. I'm just saying—"

Before Dawn could complete her sentence, Todd's huge hand had smacked the drink from her lips, and met her face with such a force that she spun around in the chair, her side ramming into the solid steel desk. The pain in her ribs was excruciating and her face stung like hell, but she was too shocked to even speak.

"Don't ever speak to me like that again, Dawn. Ever. I don't have to take this shit from you, too," Todd said, his eye twitching as he stared at her like she was a complete stranger.

Dawn rubbed her face, and tears sprung to her eyes. Her teeth felt loose and blood pooled in her mouth. "Wha- what? How could you hit me?" Dawn clutched her bruised side. "How could you?" She pushed herself away from the desk, and tried to stand, but fell forward, and had to brace herself. Her knees were slightly wobbly, and she felt dizzy and confused.

Todd's eyes blinked, like he was snapping out of a trance. "I-I told you not to talk to me like that. Okay? But, but I'm sorry, Dawn. I shouldn't have hit you." He reached for her, but she jerked away.

"Just leave me alone, Todd." Dawn grabbed her purse and took a step toward him, but changed directions. Trying to get away from him in that tiny office was not going to be easy. "I mean it." She pointed to his scribbled notes, which were now covered in dark, sticky soda. "Forget you and your article. Just leave me the hell alone."

Dawn slid past him, and freed herself from him and that office, over his protests. She went home, put ice on her face, and turned her ringer off. Todd filled her voice mail with massive apologies, and blew her cell phone and pager up. Dawn called in sick the next day, too embarrassed by her bruised face, and still nursing her aching ribs. She lost herself in the make-believe world of soap operas and let her mind vegetate when the talk shows came on. She was feeling a little better watching others whose lives were worse than hers. Unable to eat since Todd had struck her, Dawn suddenly felt hunger pangs. When Dawn ordered a pizza to be delivered, she opened her door and was shocked to find Todd standing there, holding her sausage and onion pie. And a huge bouquet of exotic flowers, which included Birds of Paradise, her absolute favorite. The gesture nearly floored her.

"Needless to say, I forgave your daddy," Dawn whispered into Asia's tiny ear. "He just didn't know his own strength," she said. Dawn, although she was almost as tall as Todd, weighed only 120 pounds, soaking wet. She was clearly no match for a rage-induced, former wrestler like Todd.

Dawn raised her daughter's arm, and it fell limply by her side. Asia snored deeply, and Dawn watched her chest rise and fall. "Well, I guess it's time for me to put you to bed." Dawn struggled to get up without waking Asia or hitting her with her sling.

Dawn managed to get Asia into her little princess bed; then she snuggled in behind her. The frilly pink ruffles from the canopy tickled Dawn's face, and she carefully placed her injured arm above Asia's head. Laying her head on a bright pink pillow, Dawn sniffed her little girl's hair. She loved the way Asia smelled of baby powder and sweet cocoa butter.

"Yes, I know you probably wonder why I forgave him, but I just did. He was so apologetic. He surprised me with this ring," Dawn said as she wiggled her fingers on her left hand, showing the sparkly, round, half-carat diamond. "He held me that day, and promised that he'd never hit me again. I really believed him. And he didn't. Well, not for a long time, anyway.

"Your father moved in with me, and he kept his word. Even though he was still pretty angry about not being promoted, within the next six months, he got offered a job working for *The New York Times*. Boy, was he thrilled! For a while, things were really going great for us.

"I went about planning our wedding, and we got a place in the East Village that was closer to your father's job. That was really nice for him, especially since he was working long hours. I was actually moving up at *The Ledger*, and I became the assistant editor of the Metro section. Todd was even happy for me, and supportive of my career, and within a year, we were married at the Manor in West Orange. It was quite an affair. Simply beautiful. Something that I'd always dreamed about, ever since I was a little girl. A wee bit older than you.

"We were quite the couple. We went to a lot of social events, and got invited to all of the nice parties. Your father was really networking with the right people, and he was getting pretty popular. He and I were also getting along so well. He got another promotion, and was really shining at the paper. He was getting quite a reputation for capturing the big stories, but things were pretty hectic for him. There were more deadlines, quicker turnarounds; everything was just kind of snowballing for him. Then the bombing of the World Trade Center in 1993 occurred, and it kind of pushed your daddy over the edge. The city was paralyzed with fear, and the police and the media were working nonstop. Your daddy clocked 14-hour days, and wasn't getting a whole lot of sleep. We were busy at my paper, too, and I was unable to help him as much. Unfortunately, your father had so many deadlines that he missed one, and he blamed me. And then, well, then he struck me again."

Todd's trance-like episodes came to dominate their relationship. "His abuse became more frequent after that. Not only physically, but mentally also. The more he stressed over work, the less supportive he was of my career. I guess he felt somewhat threatened. But, I never wanted to think that. When my editor went out sick and I was temporarily promoted to Metro Editor, he really beat me. He said that I was trying to usurp his position as the breadwinner in the family. He also said that I really didn't care about him, and that I was being selfish. But, he couldn't have been more wrong. I loved your father, and wanted nothing more than to be there for him. In every way. Even though he was physically abusive to me."

Her world became his. Todd would question any of Dawn's actions, and slowly cut her off from the few friends she had.

Todd's mental cruelty toward Dawn was nearly as severe as the physical. He would berate and belittle her, constantly undermining her capabilities. Even though Dawn knew she was a good editor, she began to question her skills, too. She was beginning to think that maybe she should quit working, and the answer came, when she discovered she was pregnant.

At first, Todd was less than enthusiastic. But for Dawn, maybe it meant that he'd stop putting his hands on her. And then, her career wouldn't be as important. She could go out on maternity leave, and just not return. That would make one of their issues go away. Or, so she thought.

She started the ritual of talking to her womb, while Todd remained detached and aloof. When her pregnancy became difficult, Dawn took an early leave of absence from her job. After her first amniocentesis, it was determined that her baby was going to be a little girl, and Dawn was elated. Being at home, when she wasn't feeling ill, Dawn was now able to again help Todd with his work, and things slightly improved between them. She had even started doing some freelance editing for Sutton House, a major publishing company in New York. When Asia was born, the world seemed to be right, for the first time in a long time.

Asia was a beautiful child, born with inquisitive eyes, a head full of thick, curly hair and a cherubic face. Todd took to her with a fascination and interest he had only briefly shown in Dawn. It made Dawn happy, though, to know that she had been able to bring this little bundle of joy into the world, and that Asia might possibly be the tool to repair their troubled relationship. Todd had been awarded a news industry prize for his article on the Central Park jogger case, revisited, and he had gotten a huge bonus and an even bigger byline. As Asia grew, they were quite the happy family. That was, until Dawn got offered a job as a full-time editor at Sutton House, and accepted. She figured that Todd would be fine with it, but he wasn't. He beat her savagely and ferociously, and never stopped.

"Why do you make me do this to you?" he'd always say after he had nearly beaten her to a bloody pulp. And Dawn wondered why she provoked him into hitting her. She never cooked well enough. She didn't make love to him often enough. The apartment was never clean enough. Her friends called her too much. She stayed on the phone too long. She went out too much. She stayed in too much. She didn't take care of him well enough. She had let her looks go. She was too fat. She was too skinny. She could never do anything right. The only thing she could do was take an ass-whipping. Black eyes and split lips were her daily accessories, like jewelry. Dawn learned to apply expensive makeup to cover the scars, and wore long-sleeved shirts in the summertime to hide the bruises, but her spirit was broken. The only real joy she had in her life was Asia, and she began to fear that Todd would want to take that away from her as well.

But, he seemed to love Asia, and treated her well. He'd lavish her with gifts, and read to her, and play funny little learning games with her. At first, Dawn was relieved by their closeness, and appreciative of the fact that he didn't hit her in front of their baby. But then Todd began to talk down to Dawn when Asia was there, and began loudly denouncing and belittling her. Despite their evening ritual together, Dawn began to feel that Asia was slipping away from her. Her daughter's little face absolutely shined when Todd was around, and even though she was only four, Dawn felt that Asia was somehow looking at her differently now. It was confirmed this evening, just before Todd left for his evening out. As Dawn stood there, her arm in a sling from her shoulder having been dislocated by Todd the week before, she witnessed an act that had spun her world completely out of control. Todd picked Asia up, and kissed both of her cheeks.

"Daddy loves you best, Asia-boo," he said. "And Daddy will always love you best, as long as you grow up to be a fine, young lady. A good girl. Not like your mother."

Dawn could barely raise her head, but did so just in time to catch her daughter's cherubic face staring at her with empty, disappointed eyes. "I will, Daddy. I will," Asia cooed, and kissed her daddy's face.

The image of Todd whisking Asia onto her feet brought a conclave of upsetting images back into Dawn's mind. They created a convergence point of her past and her present. Her father had said the exact same thing to her. When she was around Asia's age.

"Oh, I loved your granddaddy, Asia. I kind of wish that he was here to see you now, I guess."

Dawn had grown up in the early '70's, the product of an outspoken Black militant named Carl Boyer and a naïve, White flower child named Margaret. A tall, thin brunette with a thick, New England accent, Margaret Reilly was known as Peggy, and she hailed from a large, protective, affluent, Boston, Irish-Catholic family. When Peggy came to New York, she was fresh from Brown University and her equally sheltered environment. She had never had much exposure to black people, other than her family servants. When she became a social worker in the horrific New York welfare system, Peggy was both amazed and appalled. Tenements, rat-infested apartments and boarded-up buildings were a culture shock to her. The conditions she encountered on a daily basis sometimes left her shaking and unhinged, but she was determined to make a difference in the lives of the families she worked with. Her other Ivy League friends thought that she had taken leave of her senses for subjecting herself to such an unpleasant lifestyle. They figured that she'd last a few weeks against the rigors and lackluster reward of working for the system. And if that didn't do it, they knew that she'd run back home to her family's expansive Cape Cod home after stepping over bums to get to her small hovel of an apartment in the heart of grimy Greenwich Village. Peggy, unwavering in her own quiet way, refused to bow to the pressure her family and friends heaped on her. Her boyfriend of several years even threatened to break up with her if she refused to find a more suitable job, like an administrative assistant or secretary.

Peggy defied them all, and delved even harder into the public assistance programs. That's when she met Carl. He was a proud, tall, stocky, black man, who wore a huge Afro and vivid dashikis. He was a former Black Panther, who tirelessly worked in the boroughs and neighborhoods of New York, seeking change and spearheading protests. At their chance encounter, Carl was heading up a "Breakfast for the Kids" program in Brooklyn.

Even though Carl had never dated a white woman before, he was instantly intrigued by Peggy. Her naiveté and humble demeanor were appealing to his brusque, streetwise manner, and the diversity of their backgrounds was both appealing and confusing. For Carl, there was an underlying motive for brothers who got involved with white women. It was one way that the black men had of "getting back at the Man." Even if it meant that it would cause further harm or danger to them, it was worth it. It afforded him the opportunity to antagonize "Whitey." To really "stick it to the Man."

Carl's and Peggy's paths crossed again when Peggy came to check on one of the children in Carl's program, and their attraction was undeniable. For Peggy, Carl represented everything foreign and exciting. He was big, Black, dangerous and rebellious. To Carl, Peggy was a trophy. She was educated, humble and committed to a cause that even unnerved him sometimes. Theirs was an interesting union, one fueled by titillation, irony, passion, and anger. And Carl dominated Peggy, who willingly submitted to his wrath and contempt like she owed it to him. Or to his kind.

Despite the success Carl had working with the various community groups and social programs, Carl became increasingly discontent with the low pay, and sought greater status for his hard work ethic. He was a very bright man, and finished college at Columbia University, with honors. He continued working and even took an entry-level white collar job in the financial district as a data entry clerk. Peggy kept working as a social worker, while Carl went to school at night. Frustrated with his inability to advance at work, Carl took almost five years, but he graduated, with honors, from SUNY with his M.B.A., and was ready to take on the world.

Dawn was born on a snowy day: December 15, 1972. A beautiful complexion, with a head full of curly locks, Dawn was a gorgeous baby. Peggy became a full-time housewife, and the family moved out to Mount Vernon. Dawn was the apple of her father's eye, and the older she became, the more he lavished his love and attention on her. Peggy became a withered, ghost-like figure, who bowed down to her little Dawn. Though Carl was becoming more successful in his career, it didn't stop him from belittling, or beating Peggy. Dawn was his little angel, wings and all, and Peggy was the devil incarnate.

Even after Peggy gave birth to Dawn's brother Paul, their life at home went from bad to worse. The pedestal Carl placed Dawn on elevated higher and higher, while the bowels of depravation he dug for Peggy descended deeper and deeper.

"You can't ever do anything right, Woman!" Carl would yell at Peggy. Her mother's pale, milk white skin had become ashen and gray, and she looked much older than her thirty-something years. The years of degradation had taken a toll on her; even as a child, Dawn felt like her mother wasn't that close to her. And Dawn remembered not wanting to be close to her mother. It was quite confusing for the little girl when her father would shower her with praise, but in the next breath, call her mother "trifling" or "worthless."

"I don't know why I deal with your dumb ass, anyway, Margaret," her father said. He always called her Margaret when he was getting ready to take her down a few notches. "You're nothing to me. Nothing. You can't do anything right. You can't keep this house clean, and you damn sure can't cook. This house smells like an ashtray. You can't even get my shirts cleaned properly. The only thing you can do is host a damned cocktail party. I swear I don't know why I married your sorry ass."

Most of the time, Peggy would just listen quietly, as Carl vented at her. On rare occasions, she'd curse at him, in her thick, nasally accent, but that only served to make him angrier. He would surely beat her if she dared to say anything back to him.

Cowering and worn down, Peggy became a quintessential nanny to her children. She never questioned Dawn about any of her activities, just squired Dawn and Paul around while she became a chain-smoking, functioning alcoholic. Her mornings started with a huge Bloody Mary and a pack of Pall Malls. Lunch consisted of dirty, dry martinis and another pack of cigarettes, and dinner was a full bottle of wine, sometimes two, and another pack of smokes. After dinner was a stiff Scotch on the rocks and more 120's. Dessert was usually a vicious beating from Carl over some minor infraction, followed by tears, more puffs of smoke and downed cocktails.

Carl was known to take a drink or two of alcohol also, but for the most part, he remained sober. There was never any clear indication of what fueled his frustration with Peggy. He was just so irritated with her, that his verbal abuse was ever present. Caustic and relentless, he would annihilate Peggy with his inhuman words, and then he would wink at Dawn, and tell her that she had the best of both worlds. She was beautiful, and she'd be smart, like him. Not a waste, like her mother. And those words rang in Dawn's ears as loudly as they did that day, years ago. "Daddy loves you best. And Daddy will always love you best, as long as you grow up to be a fine, young lady. A good girl. Not like your mother."

"I promised not to grow up like my mother, Precious. And, unfortunately, I have. And the sad part about it is that I've turned you into me." Dawn sighed to her sleeping child.

"I grew up hating my mother. I thought that she was weak and incompetent, and just plain sorry. She couldn't make my daddy happy, and he was a good man. He really loved me. And she wasn't good for him. She didn't know how to give him what he needed. But, I knew that I'd grow up and be happily married, because I'd know what to do. I'd know how to make my husband happy. And now, I realize that I haven't been able to do that. I can't believe that I've failed so miserably," Dawn said, her voice drawn, but filled with resolve.

"But, I promise to make it right for you, Asia. I do. I can't have you growing up hating me. I just can't. My mother and I were never close, and even after your grandfather died, I blamed her for not being a better person. A better wife. A better mother. I can't have you feeling the same way about me."

Dawn couldn't believe how her life had become a near mirror image of her mother's. The sight of Todd and Asia interacting brought those memories flooding back to her. As a little girl, she idolized her father, and ignored the humiliation and degradation he subjected her mother to. She never gave her mother credit for anything, and though her mother might not have been perfect, she was her mother. And her mother never abandoned her, even if she wasn't the mother Dawn wished she could have been.

Dawn sighed again, and stroked the back of her little girl's head. Her arm was getting sore. She looked over at the nightstand, and noticed her bottle of pain pills. Sliding out of bed, Dawn went in the kitchen to get a glass of water. She stood at the sink and filled her glass from the tap, nearly over-running it. She absently walked back into Asia's room, where she quietly sat on the edge of the bed.

Instead of reaching for the pills, Dawn picked up the cordless phone and dialed it. After several rings, someone finally picked up.

"Hello?" The woman's deep, raspy voice was slightly slurred. Dawn looked at the clock. It was only eight-thirty, and her mother was three sheets to the wind already.

"Hello, Mother," Dawn said, and immediately wondered why she had called her.

Her mother coughed, a deep, hacking cough that reminded Dawn of the fact that Peggy was now battling emphysema, too. "Dawn? Is that you?" Her voice was still thick with that Boston accent.

Dawn wondered how a mother couldn't recognize her own child's voice. Dawn realized that it was the alcohol talking.

"Yes, Mother. I was just calling to see how you were doing."

Her mother hacked again. "I'm doing okay, Dear. How are you?" She finished the sentence with a long wheeze.

Dawn sighed, and just wanted to hang the phone up. "I'm okay, I guess." She hesitated, and caressed her throbbing arm. "Mother, I really need to talk to you." She paused, searching to find the right words that screamed from her heart. "Why did you allow Daddy to treat you like he did?"

Peggy hacked again, and Dawn could hear the phlegm rising in her mother's throat. Dawn also heard her mother take a long swallow. "Wha- what are you talking about, Dawn? Your father was a good man."

The denial echoed in Dawn's ears. "Good man? To whom?"

"To you, Dear. You were the apple of his eye, or don't you recall?" Peggy asked, and Dawn overheard the sound of ice clinking against a glass.

Dawn sighed again, and grabbed the painkillers. Now was the time for her to take a deep swallow as she tossed in two of the capsules and washed them down with the lukewarm tap water. "I recall. But, I'm not talking about me. I'm talking about you."

"I don't know what you're talking about, Dawn. Are you okay?" her mother asked, the avoidance and denial in her voice rising.

"You don't know what I'm talking about? How could you not know? The way he used to talk to you. The way he treated you. How he used to hit you. Beat on you. Is that bringing back any memories?"

Carl had been dead less than two years. Surely Peggy could not have forgotten the years of abuse she suffered, but she remained adamant about it. In her eyes, Carl was a saint.

"I'm not sure where you're going with this, Dawn, but this subject is closed. I don't feel like traipsing back down memory lane with you; especially if I don't have the same so-called memories that you do. Now," Peggy said, her speech even more slurred. "If you have something more pleasant to talk about, we can. Otherwise—"

"Otherwise what? The conversation is over? Mother, please. For the first time in my life, why don't you talk to me? Don't you realize how important this is? But this is always how you've been. Out in la-la land. In an eternal state of denial. Sucked down in a bottle of booze. You were never there when I needed you."

"What are you saying? I was always there for you, Dawn Lynn. Always."

"You never protected me," Dawn said, as she struggled to keep her voice quiet, but the rage was escalating her tone.

"Protected you from what? Your father never did anything to you. He never touched you. Never."

"Oh, so you remember that. That's not the point. He never did anything to me, but you let me see him do everything to you. You don't think that damaged me? Huh?"

"Oh, please. How could it? You were perfect. You were Daddy's little girl. How could that be such a bad thing?"

"It was, Mother. It was. It made me feel like you were worthless. That you were incompetent. And it made me despise you."

Peggy's line grew quiet, and Dawn heard the sound of ice cracking. She realized that Peggy was pouring more liquor into her glass.

"So, you've been carrying that around all of these years? So, you despise me, huh?" Peggy asked.

"Yes, I did. I hated you for not protecting me. And for ultimately turning me into you."

Dawn clicked the off button, and slammed the receiver down. Tears flowed down her cheeks as she stormed into the living room, where she ransacked the cabinets in the wall unit until she found a bottle of Stolichnaya Vodka. She tucked it under her injured arm, then picked up an old-fashioned glass. Through a tear-filled haze, she stumbled back into Asia's room.

"Thank you, Mother. I guess I have completely become you," Dawn said as she poured the clear liquor into the glass until it kissed the rim. She wiped the tears and snot from her face, and carefully sat down on Asia's bed. She patted her daughter on her back, and noticed that Asia's breaths were slow and shallow. "Don't worry, Baby. Mommy's not going to fail you. You'll never grow up hating me, nor will you turn out like me. I'll take care of that, Baby. I promise." Dawn sniffled, reached over and kissed the back of her baby's head.

Then she picked up the bottle of Dalmane. It was half-empty because, earlier, she had taken out ten tablets, crushed them, and mixed them into Asia's chocolate sauce. Dawn poured the remaining pills into her mouth, and held them until they slightly dissolved. She placed the glass of Stoli's to her lips, and forced the bitter concoction down her throat.

She nestled back into bed with Asia, and placed a loving arm around her only daughter. "Mommy loves you, Asia. I never want you to be like me. Never. Never." And slowly, Dawn's words turned into her second favorite lullaby.

"Hush little baby, don't you cry…"
VICTIM OR VICTOR… SOMETIMES NEITHER PREVAILS.

Collen Dixon is the author of Simon Says, Behind Closed Doors… In My Father's House, *and* Every Shut Eye. *She has just finished her fourth novel,* Relative Secrets, *which completes the* Simon Says *"quadrilogy." An avid reader, Collen enjoys Feng Shui and tending to her bonsai trees, collecting art and automobiles. She also enjoys "viewing the world from two wheels," skiing, traveling and entertaining. A huge movie buff, she recently successfully underwent treatment for an addiction to online auctions. She and Chadwick, her fur-faced little boy, currently reside in Mitchellville, MD. Her motto is "Always be grateful, never be satisfied."*

THE GRINDSTONE

NANE QUARTAY

I knew there was something desperate in the night, when I saw the brightness of the sparks that shot off the blade of the machete. And so...that night, I ran.

I ran down Upwards Alley, over to Front Street, and up the hill to my house. I only lived two long blocks up on the top of Front Street, but the street was so deep that I was catching my breath in heaving gasps by the time I made it to our front door. All out of breath and shit!

My youngest sister, Tammy, was sitting out front on a bench that sat alongside the house, watching my two-year-old brother toddling around on the ground. She barely gave me a glance as I stood there, breathing hard but trying not to show it. My oldest sister, Toby, came riding up on her bicycle, hopped off, and went inside the front door. I waited until I heard her footsteps fade away up the stairs and then I began to plot on her bike, laying there where she had let it fall. Toby's bicycle was one of those girl's bikes; no metal bar for me to fall on and hurt my undeveloped manhood. I was so small that I couldn't reach the pedals while I was sitting on the seat, so the absence of that metal bar was crucial. The missing tube created a gap that allowed me to pedal the bike while I was standing up and I triumphantly rode around and around in circles on the sidewalk. Boy! I can't wait till I'm big enough to ride a boy's bike! This delicious thought pedaled around in my head as I rode and turned on the bicycle.

The sound of breaking glass messed up my flow. I looked up in time to see my lucky horseshoe, the one I had won at school, come flying out of the window. It landed right in the middle of the street. The next thing I heard was my father's voice. He was drunk. Know how I know? He was always drunk!

"How you bring a bastard up in my house!"

It was a statement. My statement. My stepfather's description of me. When he was drunk, it was his only description of me. I wouldn't say that I hate him. There has got to be a better word for my feelings than "hate." Yet, he found his hatred of me became intensified when it was mixed with vodka. He was a big man...compared to me. He was a smart man...compared to me. He was a man...compared to me. To me, he was the evil that turned off every emotion I ever had, every feeling, the devil who endangered my very sanity and killed the childhood part of my life. He rampaged on my teenage years, that time of life when relationships develop, some in the most intimate of ways, where bits and pieces of your-self are defined by the company you keep, the friends that you make. The years when life is sweet and carefree... not just painful day-to-day hell. My father did that. My daddy.

He wasn't my real daddy, though. He was only my stepfather but what's the difference... especially if you don't know who your real daddy is anyway.

I fucking hate him. Yeah. That fits better.

I remember the first time he hit me. He tried to punch me with a man-punch, a hard man-punch, straight to my face. I was way too small to take that blow and I could see that shit comin'. I ducked away enough, but not all the way enough, and his knuckle caught me right in the eye. Shit! That shit hurt! My eye was all swollen and shit.

Maaannnn! I can't wait till I get big!

I had gone back to turning circles on the sidewalk, losing myself in the endless 'O's when I heard his voice again. "Woman! I will fuck you up!"

"WHY?!" my mother screamed.

"Stupid shit! You better—"

"So, why then?! Why you hit me?!"

"'Cause, Woman..."

For a long second, there was silence, and then the unmistakable sound of a hard, solid fist hitting soft, pliable flesh. Plappp! I paused to look up for an instant—knowing my black-ass stepfather was beatin' on my mother again. But I messed up when I took my eyes off the sidewalk. The bike swerved and I veered off the curb. To this day, I still don't know how it all happened. Next thing I know, I'm rolling down Front Street, down the steepest hill I had ever seen in my life. I didn't panic; not in my recollection. I really don't remember panicking. I remember looking down toward the bottom of that hill and seeing the houses come rushing by me. I remember seeing there weren't any cars in my lane, but I do recall a few cars coming toward me in the opposite lane. The bike began to gather speed and I felt soon I would be flying... and I didn't have wings! There was no way I was going to be able to stop that bike without fucking myself up. A random thought occurred to me. There ain't no way this is gonna end right!

In a desperate flash, Upwards Alley appeared on my right-hand side and my mind pictured the steepness of that sloping hill. If I could make that turn into the alley, I would be able to let gravity stop my momentum so I could fall off safely to the side and bring the bike back on home.

Yeah! I could do that shit! Shit?

I remember turning the handlebars to make the turn, but it was the first time I ever tried to make a real-time turn on a bicycle and I didn't quite make it. My front wheel hit the curb right in front of Donnell Shunt's house and I flipped. Well, actually the bike and I flipped through the air and I landed upside-down and totally! fucked! Up! My shoe had somehow come off in mid-air and my toe was smashed on the concrete. It was a pulpy, bloody mess. I felt the pain shooting up my leg so intensely, I was able to ignore the throbbing flare of the giant, knot swelling over my left ear. My head felt like someone had shoved a steel cue ball inside my head and left it there for me to grow on. I could feel it... expanding. I felt blood leaking through the cuts and scrapes on my body; my forearm had a deep gash that left a wicked-looking scar I carry to this day. My vision was colored by pain... but I was alive!

Donnell Shunt's grandfather was sitting on the front porch, smiling. He seemed kinda far away from me, his bony body a mish-mash of angles and sticks. Now that I look back on it, he seemed like, somehow like... distant. The porch was only three steps high but his voice always seems to come out of a tunnel in my memory.

He said, "You gonna get up from there, Boy?"

Famous last words.

There was a sharp, piercing scream, a war-chant, as his wife, Jessie Mae, came sprinting up behind the old man with the machete held high. It was held back, like Thor's hammer, and I can still see lightning in the reflection of the sharpened edge... and I can still remember when she swung it. I saw it mechanically... I saw the finer points of a perfect home run swing, the way a baseball coach would teach it. The swing started at shoulder height and went forward. Her hips opened up, building on the momentum generated... as the blade went forward. She pushed off with the speed gathered from her running start and stopped on a perfect dime, pivot and swing. It was power. Perfect execution. Pure power when the long blade of the machete sliced through the old man's neck...flesh, blood and bone... and cut his head clean off. It just lopped off from the initial "pop" of his blood, his life force, before it bounced off the ground, like, maybe twice, and rolled a little down the street. His body... his body fell out of the chair. Plop. Dead. The old lady stood there for what seemed like a silent forever, entranced by the scene splayed out before her eyes, hypnotized as reality started to materialize to her conscious mind. She saw his spurting blood.

And she screamed. And screamed. And screamed some more. "Willie Bobo, head off, mothafucka! Willie Bobo, head off!"

I remember struggling to my feet. The pain from my injuries became a mere background hum of an ache. I remember standing there. Watching. I don't remember any thought patterns. No fear. No disgust. No abject terror. I just stood there. My vision would register sensory images and send them to my brain, but there was no verbalization of ideas. I saw what was going on but, no, I can't say a single thought entered my mind. I guess life can be so random sometimes, huh?

But the old lady. Jessie Mae! The old lady lost it. She screamed like a banshee until the police arrived. When they got there, she dove, threw her body, face first into her husband's pouring blood. There was plenty of it, flowing down the sidewalk. His life's essence paying the cost of inflicting pain on another life—with man-punches to the face. Counting the cost that life is sweet, every life, and that a soul cries out to be free... no matter the cost.

It was the ending of the cycle. There would be no more pain.

The old man's body lay there, of course, but it looked like all of his blood and guts were rushing toward the opening where his head used to be. It looked like wormy guts and thick blood were pulsing, desperately straining to get loose, but only rivulets of brackish liquid oozed out. I stayed there, transfixed, until the firemen washed all the red fluid down the street. I looked down at my smashed and bloody toe. It didn't hurt anymore.

The front wheel of the bike was bent so I limped, walking the bike back up the hill, dumped it out front, and went inside our house. My mother looked at me.

"What happened to you?" she asked, mildly interested.

"I flipped my bike." I exhaled as I flopped on the couch.

"And tore your head up?"

I nodded my head in reply.

"That's what you get! Good for your ass, then," she intoned. "Didn't I tell you about that shit? You always doin' shit. You need to learn to sit ya ass down somewhere."

My insides were hollow as I told my mother what Donnell Shunt's grandmother had done to her husband's head. I had an image stuck in my mind. A picture of his guts straining to escape from his headless neck.

"She did that with a knife?" My mother looked me in the eyes.

"A machete, you know, those long knives," I answered.

"Musta been sharp, then."

"Ma, she swung that knife like she was a home run king! It was like... like... flop and crunchy when his head came off. It went... like thump and crunch all at the same time. Nasty."

I told her how I had seen Jessie Mae sharpening the blade on the grindstone earlier that day, shortly before she took her husband's head off.

I knew there was something desperate in the night, when I saw the brightness of the sparks that shot off the blade of the machete. Once again, I felt utterly alone. The flashes of light drew me like a magnet, so I crept over and watched the woman through the slats of the wooden fence. Her face was set in a mad glare as she worked the grindstone, turned the wheel, and aimed for the razor's edge, moving the blade back and forth, watching intently as a sharp point began to materialize. An old lady. New in town. She was Donnell Shunt's grandma. Her husband had recently moved with her to our small town of Hudson from somewhere down South—Louisiana, I think.

I had seen her husband sitting on the front porch a few times. He was a rail-thin old man, rather fragile-looking, now that I think back on it, and he liked to sit outside and watch the people of the small town go strolling by. He would sit there with a grin on his face, smiling and waving at folks—at strangers that he didn't even know. He seemed like a nice enough guy.

I wondered why his wife was in the backyard sharpening a knife. She was a little sturdier than her husband. Her arms had little coils of muscle that were formed with strength developed from years of labor in kitchens, laundry rooms, and other roles of servitude. Yeah, she looked quite comfortable, familiar with the feel and handle of a sharp blade. I noticed the way she held it like a hammer. No, not a hammer; more like Mjolnir, the God of Thunder's hammer... with a two-handed grip. It meant something to her.

She paused and straightened up, wiping her brow with the back of her hand as she looked cautiously around the yard. I crouched down behind the slat of the fence as best I could when she looked in my direction. Their house stood on the corner of Front Street and Upwards Alley, a full, two-family home with a small-sized yard that stretched out behind it. I stood on the Upwards Alley side, a spot that was at the dead bottom end of the hill which stretched up, high toward the sky. Upwards was our getaway alley. We used to roll car tires down the curve of that hillside and watch them as they banged real hard into the doors of passing cars. The angry driver would emerge from his damaged car and spot us at the top of the hill before we would take off running. They would never catch us. It was too steep to sprint Upwards!

"Jessie Mae! Get in here, Woman!"

The old woman froze in place.

"Jessie Mae! Don't make me come out there, Bitch! 'Cause if I do, I'll have to run yo' slut ass in that river down there! Get in here!"

The old woman turned, flung the back door open, and hurried inside. I could see them through the opened door as she ran over to her husband.

"What you want, Baby?" she stated in desperation when she stopped in front of him. He responded with a savage, straight right hand, a man-punch, to her face. She collapsed to the floor like a sack of meat. I heard her cry of pain from where I stood and then I watched him kick her in the ribs.

"What you doin' back there? Huh?"

She coughed in pain before she groaned her reply, "Nuthin'."

"How the fuck you gonna be outside doin' nuthin'! Stupid bitch."

He knelt down in front of her and crawled between her legs. He wedged his crotch in between her thighs and began a hard, dominant grind. I saw her body buck from the contact as he invaded her, and I could hear his animal grunts as he bucked up into her. His hips dipped and thrust into her with solid contact that pushed her legs further and further apart. She lay beneath him, unmoving until he pushed himself to his knees and slowly leaned back before barking out a command to her.

"Take it out!"

The old lady, tentatively, reached up and unbuckled his pants. She pulled his swollen dick free.

"Kiss it!" he barked. "Hurry up! Kiss it! Kiss it good!"

I saw the old lady's head moving around in circular motions.

"That's it, Baby." His voice was gruff. "Give me head. Let me feel some suction." His hands reached up and snaked around the back of her head. He pulled her head forcefully toward his pelvis, his hardness stabbing the back of her throat, gagging her. "Kiss it and then suck it! Head! Head!" His body bucked a few times and he gripped her head and pulled it one last time and held it there while he groaned with release.

"Damn!" he growled. "Yo' lips be pullin' on me like you gonna take the head right off my Willie Bobo. Yeah. You gonna take Willie Bobo's head off, Baby? Huh? Kiss it one more time. Now, put it back."

She deftly tucked his shrunken member in his pants and buckled him up.

"Now. Next time? See what you get!" He lashed out again and punched her in the chest. She collapsed to the side. "Next time, you better take Willie Bobo's head off, dark bitch!"

He kicked her once again, turned, and walked back out the front door. He sat back in his chair on the front porch, laughing... her prone, beaten body a forgotten afterthought. I could see her through the back door and waited in silence for a moment. She didn't lie there much longer than that. Then she was pulling herself to her feet. Jessie Mae rose silently, dealing with the pain and pushing it down into nowhere land, a place of yesterday, the ache fading, soon to be a distant thing. But Jessie Mae's face wore a scowl, an angry determination mixed with an animosity that seemed to touch her soul and harden the dark light that shone from her eyes. She limped back out to the porch and brought herself up tall, gathering her strength and looking to the sky. As I watched her face, I wished that I was old enough to read emotions. Old enough to see the emotional pain... the psychological scars, the rape and torture of the old woman's spirit and heart. I wished. But all I saw was the hard line of her tight lips, the fire in her eyes, and the hatred that radiated from her in darkness... and tears not shed. Everybody has those, though. Tears that don't show.

Her face was swollen, bruised, and busted as her lips trembled and began to swell. A dark, red splat of blood leaked from the corner of her mouth. It seemed to pulse to the time of a heartbeat. And then I saw sparkles in her eyes. A mad flame that spoke of bad things...her eyes burned. She bent over and firmly grasped the handle of the machete. Slowly, she turned and looked directly at me.

And I ran.

"He was sitting on the porch and she came out and she chopped his head off." I finished the story. I left off the part about running, though.

My mother glared at me before she spoke. "That man's head did not come off! You got to learn to stop imaginin' shit all the time. That's what you get!"

She still didn't believe me. She would, eventually, when the news got around, so I didn't even tell her all she had to do was look out of the window and she could see that the fire trucks were still there.

"For real, Ma. I ain't lyin'!"

She looked at me hard. Not as if she really thought that I was too imaginary and whatnot. Her eyes were hard. Then I remembered that my stepfather had just got up off beating on her. She wasn't in the mood for any type of talking.

"Did I say you was lyin'?" she growled.

Shit! I groaned. I just knew that there wasn't a right answer to that question. I knew my mother. I knew her looks... and the current look was red hot. But, for once in my life, I didn't care. I needed some "kid time" to think about shit. I needed space.

"I just said I ain't lyin'," I blurted out.

She slapped me. Straight to the cheekbone, nuthin' but net! Which, alone, didn't hurt that bad. My mother didn't have bruising hand speed, but this time, Ma was rocking me with electric blows. My bruised skull was ringing savagely with each stinging contact that my face was taking. My vision blurred for a second... and then I went numb. I mean, by mind went blank. It hurt a little, but I could take it. See, my mother would whup my ass in short bursts... twenty, thirty seconds of pure fury, but if I could survive that? I consider that ass-whuppin' a success! Then she slapped me again. And again. And again. In the midst of this assault, I began to notice my mother had developed a little more power—from somewhere! Her stamina was improving, too. She wasn't stopping. Slap! Slap! Slap!

"Why you hittin' me, Ma?!" Slap! "Why?!" Slap! "Go ahead, then!" Slap! "I can take it!" Slap! "I can take it!" Slap! "I look like my daddy, huh?!" Slap! "I am my daddy, huh?!" Slap! "Right?!" Slap! "I can take it!"

A lone tear welled up in my eyes, stinging but holding, refusing to creep down my face. She stopped with her hand paused in mid-air, the hatred in my stare burning with spite, me feeling like she wasn't my mother; she couldn't tell me she cared. She cried out incoherent words of pain that I couldn't even begin to understand and I wouldn't have understood them even if I could understand them. She was the reason I was always utterly alone, with no one on my side, no one to turn to whenever my stepfather got abusive. I don't know what it was. I never knew what it was, the total loneness; the disconnection between my mother and me. But, I knew she did not like me. By that, I mean that she couldn't stand me. But, she still didn't have to hit me.

I finally jumped up and ran out the front door. I limped around the house to the backyard, up the back steps, and hid on the back porch. I sat there quietly and listened. I could hear my mother through the window as she began to cry in pain and frustration. My face was still stinging from the force of her blows and all of my body's aches and pains rushed through me. I still couldn't find any vestiges of love for her...not in my heart. She knew that pain was wrong. She saw it up close and personal every day, and yet that was her gift to me. The long right hand of love. I wondered exactly how much of that torture was my mere existence costing her. I wished I could help her. But she still didn't have to hit me.

A few days later, I took my mother down by Donnell Shunt's house and showed her the grindstone. It had been moved over to the far corner of the yard, tucked, sinister in the darkness. I told my mother about the sparks and the sharp, shiny point of the blade. I told her about the strength Jessie Mae got from holding that powerful weapon in her hands. Even after her husband had held her down and violated her, she had found the control of her own destiny in the weighted heft of the knife.

Over the next three weeks, my stepfather rampaged on, beating on my mother constantly and my mother, in turn, found reasons to beat on me. But, now I understood my mother's motivation and, more importantly, I shared the passion of her need for payback, for some sense of ultimate justice, for someone to hear her cry. Subsequently, after each of the many violent episodes in which my mother was beaten and she, in turn, would beat me, I began taking her to the grindstone. While we stood in the darkened yard, I began to plant the seeds of violent retribution in her mind. I began to give form and shape to the primal urges that lurk within the psyche of the abused until, one day, I noticed a strange gleam come into her eyes;

another persona emerged as we became more and more comforted by the sight of the huge grindstone. Who knows, maybe she was having those dark matters dancing in the madness of her imagination.

One night, my stepfather came home late and pushed my mother straight to the edge of madness. He beat my sister.

Tamia was my youngest sister. She was still lost in her ignorance at times and she always managed to stay out of my stepfather's way. I will give him credit; my stepfather usually left the girls alone, physically at least. He still stomped around them with terror in his stride, but usually that was all he would do to the girls and Tamia was still enough of a child to reap the benefits of being the youngest girl. She still had the ability to sing to my stepfather, still had the ability to soothe him, to bring his anger in to where he could look at it and let it die. "I like the taste of cann-dee. Sweetness is my pool. I like the taste of caann-dee. And I like you!"

I, for one, hated that freaking song. But it worked for her...so she sang for him whenever she saw bad trouble on my stepfather's drunken radar. The big behemoth was bearing down on her now, his voice gruff and grating at the fears of his child, carrying a lifetime of trembling on its timbre.

"Didn't I tell you to bring me some algae syrup, Gurl? My chil'ren is all so stupid. Didn't I say algae syrup? Didn't I?" He was on a rant. "All my dumb chil'ren."

Tamia looked up at him with eyes widened in apprehension. Her daddy was chocolate thunder, dark lightning, and streaks of a painful storm. He was a black hulk, both dark and intimidating...the bare essence of a scary nightmare to a fragile, little girl. He bent over her, his bulk casting a huge shadow over her as he pointed a stubby finger in her direction.

"Girl, you so dumb. How you remember shit? You get it from yo' mama, though. Yeah. She stupid, too. Be like a dumb slut sometimes. Now, have you ever seen me eat anything else but algae syrup? Have you?!" He was screaming at Tamia. Each harsh word pulled an anguished cry from her as she cowered from him, her eyes darting wildly, anxiously, searching for an avenue of escape. His temper was brewing like a big, black storm...and his dark cloud was heavy with his violent nature. She was going to be drenched in the fierce downpour. His very face was turbulent. A raw mixture of a blind rage and primitive urges wrapped in the guise of a man. We could only guess that violence had always been a part of his life. After all, he was turbulent; his very nature was based on intimidation as a means of control. A tool to terrify us with. Fear.

I lived the fear as I watched him tower over Tamia. I lived her moments of paralyzed anguish as I stood witness. We both knew his movements, knew when to prepare for serious episodes from him, and we saw it in the curl of his lips that were pulled back in a sneer. I wasn't able to move as I watched him bend over my little sister and wrap his big hand around her throat. He lifted her up with no effort as she feebly kicked her legs, flailing, as he spit harsh words and spittle into her face.

"I want algae-muthafuckin' syrup! You hear me?!"

And then he flung her at the living room wall. Tamia's little body slammed face first into the wall and she shrieked in pain when she fell in a heap on the sofa. When she turned over, blood splashed from the corner of her mouth and the left side of her face was swollen and discolored with bruises. Tears streamed down her face as she pulled herself to her knees and looked up at her drunken daddy.

She began a mad singsong. "I like the taste of cann-dee. Sweetness is my pool. I like the taste of caann-dee. And I like you!" She sang haltingly; her voice strained around the pain that throbbed in her face. "I like the taste of cann-dee." Tamia wiped the blood away from the corner of her mouth. "Sweetness is my pool." My stepfather hesitated with his hand raised to strike her. "I like the taste of caann-dee. And I like you!"

I heard a piercing scream and turned to see my mother flash past me in a blur. She swung her fist and connected solidly with my stepfather's face, rocking him backwards with the force of the blow. She attacked in a mad frenzy. She was throwing punches in bunches, scratches and straight rights that rained down, but didn't move the heavy drunk and he began to shrug off her frenzied attack. He howled with rage and lashed out at my mother, catching her in the side of her head, stunning her, and then he rammed her with his shoulder, sending her body crashing into the wall.

I could tell that my mother was really hurt this time. Hurt badly. I heard her tortured breathing as she slid to the floor in a limp heap.

"Stupid whore." My stepfather looked down at her and gingerly touched his swelling lip. Then he turned to me. "And you just a bastard." I watched him. "Take your slut ass mammy in there and put her in the bed. Naw. Fuck that! Leave her ass right there."

He turned and headed to another room. I waited until I heard the noise from the television before I moved over to my mother. She turned over and propped herself against the wall with her eyes closed. Tamia slid off the couch and was pulled into a tight embrace, her cries softer now as she sobbed in the comforting folds of my mother's arms.

"And ya'll both better shut up in there!" My stepfather's voice boomed from the other room. "Um tired of hearing that noise! Ole bitch hit me in my mothafuckin' lip! I oughta go in there and bust that ass right now! Shit!"

The moments dragged by as I sat and watched my mother and my sister. That was my lot in life, it seemed. To observe as life went by, as shit happened. My mother got up from the floor. She struggled to her feet, with Tamia hugged to her breasts, and staggered into the bedroom. My mother had really been hurt. She had a large swelling on the side of her head near her temple. She held her body sort of off to the left side, as if the force of my stepfather's blows had broken something loose in her ribs. I had never seen her move with such obvious pain. She closed the bedroom door and left me outside, pondering the madness that had become my life, the everyday that spelled such lunacy, the moment after moment I was forced to endure. Maybe, just maybe, I could make sense of it all, if it all could make sense. Sometimes life simply wasn't fair at all.

I hated him. I hated that black muthafucka. I looked toward the family room, where he was sprawled out in front of the television, snoring. I hated his snore. I hated the sound of that nigga living! His very existence made me weak. Made me scared. Made me watch as he hit on my mother and sisters and brothers. Made me watch... and do nothing. At least my mother had taken a shot at him, though! She had stung him a little when she clocked him upside his head, rocked him when she had caught him by surprise with that first punch. Good to know that he could be hurt, too. I heard him rouse in the front room.

"Hey, Nigga! Get in here!" he growled at me. I ran to him and waited. "The world don't owe you nuthin', Nigga! Know that? World don't owe you shit!" I waited some more. "Look at you! You ain't shit, just like yo' daddy. The apple knocka. Yo' mama threw her legs up for him in the middle of one of them apple fields. He was... apple knockin'."

I stopped listening to him. I fazed out and into my own world as he droned on. I had heard this story too many times before and I hated the son of a bitch anyway. I wished he would stop talking to me...or at me. I wished that I could reach inside of his throat and rip his neck out. He was still talking.

"One of them old, field hand niggas got up in yo' momma's panties. That's why you got that little apple head you got! Shit! Ain't got no sense in that mothafucka neither. Shit!"

Fuck you! Fuck you! Fuck you! I glared at him. I would've been more than glad to hit him in the face with a brick as soon as he fell asleep. I should do it! I should!

"Boy!" my stepfather roared. "Why you lookin' at me like that? Huh? You betta take some of that shit outta your eyes, Boy."

I bowed my head and closed my eyes.

After a moment, my stepfather commanded me, "Turn the station on that TV." I turned to a channel with a baseball game and he dismissed me. "Right there," he said. "Now gone! Get out!"

I went back over to the couch and sat down. Moments later, my mother's bedroom door crept open and she beckoned to me from the doorway. I quietly got up, peeked over at my stepfather, and then eased inside her bedroom.

"Is he sleep?" my mother asked me.

"Yeah," I said. "He sleep."

"That nigga ain't never gonna put his hands on my baby again. You hear me?"

"Ma, you got a big bump on your head."

"I know. Ain't nuthin'. That's just gonna be my fuel. My energy I use to get this evil ass bastard. You see how hard he hit Tamia? He threw her! That's a little girl! That nigga dead! He ain't doing that no more."

"We can go get a brick!" I supplied. "Or a rock maybe."

Ma's eyes glazed over before she spoke. "Or a grindstone."

"The grindstone?" I tried to make sense of her reply.

"Yeah, the grindstone." She turned to me. "Listen to me. I got a surprise for his ass. I got a couple of knives hid downstairs in the basement. They those long, heavy hunting knives. I got them real cheap at the flea market. I'm gonna get him myself. I'm gonna get him." My mother held my hands tightly as she looked me in the eyes. "Tomorrow, we go to sharpen my shit...to make my point to that dog out there. We gonna grind."

I was with her every step of the way...but I knew it was going to cost her. My stepfather was a big, strong, slave-tough nigga. He would have to be hit hard and quick and I knew that Ma would catch hell trying to get him. Even with a knife. But I'll give her this; my mother was determined to take her husband off this earth. So, every night I took her down to the grindstone to sharpen her knife....and after she was done, I would sharpen mine.

Her knife was bigger than mine. The blade was wide and thick and it had a black rubber handle. It looked like a hunting knife, yet it held a deadly beauty; graceful but lethal. I only hoped it would inflict enough damage to finish the job. In comparison, my knife was like a kitchen knife, which I kept sharpened for those special occasions when Ma would go off into one of her stark raving fits.

I commiserated with my mother over the following weeks when we stood in the yard, late into the night, and watched the sparks shoot off into the darkness as we sharpened our knives. This was our moment...our time to bond closer, to learn to love and be loved, to find that commonality that would define our relationship for life...but my mother treated me like a red-headed stepchild.

My stepfather came home drunk one day and tried to hit my mother with a baseball bat. That night, while we stood in the dark at the grindstone, as we sharpened our knives, my mother would confirm her value of me.

She turned the grindstone. "That nigga always hittin' me for nuthin'.

Hittin' on my babies." Her eyes glared when she put the knife to the stone. "I had dem babies...not him! Fuck him and his stankin'-ass-ho-mama-ass! Shit!"

"We ever gonna leave him, Ma?" I asked.

She smirked at me...and suddenly the sparks from the grindstone began to fly. "Shit!" she exclaimed. "'You ain't no 'we.' You ain't no part of 'we' and never will be. You are the biggest piece of shit that ever happened to me, Boy." She paused to look me in the eyes. She saw right past the pain that her words inflicted on me...and she created even more. "You know how your black-ass stepdaddy, if you can call him that, you know how he keep on talking about your real daddy? Well, he don't know shit about your real daddy. Truth is, I don't know nuthin' about the mothafucka myself. You know how I met your daddy? How I had you?"

I was speechless. I mean, my mother never talked to me about serious stuff. She usually just hit me.

She took my silence as assent. "When I was young, I was wild. I was out and about and I wasn't thinkin' about that black bastard up that hill with the baseball bat. I already had two babies by him but I was still young and still wanted to be free like I ain't have no kids. So I was out at the clubs, partying, when I first saw your daddy. He had 'nigga' written all over his stank ass...and he was just what I needed. So when he came over to me, I was more than ready for him. We did a few jitterbugs and I checked out his rhythm just to see if he could swang. And then we did some slow grinds so I could check out his 'rhythm' and I knew he could swang. It was time to go. And I wanted him to be my lover." She paused to look at me. "You know what a lover is?"

I nodded my head in astonished negative. She continued anyway.

"Well, your real daddy took me. He was savage with me. I looked up that word: savage. And that's what he was...like a hungry, hard animal...and he growled as he took me. I tried to stop him but he started choking me. When I stopped fighting him, he still squeezed my neck so tight that I could hardly breathe. Then he looked me in my eyes as he took me. I still feel that look sometimes 'cause, to this day, I still wonder what he was looking for. It musta been pain he was lookin' for 'cause that's what he gave me. He was big…well, his manhood was real big, and he took me hard and vicious. That muthafucka raped me. Your muthafucking daddy!" She turned back to the grindstone and began to sharpen her knife. "I hate that muthafucka. I hate what he took. I hate what he hurt. And through him, I hated you."

Tears welled up in my eyes and I desperately tried to catch them before they fell. My pain had no place to go but inward. My mother wanted to leave me alone. As a matter of fact, I had always been alone, with nothing but hope as my companion. My life was a fucking tragedy.

"And you look just like his ass," my mother continued, grinding the stone. "Every time I look at you, I see that man. I see that man."

My mother had her back to me so she didn't see me walk up to her. I thought I saw a slight tremble in her frame as she recalled the horror of my conception and, instinctively, I reached out and touched her shoulder. She had been through more than enough pain.

She turned around and slapped me to the ground. "Muthafuckin savage!"

She spit the words at me as I lay there, her words stinging me more than the blow to my cheek. Yet again, my pain had no place to go.

We spent the rest of our time at the grindstone in silence. I watched the sparks fly and tried to imagine myself in another time, another place. When we finally made it back to the house, I went straight back to my bedroom and slammed the door. I pulled my knife from my pocket and flicked the blade out. I had been practicing flicking the blade like I had seen guys do in the movies, but I couldn't seem to master the technique of shooting the blade out in an almost magical, Houdini-type move. Next, I was going to learn how to throw the knife and make it stick in the wall like Davy Crockett did on TV. I had visions.

I heard the heavy footsteps of my stepfather as he pounded up the stairs into the house. His voice boomed. "Did you get my money for me, Bitch?!"

I eased my bedroom door open a crack and watched them.

"I told you that I couldn't get no money," my mother said. "You know nobody ain't got no money. You know that shit. You ain't got none neither."

"I know I'd have some more money if I didn't have to put out no money for that bastard you got up in my house. Where is that skinny little nigga you call a son anyway, slut. Where his ass at? Where that motherfucker?"

"I don't know!" she screamed. "I don't fucking know, alright!"

A shocked second of silence hung in the air. The next sounds I heard were the utterly identifiable sounds of violence. My stepfather was enraged. He punched my mother to the floor and then he began picking up things and hitting her with them as she lay there. When she finally lay still, beaten and whimpering, he began asking her questions and kicking her to make her answer. When he began to tire, I heard my mother, in a very weak voice, begin murmuring her apologies, begging his forgiveness. He was drunk. It was always the same.

He plopped down on the couch and I heard his heavy breathing from my doorway.

My mother crawled over to him, crying in pain. "Why you got to beat on me all the time?" Her voice was heavy with desperation. "Why?"

My stepfather ignored her and picked up the remote control from the end table.

"Why?" she asked again.

"Bitch, I know you see me finna watch this program, right?" he replied as he flipped through the channels.

My mother curled up in a ball on the floor and I watched as she deftly reached under the sofa and dragged the knife over to her. The blade looked ominous. Its edges looked sharp as she tucked it down by her side, hidden from my stepfather's view when she turned back to him.

"I just wanna know why," she said. Her voice was much clearer when she spoke. "You been hittin' on me for years…and for nuthin'. I do everything I can and you still beat on me. Why you do that?"

"Bitch! If you don't shut yo' ho mouth while I'm watchin' my program…"

"I just wanted to know," she said, "before I stick you."

And then my mother plunged the knife into his leg. He howled in pain and tried to scramble away but my mother had his leg locked in an iron grip. She swung the blade again, sinking it deeper into his thigh. My stepfather clubbed my mother in the head with both fists until her grip loosened. He tried to dive on top of her but his damaged leg wouldn't cooperate. He fell in a heap on the floor next to her and my mother rolled away from him. He reached over, grabbed her arm, and pulled her back toward him, but she had the knife in the other hand and she swung it at him. The knife sunk into his chest to the hilt and my mother froze in terror. He looked down at the knife, buried to the hilt in his flesh, then he looked at my mother with a look of disbelief. An animal cry escaped his lips and he reverted to the monster inside.

He seized my mother by her neck with both hands and began to squeeze. She was powerless in his chokehold and he began slamming her head into the floor. I stood there, in shock, as my mother's body went limp, as her life left her, and I could only wonder why my stepfather wasn't dead. It looked like my mother had stabbed that man right in his heart but he was still sitting there, living and breathing. I watched him for a second as he sat there next to my dead mother, as his chest heaved and blood leaked down the front of his shirt. I just knew that he was going to die but as I fingered my knife...I decided I couldn't wait.

I flung my bedroom door open and charged toward him, knife extended. He barely moved when he saw me coming for him and I swung my blade at his chest and face repeatedly. I realized it was my life or his, so I stabbed at him with blind rage. He was weak. All of that power, his vaunted power, the force that he had hammered me and my brothers and sisters with, that was all gone as he tried to fend off my attack by blocking my stabs with his arm. Each strike that landed drew blood and I vaguely heard his voice as he began to beg.

"Stop...it. Don't...hit. You...hurt...me. Stop."

I was covered in his blood, but the sound of his voice froze me. I stepped back from him. "What? What you say?"

"You hurt...me." I watched his chest rise and fall heavily with the handle of the knife poking out at an angle. "You hurt. Me." His head lolled to the side but his eyes were still on me. In that instant, I knew he was going to live if I let him, and I vowed that he wouldn't ever rise from that floor. My stepfather was a big, strong man and the hatred he had placed in my heart now turned to fear, which drove me to the brink of desperation. He raised his hands to the handle of the knife, got a good grip, and violently ripped it from his chest. He howled in pain as the knife fell to the floor by his side and deathly coughs began to rack through his body as he spit up blood. I just waited and hoped for him to die.

"Hurt!" he screamed. "Hurt!"

"Shit!" I screamed back at him. "That's what you did to us! I ain't never hurt you before! I ain't never do nuthin' to you! But all I am is a bastard, right? All I did was be born, right? Every day! Every day, I hated you. Every day, I was wishing you'd walk out that door and never come back. That we could make it without you...without you comin' home drunk and beatin' on me. And for nuthin', Nigga. For no-thang!" My mother's body lay on the floor next to him, lifeless. "And look what you did to Ma," I ranted on. "Look what you turned her into. Look what you did to her! She dead, Nigga! Dead! You turned her heart against me. Her own son. But that's all right, though. That's a-okay with me, 'cause you know what? Inna minute you is just gonna be another nigga, dead. Even if I have to do it myself."

"Boy," he managed to get out before his body exploded in coughs of pain. "Boy, I ain't never...gonna die. I'm gonna always get your punk ass. You ain't shit...just like yo' apple knockin' daddy. Yo' slut ass mama threw her legs up in an apple field to have you...and umma end up fuckin' you just the same. Shee-it."

"Fuck you!" I screamed and charged him again. I stabbed him and stabbed him and stabbed him until his lifeless body was slumped face down on the floor. I stood up and caught a glimpse of my reflection in the living room mirror and saw a grisly-looking kid staring back at me. There was blood all over my body and there was a madman dancing in my eyes. My torture was over but my tragedy had just begun.

I arose from the grisly scene in a trance. I plodded out of the house and walked down the hill to Upwards Alley. It was nighttime now and the streets were quiet. I snuck around to the back of Donnell Shunt's house and hid behind the fence. The grindstone was still there and I watched it for a while...harboring cruel visions accompanied by dark thoughts, the pair playing with each other on a jungle gym in the twisted playground of my mind.

I look back now at the detritus of my life, at the mess that was my misspent youth and I can only feel wondrous justification. My existence is a fractional cycle, ending and beginning in shattered bouts of hopelessness. My memories are like that also; violent images that push themselves to the forefront of my consciousness in staccato rhythms of madness. Images of blood and guts, fists and knives, pain and agony, flash across my mind and cause me to, temporarily, push against the restraints that bind my mental state.

My agony sometimes comes in the terrifying form of questions: Did I let my mother die? Did I really bring about my stepfather's bloody demise? Was my childhood pain only a youthful nightmare? I don't really know the difference between illusion and reality anymore. They keep me locked up most of the time but the pills and medication are my real captors. I've been a functional zombie for so long that I've lost touch with the warmth of humanity, the sound of the human heart, and the joy of laughter. Through the haze of my insanity only one light shines for me to hold onto; sometimes violence is the only answer to violence, and blood is the only detergent that has washed my soul clean. Forever.

Nane Quartay was born in upstate New York and attended Augusta College in Augusta, Georgia. After a tour in the United States Navy he traveled extensively before returning to New York to begin writing his first novel Feenin. *His next novel,* The Badness, *is due out this spring. He now resides in the Washington, D.C. area.*

SILENT SUFFERING

SHONDA CHEEKES

CHAPTER ONE

I don't condone violence of any kind. But I think it's really embarrassing when it happens to a man. I'm basically treated like a helpless, punk ass bitch in my own house.

Candace, or Candy as she's known, is the inflictor of my pain. I've suffered unthinkable pain at her hands for more than a year. I bet the question in your mind is why do I stay and take it. I guess because I feel a connection to her in some sort of sick and twisted way. Let me elaborate a bit to give you a better understanding.

Candy and I are both products of what happens when you're raised in an abusive environment. Her abuse was experienced secondhand. Her father would beat her mother unmercifully on any given day. A personal punching bag for the old man. Candy promised herself that would never be her lot in life. She'd always be able to take care of herself. Never have to put all of her dependence in a man in order to make it. But in her effort to protect herself from becoming a victim, she learned to victimize.

The abuse in my house stemmed from a woman scorned. When I was four, my old man left one evening for the corner store. I guess he never found it. Since I was a near replica of her source of pain, Mama took it out on me whenever the feeling struck her. A slap across the face; a punch to the head. After a while, she started tying me to the bed. Dared me to make a sound or piss. As hard as I tried, by the second day, I would lose my bladder control and she would lose control on me.

One episode that has stayed prevalent in my memory happened around my fourteenth birthday. I don't remember exactly what it was that set her off. It didn't take much anyway. I just remember the situation almost landed me in the hospital after being horrendously beaten. Tired and breathless from beating me with a belt and being that I hadn't given her the desired reaction of crying, she searched around for something that would surely get those tears out of me. That night it happened to be a hammer. I remember the feel of the metal making contact with a piece of my skull with a frightening thud. I ran as fast as I could out of the house in search of a safe haven. Ms. Johnson opened her door as soon as she heard the lock click. I ended up at her house for the next week, until she couldn't afford another mouth to feed.

Soon the prospect of going off to college became my escape plan. Tessa would laugh and tell me there was no way I was going to make it at a four-year school.

"Yo' dumb ass might as well go on down to the nearest trade school and call it a day." She'd laugh that wicked bone-chilling laugh I'd grown to hate as she lay up on the sofa watching her favorite soaps.

In spite of her, I made it further than the four-year college and attended dental school where I trained to become an oral surgeon. See, I learned to take that negativity she fed me on a regular basis and turn it into fuel. More than anyone in this world, I was going to show her.

But there was that side of me that couldn't completely cut her off. She was my mother and had given me life. I'd sit around and wonder if he hadn't walked out and left us, would my relationship with her had been different. Would she have been the loving and nurturing mother I'd seen growing up watching the Cosbys and other television shows?

Candy once asked me if I had any desires to find my father; just to let him know the hell I had been put through because of his shortcomings. My answer was a simple "no." I'd long given up that fantasy. And at this point in my life, I don't know if I would be able to control my anger.

I used to worry that the abuse I endured at the small hands of my mother would eventually turn me into an abuser myself. But it was the opposite. I had grown into a weak man where women were concerned. Went out of my way to please a woman; especially my woman.

Candy blew into my life after a breakup with a married woman. After I wined and dined her and uplifted her from the depressive state she was in when we first met, she decided to go back to her husband. "Glad I could be of service," was the best response I had. Instead of telling her how used and betrayed I felt, I helped her move her things back to his house. Yeah, stupid me.

There's no truer statement than the one about how we attract certain types of people at certain times in our lives. Candy happened to be another stop on the train of destruction I was riding. I remember the first time the monster that lived hidden under the big brown eyes and not quite perfect, but beautiful, smile showed its head.

"Eddie, what the fuck is this?" she asked about the piece of paper in her hand.

I walked closer and she handed the paper to me for a closer inspection. As I read the letter, the contents of it became clear—it was a thank you note from one of my patients. The woman had been petrified about having her wisdom teeth pulled. I assured her that I would be extremely gentle during the procedure, making sure the discomfort she experienced was minimal. While the content of the letter was nothing more than a thank you, Candy seemed to be reading something that was supposedly between the lines.

"Are you fucking her?"

"Candy, you've got to be kidding? This woman is—"

Before I could get the rest of my statement out, she smashed her fist into the side of my head; hitting me hard enough to make me stumble and my teeth rattle.

"Don't think you're going to stand up here and tell me a blatant lie. I told you when we got together, cheating is the one thing that I won't tolerate in any shape, form, or fashion!" Her hand quickly found its way to my family jewels and grabbed a handful. "This is my dick! Don't you ever forget that, you hear? Before another bitch gets it, I'll Lorena Bobbitt your ass!"

Her eyes glazed over with anger. My fear paralyzed me momentarily. All I could see was Tessa. Tessa with the unfeeling eyes that bore through to my soul. Tessa with hatred for the hurt one man had placed on her; hurt she tried to take out on the one person in the world who loved her more than breathing.

Once Candy loosened her grip, she methodically undid my belt and zipped my pants down. Fear of not knowing what was going to happen next kept me from getting the instant arousal most men experience when a woman strokes their dicks the way she was stroking mine. Knowing that if I didn't reach that erection she was in search of, I would surely be accused of the cheating she was insinuating, I put a mind trick in place to help the process along.

Candy fell to her knees and kissed the head, all the while praising how much he meant to her. She loved him and didn't want him near some foreign pussy. Being inside her mouth and pussy was the only place on earth for him. When she finally inserted me fully into her mouth, I relaxed enough to enjoy the oral pleasure. She sucked and slurped until I reached the climax she desired.

She regained her standing position and wiped the remnants of the short escapade from her mouth as I stood there helpless with my pants around my ankles. I stumbled toward the nearest couch and collapsed onto it. She walked away and returned with a warm rag and threw it at me.

"Clean yourself up."

I obeyed and fastened my pants up. Like a puppy, I followed her into the bedroom and sat on the bed until she came out of the bathroom.

"What was that about, Candy?"

"Just wanted to let you know who's running things."

"Why couldn't you simply believe me? Candy, I don't want anyone but you. I need you to trust me when I tell you that."

"The one thing I've learned about trust is you can never completely trust anyone. My mama trusted my daddy and he did everything he was big enough to do and then some. Unlike Mama, I know how to please my man. So, next time you get the urge to seek pleasure elsewhere, keep in mind the things I'm willing to do for and to you." She walked over and kissed me on the lips before disappearing out the door.

The next episode came a month or so later. We were at the annual function for black dentists when I was approached by an old schoolmate.

"Eddie? Eddie Adelson, is that you?"

I turned to find myself on the receiving end of the person who had played a major part in my finishing dental school. Nisha Von had been more than a friend to me while we were in school. She'd been my crutch, my sounding board, and study partner. I owed much of my success to her.

"Nisha, it's so good to see you." I instinctively reached out to hug her.

"How long has it been? Three or four years? How are you? How's your practice?"

"Everything is great. I can't complain. What about you? Did you open your own practice? Or are you still over there with the group?"

"Actually, I went back to school to become a hygienist."

"A hygienist? What prompted that?"

"After the baby, I wanted to be able to devote more time to her. The decision wasn't a hard one."

"A baby? Wow, that's wonderful! So, I take it that you're married now? Or are you one of these new independent women who doesn't have a problem with being a single parent?"

"No, I'm happily married."

"A dentist?"

"Heavens no! One dentist in the family is enough. Someone needs to be able to let the child get away with eating sweets every now and then."

We both laughed.

Candy strolled over to where we were standing, wrapped her arm around mine, and brought her body up close to me.

"Nisha, I'd like you to meet—"

"Candace. Candace Knight," she said in a dry tone.

Nisha extended her hand to Candy, who glared at it and then kissed me. "Eddie, let's get out of here. There's nobody here but a bunch of buppies. I'm so tired of hearing about teeth. I swear I'll throw up if another person walks up to me to inquire about my dental work."

Nisha looked down at her hand, the one Candy pretended not to see, and then pulled it back to her side. She shook her head and smiled uneasily.

"Well, Eddie, you must promise to keep in touch. Maybe you and…" She paused, more for effect than anything. "…Candace can come over to the house and join Mike and me for dinner. I grill a mean steak."

"While that sounds all nice and well, Nashae, eating steak gives me heartburn," Candy replied sarcastically, misstating Nisha's name purposefully.

I cleared my throat. "Nisha, it was really nice seeing you again. I'm happy to hear about the baby and your marriage. Maybe some other time, though."

"Yeah, maybe." Nisha gave me a pity stare as she slid her business card in my coat pocket without Candy seeing her. She mouthed the words "call me" as I glanced back while Candy yanked me toward the exit.

I was still hot under the collar once we got home. "I can't believe you embarrassed me like that. Nisha happens to be—"

"Yes, you told me; an old college friend. Umm, hmm, like I'm supposed to believe there was nothing more between y'all."

"Candy, I've never kept anything from you. You know the gruesome details of mostly everything else that has happened in my life. Why would I lie to you about something as trivial as an old girlfriend? If that were the situation between me and Nisha, I would've told you, but it wasn't. She and I were more like—"

"Brother and sister. Yeah, I've heard that line before."

"You really need to seek some counseling about your problems with infidelity."

"What did you say?"

I could feel the hairs on the back of my neck stand up. I knew the monster was going to make an appearance that night.

"I'm not the one with a problem, Mama's boy. You don't know what the fuck you're talking about."

"I didn't mean anything by it, Candy. I was simply trying to say that I'm not like your father."

"You're damn right; you're not my father."

"Candy, look—"

I went to walk out of the room and turned around to catch the TV remote with my forehead. Just like in a Looney Tunes cartoon, the hickey quickly rose up. I stumbled my way out of the room and into the guest bedroom where I fell on the floor. I could feel a trickle of warm blood as it snaked its way down the side of my head. Before I could recover, she was on me, punching and slapping and pulling at my clothes. This time she undid my pants and pulled them and my boxers completely off. She hastily slid out of the black slinky dress she was wearing and removed her thong. Then she ripped open my shirt, sending the buttons flying across the room. With nothing on but a pair of stilettos, she slid on top of me and began to ride her way to ecstasy. The harder she pushed, the more she cursed.

"I keep telling you, this is my dick. No other bitch is going to get any part of my dick. Lil' skinny yella bitch all up in your face grinning. Was her pussy as good as mine? Could she fuck you like I do? Answer me, Eddie! Tell me how much you love my pussy and how good I fuck you! Tell me this is the only pussy you want! Tell me, Eddie, that you'll never leave me or do me wrong! Tell me! Tell me!"

I couldn't bring a response out of my mouth if my life depended on it. I couldn't believe how hard she was humping on me, in an attempt to punish me and teach me that I wasn't to look, let alone talk, to another woman.

Once again, when we were finished, she calmly walked into the bathroom and returned with a warm rag for me to clean myself.

From then on, the encounters worsened. Whenever we had a problem, it would start with a physical confrontation, more than likely to be followed by rough, aggressive sex. My only use was that of a prop.

CHAPTER TWO

Candy was holding me hostage on the phone while I had a lot of work to do.

"What time you finish today?"

"I'm not sure. I still have quite a few patients in the waiting room. We're extremely busy today."

"Things are pretty much the same around here. Muthafuckas complaining about waiting in line. Complaining about the service. I mean, what do they expect when they wait until the last minute to come in and get their shit taken care of?"

"You know that's human nature. Seems like once we see that final notice or deadline date, we get the fire under our asses that we should've had from the beginning."

"I can understand that, but to wait until your tag or license is expired makes you really stupid. In the middle of the month, you can damn near walk in and out. You'd think everyone else would know that by now."

Lana poked her head into my office. "Mr. Harris is prepped and waiting in room five, Dr. Adelson."

"Thanks, Lana. Let him know that I'll be there in a minute."

"I guess duty is a calling."

"Got to finish up so I can get out of here. Do you want me to pick something up, or were you planning to cook?"

"I was hoping we could get dressed and go down to Preston's. I really have a taste for the seafood dish I love."

"I'm really tired, Candy. Can I get a rain check?"

"Damn, Eddie. I was really looking forward to it," she said in a whiny voice.

"I'll make you a deal then. If you let me slide tonight, we'll go to Preston's on Friday and stay in a hotel. How does that sound?"

"I guess that's a fair deal. Just make sure you get a suite. I love the ocean-front view."

"I'm not sure if we can get a deal on a suite on such short notice, especially this time of year."

"For someone who makes good money, your ass is so cheap."

"That's the only way I'm going to keep my money."

"See what they say first, before you start talking against it."

"I thought you could call, since you're going to get home before me."

"Why is it that you suggest something and then I get stuck having to do all the footwork? Which hotel were you talking about? I know how much of a penny pincher you are, but since we're going to Preston's, it would be nice to stay at the Loews. I mean, it's what? Only a few bucks more than the Palms."

"Call both hotels. See if they have any kind of specials for this weekend. Better yet, go online and see. I know the Royal Palm gives better rates online. Maybe the Loews does the same."

"Do you want me to go ahead and put it on the credit card?"

"If you have to. Candy—"

"I know… call you first. Go see about your patient."

I'd almost forgotten about Mr. Harris.

"Okay, I'll see you when I get in."

"Yeah, okay. Bye."

She hung up before I could reply.

Things between us were unpredictable most days. I was trying my best to keep her satisfied, in more ways than one. Didn't flinch when she asked about bringing her prized vibrator into our action. Using it on me was a definite no-no, but we discovered a few ways to please her by adding it into the act.

"Mr. Harris, how are you today?"

"Seeing that I'm sitting in your chair about to be put to sleep so you can pull my tooth out my head, I'm not sure I'm doing all that well."

I laughed at the irony and continued to prepare for the procedure. "Don't worry. I'll have you feeling brand-new in no time."

I had my assistant start the drip. Within seconds, he was out.

"Can you believe that Mr. Harris thought he could drive himself home after his procedure?" Lana asked.

"I guess it helps to have an arsenal of women to pull you out of a crunch. I didn't want to leave him here, but it's time to go."

"A man with his credentials? Plus he's single? I would've driven him home in that nice, new BMW he had out there."

"Is that all that's important to women nowadays? I mean, what about what's in his head and in his chest?"

"Those things can be worked on. Relationships are something you have to put in time and effort on."

"Is that right? How about being happy with them as they are? Why would you have to change someone in order to be happy with them?" I ran my tongue over the spot I knew was still there; no matter if the swelling had gone down. A busted lip; courtesy of a flying shoe.

"That's not what I'm saying. You should never compromise your happiness for someone else."

"So, that brings us back to your statement about Mr. Harris. Isn't wanting him because of his money, nice house, and nice car, despite the fact that he may not be your Prince Charming, a compromise?"

"I guess, but those things let you know if you want to get to know someone."

"Now, that's shallow."

"Hey, what can I say? Women have been known to be that also." She laughed and walked out the door.

Never compromise your happiness for someone else, echoed in my head while I set the alarm. That one simple phrase was food for thought.

CHAPTER THREE

"Are you sure you couldn't get a room next door?" I hesitantly asked Candy later that evening.

"If you feel I'm lying to you, why didn't you make the reservation yourself? I don't need this aggravation."

It wasn't that I couldn't afford to pay the two hundred dollars-a-night room rate; just the principle of whether or not I had to. Although the Loews was by far the more extravagant of the two, the Palms was nothing to bat your eyes at and usually had more affordable rates. While it was touted as the black hotel, you couldn't tell by the people working behind the counter, or anywhere else in the hotel for that matter.

I decided to give in, once again. "It's been a long day for both of us and I want this to be an enjoyable weekend. So, the Loews it is."

I pulled under the overhang and unlocked the doors. Candy waited as the valet ran over and opened the door for her. She seemed to switch into another mode once her hand hit his. Yeah, my Benz was nothing shameful to get out of, but it was like she was a star or something.

"Will you be with us this evening?" the valet asked as he stood waiting for me to turn over my $50,000 car to him.

"Yes."

He pulled a card from his shirt pocket and wrote something on it before tearing off one part and handing it to me. He went on to explain the price of the valet service per night and instructed me to have them put the room number on it at the front desk.

"Thank you for choosing the Loews. Enjoy your stay."

Candy stood waiting on the curb as the bellhop pulled the last of our bags from the trunk. We followed him into the grand lobby and made our way around to the check-in counter.

As the bellhop placed the last of our bags into the room, Candy walked over and drew the curtains back to reveal the breathtaking view of the Atlantic Ocean, which lay just beyond the white sandy beach. I placed a bill in his hand and he quietly thanked me and slipped out the door.

I walked up behind Candy and slid my hand around to her flat stomach, kissing the back of her neck. "Where to now?"

"I was thinking we could get dressed and either head down to Preston's or Emeril's. You know, they opened his restaurant a few weeks ago? With his reputation, it has to be nice." She turned around and kissed me softly on the lips.

"This weekend is for you. Anything you want to do, simply ask and I shall try my best to oblige." I gently kissed her, realizing those were the words she wanted to hear.

"Then, let me oblige you."

She sauntered over to the bed. Slowly and methodically, she began to remove her clothing. The white midriff shirt with the flowing, wide-cuffed sleeves. The khaki cargo pants and black satin bra soon followed. With the sexiest of walks, she closed in on me and slipped her hand into my pants, caressing my manhood that was already at attention and waiting for the command. Her eyes never leaving mine, she undid the belt of my khaki shorts as I slid the white polo over my head. I kicked my leather slides off as she slid my pants and boxer briefs to the floor.

"Lie down," she commanded.

Like an obedient child, I followed her orders and moved to the middle of the king-sized bed. She reached over to the nightstand and turned on the CD/Radio/Alarm Clock.

"Give me one second."

She walked away and grabbed a CD from the case she traveled with. She placed it in the player and clicked it to the cut she wanted to hear. No sooner than she hit play, the room began to fill with the melodic sounds of Floetry's erotic tune.

Candy sang along. "There is only one… for me…"

She knew it was a song that got me hot and bothered. I was ready to explode as she sang and did a sultry dance. One that ended with her slipping her thong seductively off to the music.

By the time the second chorus of "Say Yes" filled the room, Candy had straddled me and was riding off to ecstasy. She moaned along with them. Told me where her spot was along with them. Even erupted on cue with them. She collapsed on my chest as we both worked on composing our breathing, slowly coming down from the high we'd just experienced.

Why couldn't it always be like this?

"Isn't this place just gorgeous?" Candy's head turned, scanning the room from one end to the other.

"Good evening. Welcome to Emeril's. How many in your party?"

"Two," I replied.

"How long is the wait?" Candy asked.

"One second." The hostess looked over her seating chart. There were people in there, but it wasn't what I would call packed. The hostess grabbed two menus and asked us to follow her.

"This is so nice. I wonder when he's going to come back. You know he was here for the grand opening? I wanted to make it down here, but… Damn, I can't remember why I didn't."

I looked over the menu and noted the prices. Not too over the top, but not all that inexpensive either. "You sure you don't want to go to Preston's? You did say you were craving it the other night." Not that Preston's was any cheaper; it's just hard to find something to eat whenever you go to a restaurant for the first time.

Candy leered at me. "I'd much rather be here."

"Now that was a real nice experience," Candy said excitedly after dinner. "I must say, the food was excellent."

"Yes it was," I agreed. "Now, where to?"

"Hmm, let's see…" She placed her finger to her chin. Pretended to be deep in thought.

"You know…" I kissed the back of her neck. "We could go back upstairs to that beautiful room we have…" Another kiss. "And make use of the bed…"

"Now, what fun would that be? We do that all the time. I want to go to a club. Oh, I know… Let's go to Club B.E.D."

"Why there? You know ain't nothing there but a bunch of people trying to be seen by a bunch of other people who really don't care about seeing them at all."

"And what's wrong with that? That's what this entire scene is about any-way."

"You mean, like staying in one of the most expensive hotels out here? Dining at one of the trendiest restaurants?"

"First of all, if being seen was what it was about for me, we would be at the Delano and not the Loews. Instead of the measly two hundred, you'd be really dishing out the dough."

I knew the evening wasn't going to go the way I planned from that moment.

"Are we going to the club or not?"

I realized if "no" had been the answer, the fate of my weekend would've been sealed. So, against all that raged inside of me, I followed as she made her way around to the valet stand.

"Why can't we walk over there?" I asked.

"Walk! You must be crazy if you think I'm going to walk all the way over there in these!" She lifted her foot to show me the four-inch skinny heel of her shoe.

I pulled the valet ticket from my pocket.

We pulled up to the club where there was another charge for parking. Finding parking anywhere along Washington Street was a challenge, so it seemed fruitless to argue. We walked to the front of the club. A few people were standing around in hopes of being allowed the opportunity to party with the "in crowd" of the moment.

The cover charge was a ridiculous price. I looked at Candy long and hard. Never compromise your happiness for someone else, came to me loud and clear. Here I was doing exactly that. It didn't matter that I could more than afford it. What weighed heavily on me was the fact that it came back to everything being about what she wanted. Never was it about me, or we.

As bad as I knew things could end up, I stood back at the door as she started to walk in. "Candy…"

She looked back at me like I had lost my mind. Then she slowly made her way back to me. "What?!" she said between clenched teeth. Clenched fists at her side.

"As much as I know you want to be here, I'm really not feeling it. I mean, I can't see shelling out that type of cash just to say I was here. Can we just go?"

I was given the kiss of death when it comes to looks. I should've rolled with the flow in order to keep the peace, but I had been doing that for far too long.

"I can't believe you're going to embarrass me like this." Her response was more of a hiss than anything else.

"Do you have money to pay for this? I mean, if you do, I'll go in and we can hang all night."

"So, we meet again," a voice called out from behind us.

I turned around to find Nisha walking up behind us. "Hey, you!" I gave her a slight hug.

"Eddie, this is Mike, my husband. Mike, Dr. Eddie Adelson—the old friend from college I was telling you about."

"Hey, Man. Good to meet you." He grabbed my hand in a firm handshake.

"What are you doing here?" Nisha inquired.

"We were about to leave. It costs a pretty penny to hang out in here."

"Don't I know it, but Mike knows the owner and—"

"You guys are more than welcome to join us," Mike interrupted and added.

Before I could decline, Candy came to life in a way that was so like her.

After the cold reception she'd given Nisha the night of the dinner, you'd think she was the last person she would want to be indebted to. Strangely enough, Candy acted like she and Nisha were the best of friends. Being invited into a circle that would've been elusive to us otherwise seemed to animate her.

Mike, a successful movie editor, was privileged enough to be a part of the very "it" crowd. When you have extremely well known people walk over to you to speak, it's a definite sign of some sort of royalty. Candy ate the semi-attention up she received as a result of being with Mike.

Candy excused herself to the restroom while Mike walked over to another bed to speak to some friends.

"Now, that was a switch," Nisha commented. "I remember home girl look-ing at me the other night like I had the plague or something."

"What can I say?" I shrugged. "She's an opportunist."

"You looked like you were ready to jet when we first walked up. What's going on with you? Why haven't you called me?"

"Just been busy, is all."

"You do remember I'm a good listener."

I definitely remembered. The long nights we used to have; sitting up shooting the breeze. Nisha had always been eager to lend an ear; dishing advice only when asked.

"I may take you up on that," I said.

"You still have my card?"

"Of course I do."

"Why don't you give me a call Tuesday? It's my day off. Maybe we can meet somewhere and have lunch."

"That so happens to my day off also. Sounds like a plan."

"You can unburden your soul over a plate of soul food." We both laughed. "Seems your face just found a missing friend."

"Haven't had much to smile about lately."

"Then you need to change that."

"Trying to. It's complicated."

"I don't think it's complicated," Nisha said. "You're probably making it more complicated than it has to be."

"You know me, a glutton for punishment." I gave a nervous chuckle and waited for her to join me.

Her affirmation never came in the form of a laugh, but rather in a soft reassuring touch. "You'll get through this like you've done before. You're a survivor. Remember that."

"This has been one of the most exciting nights of my life." Candy smiled as she slid out of the micro-mini. Her shoes had landed in the corner when she kicked them off. "Why didn't you tell me your girl was hooked up like that? If I'd known, I wouldn't have treated her so funky the first time."

"You shouldn't have treated her that way regardless. She's a friend of mine. That alone should've been enough for you to treat her decently. Why does a person have to have some type of worth for you to be civil?"

"I'm not about to let you ruin my night with your bullshit. You might as well climb into bed and call it a night like I'm about to do. You better be glad they came along and saved us from the embarrassment you were trying to put me through."

She turned her back and slid on the oversized nightshirt. Clicked off the light like I wasn't even in the room. Leaving me to undress in total darkness.

CHAPTER FOUR

"So how long has this been going on?"

"It started about two months after she moved in with me. I was trying to help her out after she got put out by her roommates. Now, I understand why they dropped her."

"Yes, she definitely seems to be a piece of work." Nisha stared at me with compassion. "Eddie, you've got to get away from her. She's bringing you down and someone's going to end up getting hurt really bad."

"But how can I just leave her?" I asked in dismay.

"There are ways, Eddie. Maybe you can sit down and talk with her. If you're afraid of having the conversation alone, find someone to be a mediator. Here…" She reached into her handbag and pulled out a card. "This is a good friend of mine. He's a really good therapist. His specialty happens to be abusive relationships."

"Yeah, but abusive relationships where men are the victims?"

"Especially those types. After doing research for a project, he noticed there were a lot of men in abusive situations who had no outlets to lay down their burdens or their pain. They were afraid to share their stories because people would either laugh or call them wimpy, or punks. So, he decided he would be the ear they needed."

"How long has he been doing this?"

"More than ten years." She could see the doubt on my face. "Look, if you want, I'll go with you. I promise; you won't regret it." She squeezed my hand in a reassuring gesture.

"Dr. Adelson, how are you? I'm Dr. Griffith." He extended his hand toward me.

I was still a bit reserved about the entire thing, but anything was better than the nothing I'd been doing.

"Dr. Griffith." I shook his hand. My palms were a bit clammy. I swiped them on my pants as I took a seat in the leather chair. "Nisha told me that you specialize in this sort of thing."

"What thing would that be?"

"You know…" I paused and looked at him.

"The first step of working through any problem is being able to admit it." He looked at me as I adjusted in the chair.

"I'm…" I swallowed hard. "In a relationship where my…girlfriend abuses me mentally and physically."

I took a deep breath. I suddenly recognized what Terry McMillan meant about exhaling. With that confession, I felt like I was breathing deeper than I had in over a year.

"When did this all start?"

Dr. Griffith turned on a mini tape recorder as I unfolded the story of the hell that was going on in my life. His dark, intense eyes stared at me from behind a pair of stylish frameless glasses. His well-groomed appearance was non-threatening. The more I talked, the more I relaxed, allowing every horrid detail to spill from my lips.

"Here are a few numbers I think would be helpful for you. Remember, any type of abuse is bad. Be it emotional or physical. Just because you're a man does not mean you should be ashamed. You have done nothing wrong, so never be ashamed." He reached out and shook my hand again as I stood to leave.

"So, is this it?"

"Don't we wish it were that easy?" He laughed. "No, I'll see you this Friday. You can make an appointment with Francine on your way out."

"Okay. Thanks again."

"Remember, you are the victim here. If things get to the point where you feel they're about to boil over, leave and call the police before going back. Make a paper trail."

"I'll try and remember that."

I walked out to the front desk and waited for his assistant to pencil me in. Never compromise your happiness for someone else.

CHAPTER FIVE

I could feel the chill in the air the moment I opened the door. The missing odor of something cooking was a sign that all was not well. I braced myself for what was to come.

I placed my keys on the table and picked up the stack of mail sitting there. I flipped through it quickly and continued my way into the kitchen. I placed the mail on the counter and went in the fridge for a cold drink and to see if I could find something to snack on until dinner plans had been figured out.

Dr. Griffith's words danced in my head as I pulled things out and sat them on the counter. Our entire relationship had been about control from day one. She suggested where we would go on our dates. When we would go on dates. I was nothing more than a yes man to her.

"I guess you couldn't come in the room and say hello."

I damn near jumped out of my shoes. "I just walked in."

"Why you acting like you're guilty of something?"

"What?"

"I called your office today, only to find out that you'd left early. So, I rushed home thinking that I would surprise you."

"I had an appointment…"

"An appointment? You didn't tell me anything about an appointment. I'm starting to feel that you're lying to me."

She stepped closer to me. My defense mechanism kicked in as I braced myself for the terror I could see growing in her eyes.

"Look, why don't we go over here and sit down and talk so I can tell you all about—"

Her balled fist hit me dead in the mouth. I felt my lip beginning to swell.

"You think I'm stupid or something?! If you think you're going to play me like that, then your stupid ass better think again! I keep telling you, don't fuck with me!"

She grabbed the egg pan from the stove she had used earlier that morning. Still recovering from the first blow, I didn't have my bearings together enough to fend her off. My ears rang from the two swift hits she landed upside my head. No longer could I hear the ranting of the mad woman who stood before me. By the time she connected the final blow, darkness was taking over.

A sharp pain shot through my head as I tried to lift it. I reached out and felt the cold metal railing of the hospital bed. Brief spurts of what had transpired between Candy and me played out in my nightmares. When I tried to raise my left hand, I couldn't. Panic set in when I realized the reason behind it. Every time I moved it, the metal bracelet that chained me to the bed made a clinking sound.

I frantically searched for the button to call for the nurse. Must've pushed it fifty times once I found it. Three people ran into the room and only one of them was the nurse. The blue suit and uniform told me who the other two were without words. I looked down at my wrist again. I tried to open my mouth and speak, but no words came. My tongue felt heavy and pasty and my throat tightened as I thought about the possibility I could actually be convicted of something I was actually the victim of.

"Dr. Adelson, we'd like to ask you a few questions," the detective said as he pulled up a chair next to the bed.

I looked down at my wrist again and then back at him. My eyes began to fill with water, water that represented the anger and shame I was feeling inside.

"Dr. Adelson, I truly apologize about this, but we have procedures we have to follow when a case is under investigation."

Just then the door opened and in walked a female, dressed in a tan pantsuit with a brown shirt. Her shoulder-length hair was parted down the middle.

"This is my partner, Detective Thomas. As I was saying, we need to ask you a few questions so we can get to the bottom of this. We arrived at the scene after you were taken away in the ambulance. From the information we gathered from Ms. Knight, there was some sort of struggle between the two of you. She claims to have struck you in self-defense."

My eyes widened at the blatant lie she had told them.

"Is there something you would like to say, Dr. Adelson?" Detective Thomas moved a little closer to me.

I blinked back tears as I tried to gather my thoughts about what had happened the night in question. I swallowed hard before I was able to get one word out. "Sh-sh-she…" I took another breath.

"Take your time. We understand," Detective Thomas said.

"Our relationship…" My eyes frantically searched the faces of both detectives. What would they think of a man who allowed his woman to beat him? My chances of avoiding any prison time relied on me telling the truth, no matter how embarrassing.

I slowly relayed to them the events of that night, at least the ones that I could remember. Telling them of incidents before. Sounding like the stories told by women countless times before. Women that had been labeled crazy because they stayed in the relationship. Here I was, living proof that it didn't only happen to women.

"Dr. Adelson, you're not alone," Detective Thomas said reassuringly.

"I know it now."

"Since she's accusing you of attacking her, we still have to look into it further. Is there anyone we can talk to who will confirm what you're telling us?"

Detective Thomas took out her notepad and wrote down the information as I gave her Nisha's and Dr. Griffith's phone numbers.

"What exactly did Candy say happened that night?" I asked.

They both looked at me with a sense of pity.

"While we can't go into details, we can tell you she's accused you of attacking her, thereby justifying her reasoning for damn near beating your brains in with a pan as self-defense."

"And people wonder why abuse is never reported." I gestured toward my shackled wrist.

"We can take care of that." Detective Thomas pulled a set of keys from her pocket and undid the handcuffs. I rubbed the sore spot and thanked her. "We're going to give them a call and then we'll get back to you."

"How long have I been here?" I rubbed the stubble on my face.

"About three days."

"Three days?!" The pain in my head came back quick and strong. I blinked in an attempt to keep it at bay.

"Okay, I have to ask that you let Dr. Adelson get his rest." The nurse ushered them to the door. Detective Thomas left her card on the bedside table.

"We'll be talking to you soon."

I slightly nodded my head.

I had attacked her. Wow, I couldn't believe she would even think to say something like that. After all of the pain I had suffered at her hands, she had the nerve to flip the script on me.

I picked up the phone and dialed my house. She picked up on the third ring. I was furious that she was still in my house.

"What are you doing there? Why would you want to be in the house of a man that attacked you?"

"Eddie, Baby, I was just on my way to see you and—"

"Save it, Candy. The police are on their way there now. So, don't get any ideas about destroying or taking anything. I never thought you'd lie like that on me. The best thing right now would be for you to gather your things and leave. For good."

"Eddie, just hear me out. You know I love you. Baby, we can work this out—"

"Work it out? What is there to work out?" The more we talked, the more my head throbbed. "Candy, before you take the baggage that you're carrying into another relationship, you need to get some help. Goodbye." I hung up without another word.

CHAPTER SIX

"I'm Edward Adelson and I was once the victim of abuse. After waking up in a hospital near death and being accused of attacking her, I decided I had to make a change. That's when I found Men Against Abuse and realized I wasn't alone. There were plenty of men who were going through the same thing as me. When I first started coming to these meetings the group was very small, but we have since grown into a family of over two hundred. As far as the numbers go, that is only a drop in the bucket.

"Men Against Abuse's goal is to let other men know they are not alone and should never feel ashamed of their situation. Most importantly, we want them to know there is a place for them.

"Together we'll expose this dark secret and get the help that is needed to those in need. Thank you."

The crowd erupted into thunderous applause as I made my way from the podium. It had been two years since I put Candy out of my life. In doing so, I had to make drastic changes. I closed my practice and relocated to another state. I was even tempted to change my name.

Before I left, I wrote her a letter, again suggesting she get help. Whether she did or not, I'll never know.

I finally realized she had to deal with her shortcomings, like I had to learn to deal with mine. By taking control of me, it gave her the sense of security she lacked in her relationship with her mother, the relationship Candy swore would never be hers.

I'm in a new relationship now with a wonderful woman who appreciates me, as I do her. While we're taking things at a leisurely pace, I have a feeling this one may be the one to last a lifetime. Never again will I allow someone to make me feel unworthy.

Never compromise your happiness for someone else.

Shonda Cheekes is the author of Another Man's Wife *and the upcoming sequel* In the Midst of It All *coming in May from Strebor Books International. She is also the author of the novella* "Lessons Learned" *in* Blackgentlemen.com. *She resides in Atlanta, Georgia with her husband and children.*

VICTORY
BEGINS
WITH ME

DYWANE D. BIRCH

How did it all begin? Well, I know the answer. Still, I've often asked myself that question over and over, trying to make some sense out of the craziness I allowed—yes, allowed being the operative word—myself to live through for almost three years of my life. You see, I had willingly given away my heart, body, and soul to a man who was controlling, verbally abusive, and physically combative. In other words, he beat the shit out of me. Excuse me for cursing. But I don't know any other way to say it without sugarcoating it. In a nutshell, the bastard would beat me with his fists like I was a man on the block. He was a man who hated women. And I was, ironically, the woman who loved him.

You see, I spent those horrible years of my life covering up bruises, and telling many stories to explain my misery away. I was scared to tell anyone the truth—let alone face it—that I was a victim of domestic violence. Out of embarrassment. Out of fear. I closed the windows to my soul, losing myself in a kaleidoscope of emotions. I foolishly gave a man I loved—a man who knew nothing about loving me—the license to control, intimidate, and threaten my total being as a woman.

Why? Because I allowed myself to get sucked into a disturbing fantasy that he was the only man for me. I allowed myself to believe that without him in my life, I would be nothing. But the truth of the matter was: I was someone who allowed him to treat me like nothing. I didn't demand he respect me. Instead of walking away the first time he raised his hand to me, I stayed, hoping it was an isolated incident. But it never was. And still I stayed.

For those of you who may not know, time clock statistics state that every nine seconds a woman is abused in the United States. It is also said that one-fourth of all women in the U.S. will be abused by a boyfriend or husband sometime in their lifetime. And that thirty percent of all women who die—by homicide—are killed by the men in their lives. It's disheartening when I think back on how I was one of those women. Battered, frightened, alone, and on the brink of death. Stripped of my self-worth, and robbed of my dignity. But somehow, somewhere, I found the strength, and courage, to break free from the grips of abuse. And became a survivor.

And so here is where my personal journey through pain and abuse ends, and my humble road to self-discovery begins…hopefully, my story—the tears I shed, the hurt I felt—will free another life from the chains of domestic violence.

So, again, how did it all begin? It began with a dance: A rump-shaking, finger-popping, hip-grinding, sweat-it-all-out night on the dance floor at the Freehold Elks with one of the finest brothas in the place. Tyquan Arlington. Six-four, chiseled, dark-chocolate coated, with piercing brown eyes, and a smile that would melt the snow-capped Alps. But little did I know that beneath the surface of his playboy charm was the temperament of a rattlesnake. Dangerous.

One dance led to another, then another, and before I knew it, it was "last call for alcohol" and time for me to go. Ty, as he liked to be called, walked me out to the parking lot to my car where we stood for another half-hour talking and laughing.

"Damn, Girl," he said, licking his lips. "I'm really feelin' you. I dig your style."

I smiled. "I'm feeling you, too," I responded, looking him dead in his dreamy eyes. "But I'm not in the mood for no drama."

"Nah, Baby. I don't come with drama. Just a whole lot of good love."

He smiled, flashing his pearly whites. He was sexy. And I definitely wanted to get to know him better. But I wasn't going to press it. I had recently gotten out of a two-year relationship with an idiot who actually thought he could have me, along with his three babies' mamas. Wrong answer. I was tired of wearing my heart on my sleeve and having it stomped on, then thrown in my face. A relationship with another man was definitely out of the question for me. Period. But here it was, almost two a.m., and I was standing outside flirting with a man I'd known for less than three hours.

Anyway, I already knew if he pushed up and wanted the digits, I'd hit him with them. If not, oh well. I'd catch him around some other time.

"Well, it was nice talking to you," I said, pressing in the code for my car door.

He held it open, then closed it once I had slipped in behind the wheel, and rolled down the window. I started up the engine.

"Damn." He sighed, leaning his body into the car. The crisp scent of his Dior cologne enticed me. He lowered his voice. "I can't let you get away just like that. Let me get your number."

I grabbed a pen from out of my glove compartment, then took his big, warm hands into mine and wrote my numbers—home phone and cell— down in his palm.

"Yo, that's wassup," he said, grinning. "I'ma holla at you." He lifted my chin with his finger, then kissed me lightly on the mouth. "You gonna be mine," he said, kissing me again before stepping away from the car.

I smiled, licking my lips, then slowly backed out of my space, pulling out of the driveway and heading down Throckmorton for Rt. 9 North.

The next day, he called and we talked on the phone for almost three hours. I learned he was originally from Brooklyn but had been living out here in Jersey for the last two years. He was single. Had a J-O-B. Had a car, and his own place. No children. Hmm. No woman, no baby mama drama. The more he talked, the more I liked.

By seven o'clock that night, I was sitting across from him at Freshwaters in Plainfield, having a delicious soul food dinner. By eight-thirty, we were off to a movie at Perth Amboy Cinemas and by midnight, I was back at his townhouse in Matawan being licked from head-to-toe, from front to back. He had loved—let me rephrase that—sexed—every inch of my body incredibly.

However, had I known my whirlwind beginning would have a tumultuous middle and a devastating ending, I would have run for cover without blinking an eye. But he was smooth. In a matter of weeks, I had gone from being single and free to being Ty's girl. We were inseparable. He'd say all the right things, and do all the right things. He'd tell me how beautiful I was, how I was the only woman for him. He wined and dined me constantly, and bought me flowers "just because" almost every day. He held open doors for me, rubbed my back, massaged my feet, and continuously made love to my mind and body all night long. There wasn't anything he wouldn't do for me.

Then as the weeks collided into months, the flowers stopped, and all of his gentlemanly qualities seemed to slowly disappear. He became more demanding, and increasingly possessive. The signs—no matter how subtle—were definitely there. I just refused to see it for what it was. At first I thought his jealousy was cute. But then it became aggressive and began to border more on the crazy end of the spectrum.

He didn't care where we were. In public, behind closed doors, it didn't matter—he'd make a scene if he thought I gave another man eye contact or if a brotha spoke and I cordially smiled. He was really beginning to wear my nerves thin with his constant accusations. No matter how many times I tried to reassure him that I was committed, and faithful to him, he still questioned my trust. I was in a no-win situation.

But instead of leaving him, I proceeded with caution and kept giving him my all. I didn't see his combative, and argumentative, nature as abusive. He hadn't hit me, yet. But his habit of snatching me by the arm whenever I tried to walk away from an argument should have been a red flag for me. It wasn't. I pressed on.

Then one night—about a year into our relationship—I was on the phone talking with one of my girlfriends, getting caught up on all the girl stuff we normally did on our girl's night out. Since I didn't go out now that I had a man in my life, there was a lot of gossiping and cackling to do. The call waiting beeped. I ignored it and kept on talking, since my call was to Maryland. Finally, after the tenth time the line buzzed through, I clicked over. "Hello."

"Yo, what the fuck took you so long to answer the damn phone?" he asked in a tone that told me he was pissed.

"I'm on the phone long distance with my girl Velvetta," I said, keeping my voice calm and steady, trying to keep my attitude in check. Ty and I had already had an argument three weeks prior about me being too "damn mouthy" as he kindly put it. So I was making a conscious effort to keep my attitude in check.

"Yeah right. You probably on the phone with some nigga," he snapped. "Let me find out."

I rolled my eyes. "Ty, please. Where are you?"

"Why?"

"'Cause I wanna call you back."

"Fuck that. You tell that bitch you'll call her back."

My first instinct was to tell him to kiss my honey-dipped bottom, and hang up on him. But I didn't feel like beefing with him for two days, then him giving me the silent treatment like I was the one who had done something wrong.

"Hold on," I replied, clicking the phone over before he could say another word. "Hey, Vetta, let me call you back. Ty is bugging again."

"Humph. What else is new?" she said. "Go do you, Girl. I got my own man drama to deal with. Call me when you can."

"I will," I said, then clicked back over. "I'm back."

The phone line was dead. He had hung up. And I was pissed.

Twenty minutes later, there was a knock on the door. It was Ty, standing there with his face all bunched up. His jaws were clamped tight. Just by his posture, I knew there were gonna be problems. I took a deep breath, opening the door.

"Don't you ever do that shit again!" he shouted, pushing the door in. He took off his leather coat, tossing it across the leather ottoman. I shut the door, counting to ten.

"Do what, Ty?" I asked, scooping up his coat from off the chair and walking over to the closet to hang it up.

"Yeah, aiight. Play stupid if you want. But let me call here again, and you don't answer and…"

The nerve of him, I thought. The last I checked, it was my name on the bill, and I was the one paying it.

"Look," I said, feeling myself lose it. "Don't come up in here with your bull. I'm not in the—"

Before I could get the rest of my words out, he was hovering over me and had slapped me. His hand burned a print into the side of my face. I couldn't believe he had raised his hands to me. This couldn't be happening to me. Not to Persia Monae Swanson. No man had ever hit me before. Not even my father. I didn't grow up around men beating on women. I wasn't raised in a home where there was violence. Or strings of expletives hurled at you. I had been fortunate throughout my life to not be a victim of abuse on any level, be it emotional, physical, or mental. But with the strike of a hand, I was now on the receiving end. I was hurt and in a state of shock.

"I don't believe you just hit me," I said, holding my face. It stung. I fought back my tears.

"Baby, I'm sorry," he said, trying to touch the side of my face. "I don't know what came over me."

"Get out!" I yelled, backing away from him. The wells of my eyes were beginning to open. I willed them shut.

"Come on, Baby. I didn't mean to hit you. It just happened."

"I don't wanna hear it," I snapped, snatching his coat off the hanger and throwing it at him.

"I'm sorry, Baby."

"Just get the hell out!"

He reluctantly left, but kept calling me and calling me. And I kept hanging up on him until I got tired of it and turned the ringer off. I didn't want to hear anything he had to say. He had crossed the line. And I had no intentions of putting up with it.

I crawled up in my queen-sized bed and cried myself to sleep, waking up in the middle of the night to someone stroking my face and hair. I screamed. Ty had found a way to break into my apartment, leading me to believe I didn't know what else he was capable of. But little did I know, I'd find out, sooner rather than later.

Nevertheless, he apologized relentlessly, and after two weeks of giving him the cold shoulder, I ended up giving in. I missed him. Besides, he said he'd never do it again. And I wanted to believe him. I needed to.

Weeks slid by without any further aggression. And in the midst of us being the loving couple again, he somehow convinced me to give up my place and move in with him, saying he needed to wake up to me in his bed every night. He professed his undying love for me on bended knee, slipping a beautiful engagement ring on my finger, then making spectacular love to me. I was strung. And against my better judgment, I did just what he wanted. I gave up my own space. I didn't realize how big of a mistake I had made until it was too late. Unfortunately, I was already playing housewife. I had already given him control.

Interestingly, he did everything he could to make me feel comfortable. He even went as far as getting rid of most of his furniture and allowing me to decorate the house the way I wanted. I had to admit, the first six months were wonderful. I was truly happy. Or so I thought. But when you're blinded by what you think is love, you can only see as far as your heart will let you. Which, in my case, wasn't very far. I was looking at life—my life—through cloudy, smudge-stained lenses.

You know. I realize now that Ty was a really disturbed man. But back then, I justified his behavior, believing he'd see how much I loved him once we were married. Once we made our vows to love each other til death did us part, he'd see that he was the only man for me. Silly me. Humph. I can vividly recall the first time he looked me in my eyes, after rocking my body for the third time that night, and whispered in his deep, delicious voice, "If you ever try to leave me, I'll kill you."

I nervously laughed. "Ty," I said, slapping his arm, playfully, "you so silly."

He didn't crack a smile. His eyes bore into me, causing a chill to go up my spine. "Nah. Word is bond. I'll kill you before I ever let you leave me." He spoke deliberately. Purposefully. And it frightened me. But I let it pass the minute he climbed back on top of me, slipping his manhood back inside of me. I gasped. However, the look on his face told me he'd love me to death, or at least try to—figuratively and literally.

Two weeks later, he threw—Umm, maybe threw is the wrong word to use. It sounds a bit harsh. Let's use his words, he accidentally pushed—me down the stairs, causing me to break my arm and ankle. When he drove me to the hospital, I lied about my injuries. I told them I had fallen down the stairs. The doctor looked hard at me, then shot a look over at the nurse, but neither said a word to contradict my story. Nevertheless, I spent eight weeks with both my arm and foot in casts because I didn't feel like having sex.

Even after that, I hadn't planned on leaving him. Not yet, anyway. A part of me still wanted to believe that he would change. That we could get through this. If I just didn't do anything to upset him. Time and time again, I rationalized his anger and resentment. His quick and sudden mood swings had to be because of something I said, or didn't say. Something I did, or didn't do. Something I forgot to do. Something I forgot to say. There was never any rhyme or reason for his rage. It would come in cycles.

We could go for weeks, even months, without any arguments. He'd be the most loving and attentive man I could ever ask for. Then, out of nowhere, something real or imagined would trigger his rage, causing the gates of hell to open and ending up with me being thrown around, kicked around, and beat around until he tired out. It was a ritual that I had numbed myself to. If I could just weather the storm, I kept telling myself, there'd be brighter days. But each time he slapped me, punched me, or stomped on me, he'd rip away another strand of my being.

I had had enough of his abuse. I was tired of being his punching bag. So, I gradually withdrew from him emotionally and mentally. I became detached. But it only heightened his paranoia, and fueled his insecurities. He must have known something was going through my mind because he had taken all of my clothes—every stitch I owned, including shoes and underwear— and either ripped them up or cut them up before throwing them in the trash. When I confronted him, he punched me in the mouth, splitting my lip. Blood spurted out.

"Owww!" I cried out, grabbing my mouth with my hand. "Why do you have to always put your hands on me? Why?"

He hit me again. I screamed. He hit me again, causing my head to hit the wall. He ripped my clothes off of me, then dragged me down the stairs by the back of my hair.

"You wanna leave. Then take your bare ass on," he said, opening up the front door. I screamed in agony. He kicked me in my back, then continued punching me until I lost the will to fight back. He was going to kill me. And I had no clue why. He picked me up and tossed me outside in the snow, butt-naked. As if that wasn't enough, he spit on me. "Fucking bitch." He walked back inside, slamming the door and locking it, leaving me out in ten below zero weather to freeze to death. Humiliated.

I remember lying in that snow, promising myself he'd never put his hands on me again. I half-crawled and half-dragged myself across the ice and snow to the next-door neighbors' and banged on the bottom of their door, pleading for someone to help me.

Finally, the door opened and I passed out. When I came to, I was in the hospital suffering from a concussion, two broken ribs, and hypothermia. The doctors probed me. The social workers interviewed me. The police interrogated me. Everyone wanted to know what had happened to me. But I refused to give them any information. You see, New Jersey has very strict domestic violence laws. If there are any signs of physical injury, the police must arrest the abuser. Even without witnesses, or injury, the abuser can still be arrested. I didn't want to see Ty in trouble. I just wanted the fighting to stop. Was there anything wrong with that?

Well, Portia, my sister, thought so. She was livid. "What the hell you mean, you don't want to get him in trouble? Fuck him. He could have killed you."

"But he didn't," I rebutted, desperately trying to reason with her. "I made him angry and things just got a little out of hand."

"A little out of hand," she repeated, clearly disgusted. "He beat you, stomped on you, ripped your clothes off, then threw you outside in the fucking snow. I'd say that's a whole lotta 'out of hand' as you say. You have nothing to do with how he acted. His anger is his shit. Not yours. Angry or not, he had no fucking business putting his damn hands on you. If you won't do something about it, I will."

"Portia, please," I said, crying. "I don't want to rehash this. I don't want the police involved. I just want to go on with my life and forget it happened." A waterfall of tears fell from my puffy eyes.

She sat on the edge of the hospital bed, wrapping her arms around me. "I know, Sweetheart. It's gonna be okay." I started bawling. "That's right, let it out. I know it hurts. If you don't want to sign complaints right now, it's okay. You just get some rest, okay? We'll talk tomorrow."

I nodded, my head in her chest. My spirit was crushed. My heart ached. How could he do this to me? Why? What did I ever do to deserve this? I must have cried for another half-hour or so before Portia left me. She didn't want to leave me alone, but I promised her I'd go back to her place once I was discharged. Sadly, I didn't. Ty had waited until she was gone, then came into my room. He broke down in tears, begging me not to leave him. Pleading with me to give him another chance. Asking for my forgiveness. My heart went out to him. For the two years we had been together, he had never cried before. Had never shown any emotion, other than anger. His tears seemed genuine. His promises seemed sincere. I loved him.

Unfortunately, my decision to stay with him put a wedge between my sister and me. She thought I was a "damn fool" but it didn't matter. I was a grown woman, and I was going to do whatever I wanted, with whomever I wanted. Regardless. No matter what she said, I was going home to my man. She hugged me, and handed me a card. I glanced at it before stuffing it into my purse. It read: 1-800-799-SAFE. It was the number for the National Domestic Violence Hotline, a hotline center that provides victims of abuse, information about resources available to them to ensure their safety. I hugged her again, hoping I would never need to dial the number.

The beatings stopped. But the verbal and emotional abuse continued. His behavior and moods were unpredictable. One minute he was ranting and raving about how much he hated me. How sick I made him. The next minute, he couldn't live without me. He'd smother me with affection. I thought I could handle it. But his words would cut into me worse than his fists ever did. Those wounds were always much deeper. I was sick of riding this emotional rollercoaster with him. I was ready to get off. I had had enough.

The straw that broke the camel's back was the night he came home in one of his oversized toddler tantrums, cursing and screaming because I hadn't gotten around to cooking dinner.

"Ty," I said, heaving a sigh, "I'm not feeling well. I've been throwing up all day."

"And?" he asked. I leaned over the kitchen sink, holding my head. "What does that have to do with your lazy ass not having dinner cooked?"

"I'm tired," I explained.

"And I should fuck you up," he snapped.

Right at that moment, my sister's last phone conversation played in my head. "Girl, if you don't leave his ass, he's gonna end up killing you." I tried to brush off her remark, but something I had read in a pamphlet she had given me a few months back flashed at me: Women who leave abusers are at seventy-five percent greater risk of being killed than those who stay. I shuddered. If this were true, then it was safer for me to stay.

"It's not that bad," I said, trying to minimize, once again, his aggression. "He's just under a lot of stress at work. No relationship is perfect."

"Yeah, whatever," she snapped. "When are you gonna stop making damn excuses for his sorry ass?"

"Well, at least he's not running around cheating on me like Lester," I retorted, feeling like a fool for letting the words fall from my lips. I could visualize her rolling her eyes up in her head.

"Ugh! What's worse, a man who cheats on you or one who beats on you?"

Sadly, I didn't have the answer.

"Can we not get into this right now?" I said, getting frustrated. Nothing I said would make sense to her. She'd just never understand. "He loves me."

"Persia, that man doesn't know the first thing about loving you. The only thing he loves is controlling you. You need to wake up."

"No, Portia," I said, getting frustrated, "I just need you to be there for me."

She sighed. "I am. But I'm also worried about you. Persia, you need help. I only hope you realize it before it's too late."

A part of me knew what she was saying was true. I was aware of the fact that domestic violence was the leading cause of injury and death for women in the U.S. But at the time, I couldn't let go. I wasn't ready.

My reverie was broken by the slamming of his fist into the back of my head. He yanked me around. "You hear me talking to you?"

"Oww, Ty," I said, trying to squirm my way out of his grasp. "You're hurting me."

He raised his hand over his head, then stopped in midair. "I should break your damn face."

"Please, Ty," I whined, raising my arm to shield myself from any potential blows. "I would have had dinner cooked for you, but I've been in bed all day. I'll cook something now. It'll only take a few minutes."

He sucked his teeth. "I don't want you cooking shit until you go wash your stinking ass. You look a mess." He let go of me, walking into the living room. He plunked himself down on the sofa, fuming. "Ugly ass bitch can't even have my damn dinner cooked. What the fuck."

I cringed. Ugly ass bitch, I repeated the words in my head. It wasn't so much what he said that hurt because he had hurled hurtful names at me in the past out of anger. It was the contempt in his tone that stabbed me, piercing open new wounds and reopening old ones. I was sick as a damn dog. And he could care less. My sister's voice followed me, trampling through my thoughts as I dragged myself up the stairs with tears swelling in my eyes. Persia, when are you gonna wake the hell up? You deserve better. Look what he's doing to you. I went into the bathroom, flipped the toilet lid up and hugged the bowl, throwing my guts up. "Oh, God, please don't tell me I'm pregnant," I mumbled before quickly dismissing the thought. We always used condoms. It had to be a stomach virus. I got into the shower, wondering how one goes from loving everything about you to saying hateful things about you. It just didn't make any sense to me. I was leaving him. I had to. For my own sanity, I had to find the strength to walk out that door and never look back.

For months, the idea of leaving him had surfaced and resurfaced, twisting its way through my subconscious. But I was afraid. So, I'd shake it off, pushing it far back in the corners of my mind. Out of fear. You see, I had tried to leave him once before, about a year ago. But he followed me everywhere I went, badgered and harassed me. Came to my job, hid in bushes, even broke into my apartment. He did everything he could to make my life miserable. Finally, I ended up giving in. I didn't want to see him in jail. And I was afraid he'd carry out his threats, particularly the one to hurt my sister and her children. I believed him. Portia was fourteen years older than me with two daughters, ages twelve and ten. Since both our parents were deceased, Portia and I were all each other had in terms of family. And he knew this.

He knew how close we were. And how I'd do anything to protect them, even if it meant sacrificing my own life. He knew I could never live with myself if something happened to her or my nieces. So I went back to him. Hoping. Praying. Willing myself to believe that he'd never have another reason to blacken my eyes or bust my lip again.

To keep peace with him, I made myself crazy trying to figure out what would or wouldn't set him off. If I wore makeup, he'd think I was out hoeing around. If I didn't wear any, he'd say I looked like shit. If I cooked something he didn't like, he'd dump it in the sink or in the middle of the floor. If I asked him what he wanted me to cook, he'd tell me to get a brain. I was damned if I did, and damned if I didn't. There was just no winning with him. Something had to give.

I stood in the middle of the shower that night and sobbed uncontrollably. My life had spun out of control. I didn't know why I had let it happen. I didn't know how I was going to undo what had already been done. But the one thing I knew, I wanted my freedom. However, every time I thought about my life without him, I'd get a sharp, agonizing pain in my heart. It hurt more than the beatings. I loved him more than I loved life.

Then I got a phone call that would change the course of my life. My sister was moving to Atlanta in three weeks. Her job had relocated and she was offered a management position in Marketing and Advertisement with Coca-Cola. Hearing that was like music to my ears; a ton of bricks had just been lifted off my shoulders. She and her children would be far away from Jersey and out of harm's way. Ty would never be able to threaten their lives again, if and when I decided to leave him. But right at that moment, things were going well with us. I was staying. And yes, I was confused.

"And I want you to come with us," she added.

I was stunned. "Thanks, Portia," I said, mentally preparing my list of excuses as to why I wouldn't be able to relocate. "But Atlanta is just a bit too far south for me. I'm a Jersey girl." I couldn't come out and tell her that there was no reason for me to leave right now because Ty hadn't raised his hands to me or cursed me in weeks. I couldn't tell her that I was getting married. Not yet.

"Look, before you write the idea off, come out and see for yourself. Stay a few weeks, then decide. If you don't like it, you can always come back. At least think about it."

"Okay. I'll think about it."

"Promise."

"Yes," I said, crossing my fingers. "I promise."

"The change will do us both some good," she said, smiling through the phone as if I had already agreed to pack up and go along. "You just wait and see."

I nodded. "Change is always good. I'll give you a call in a few days."

"Persia."

"Yes?"

"I love you."

"I love you, too."

We hung up. But the thought of leaving Jersey stayed with me. If I did leave, maybe I would like it. I had heard Atlanta was the metropolitan Mecca of the South. But what would I do, if I didn't like it? Ty probably wouldn't take me back. And if he did, my life would be three times worse than what it had been. If I wanted to come back to Jersey, I'd have no place to stay. I'd be homeless. Or I'd just have to stay there and try to make the best of it until I was able to get back on my feet. I was so deep in thought about the prospect of finally breaking free from Ty, that I didn't hear him walk in. He startled me when he spoke.

"Who was that on the phone?" he asked, standing in the doorway, barechested with a pair of sweats on. Oh, how I loved that body.

"My sister," I responded, turning my back on him before I weakened.

"What'd she want?"

"Nothing. She was just calling to see how I was doing."

He grunted. "I'll be glad when she gets a life of her own," he said, walking up behind me. He pressed himself into me, wrapping his arms around me and kissing me on my neck. His hands found their way around to my breasts, where he gently kneaded them. My nipples perked up. "Come on, Baby. Let me make love to you."

He smelled good. He stuck his tongue in my ear, nibbled on my earlobe, then reached down and slid his hand between my legs. I widened my stance. I was slipping. And didn't care. I needed him. I bent over, pulling up my nightgown, willingly offering myself to him. He pulled his erect manhood out over his sweats, then entered me, temporarily erasing all my troubles. I didn't know what the morning would bring, but right at that moment, the only thing that mattered was, him loving me—no matter how slight.

Two days later, I returned home from my doctor's appointment, knowing just how much control Ty really had over me—emotionally, mentally, and physically. The thought of needing to take birth control had never crossed my mind. Why should it? We always used a condom. Well, little did I know Ty had been poking holes in them for months, trying to get me pregnant! His plan worked. I was three months pregnant. And feeling more trapped.

I prayed, asking God to guide me in my decisions, to give me the strength to live my life according to His plan, and to keep His blanket of grace and mercy on me. I needed a sign. The only person I had told about my pregnancy was my sister. I drove straight from the doctor's office to her home, crying.

"Does he know?" she asked, hugging me.

I shook my head in her chest.

"What are you going to do?"

"I don't know," I whispered. "I love him, Portia." We let silence take over for a beat. She just listened. Waited patiently. "I'm so confused. I don't think I can live without him. We have our fights. But he loves me."

"Persia, sweetheart," she said, rubbing my face. "He doesn't love you. No man who loves you hurts you the way he does. And beating on someone who you supposedly care about is not love—it's abuse. You don't deserve that. No woman does."

"But I can't leave him," I said, wiping my face with the sleeve of my shirt. "Not now. I don't want to raise a baby by myself."

"You can leave him," she said, reassuringly. "You can pack up and leave with us next week. And you won't be raising your baby by yourself. I'll help you."

"But I'm carrying his child. I can't keep it from him. He has to know."

"Then tell him."

"He won't let me leave him."

"What do you mean, he won't let you leave him? If you want to leave, there's nothing he can do to stop you."

I sighed. "Portia, you don't understand—"

"No," she snapped, cutting me off. "I do understand. He's a damn nut. And that's all there is to it. I understand that he has you living in fear, walking on eggshells. Not knowing when the next bomb is going to go off. I understand all too well. But you understand something. I love you. And I know I can't tell you how to live your life. But it's not about you anymore. You have a child inside of you. What good is it going to be if you stay with a man who beats on you whenever he feels like it?

"If that's the life you want. Then fine. But no child deserves to be witness to that. You want to stay with him, then you stay. But what happens when he kills you, Persia, huh? What happens when your unborn child doesn't have a mother because his father beat her to death? Please tell me, Persia. What happens then?"

Her words slapped me, forcing me to take a sad look at my reality. I burst into tears. "I can't leave him, Portia. He's really trying. We haven't fought in months."

She rolled her eyes up in her head. "So now I guess you think he deserves a medal. Wake the fuck up, Persia. He had no damn business putting his hands on you in the first place. If you're afraid of leaving him, then sign a damn restraining order against him."

I shook my head. I heard everything she said. But I couldn't respond. My emotions were stuck in my throat. I coughed up a ball of pain, sobbing. I cried until my chest hurt. The air around me was thinning. I was feeling lightheaded. "I can't live without him. I need him."

My sister stared at me with sadness in her eyes. Her tone softened. "You don't need him or any other man. I'm telling you, Persia, you can do it. Look at me. I've done it."

I stared into my sister's almond-shaped eyes, lovingly admiring her beauty and strength. And wished I could have been more like her. Independent. Focused. Self-defined. She refused to settle for anything less than what she demanded. And she refused to let a man define who she was as a woman. Period. She had caught her husband with another woman and walked out on him after ten years of marriage and two small children, never looking back. And was happy. I wanted to feel what she felt.

We talked for another hour or so before I headed home. I didn't know what I was going to do, or how I was going to do it. But one thing was for sure: I had to do something, soon. I saw Ty's car in the driveway, glanced down at my watch. It was 9:30 p.m. I had been gone for over six hours and had forgotten to call home. Anxiety beat in the pit of my stomach. The house was pitch dark. I peeled myself out of the car and made my way to the door, hoping he was asleep. I stuck the key in the door, turning the knob, then walking in. My heart was heavy. I flipped on the light.

"Where the fuck you been?" he snapped, jumping up out of the chair. He lunged at me. I backed away.

"I-I—"

"I've been fucking calling you all damn day." He grabbed me by the arm. "Where the fuck were you?"

"Ow, Ty. You're hurting me," I said, wincing. "I was with Portia."

"All damn day?" he barked, glaring at me. Twisting my arm.

"Owww. Yes."

"Then why didn't you answer you cell?"

"Because I forgot to bring it with me."

"Bullshit!" he snapped, slapping me. "I wanna know who the fuck you out there whoring with." I held the side of my face in my hand.

"No one," I said, holding back tears.

Everything my sister said pounded through my head. No matter what I said, or tried to do, Ty would never change. He would continue to treat me like shit, as long as I let him. I yanked my arm from his grasp.

"I'm tired of you putting your hands on me, Ty. I'm tired of you accusing me of doing things I'm not. I'm tired of you mistreating me. And I'm sick of you talking to me any kind of way. I'm leaving you."

The veins in his neck and forehead expanded. His eyes dilated. I held my breath. And stood my ground. I was through. I tried to open the door to get to my car before he hit me again. But he caught me, swinging me around, then punching me in the face.

I screamed. Yelled for help at the top of my lungs. "Please, Ty. Stop! Help me." He hit me again. Blood splattered from my lip.

"You wanna talk slick, Bitch. You wanna get brand new, talking 'bout you leaving me. Didn't I tell you I'd kill your ass before I let you go?"

His fist felt like steel pipes hitting against my flesh. My vision blurred. He wrapped his hands around my throat, choking me. I gasped for air, felt around for something to grab, anything to get him off me. I felt something. I reached for it, fighting for my life. It was a crystal ashtray. I grabbed hold of it and smashed him in the face with it. He let go of me. I hit him again, then ran out the house, yelling for help. He ran after me. But I was already at the neighbor's door, banging. Kicking. Screaming. No one answered. He yanked me by the back of my hair, punching me.

"Please, Ty, stop! I'm pregnant. You're going to make me lose my baby!"

He just blocked everything out and continued to beat me, slapping and punching me. All my sister said was going to come to pass. I would never live to see the birth of my child. He was going to kill me, and there was no one around to save me. Everything began to fade in and out. In the distance, I thought I heard the faint sounds of sirens. A burst of colors swirled through my mind. My life was about to be taken from me, along with everything else. What did I do to deserve this? Nothing. I was slipping. The only thing I did was love a man who didn't love me. I closed my eyes, preparing to embrace death.

"Stop! Police!" is the last thing I heard before the world around me darkened.

It's been well over a year since that whole ordeal. And I'm happy to say that I'm safe and sound in Atlanta, and thankful that I'm here today to share my story. I'm grateful the neighbors called the police. Had they not gotten there when they did, not only would Ty have taken my life, he would have taken the life of my beautiful son. Yes, I had a healthy baby boy, Parrish Arlington Swanson. He is my pride and joy.

Although my physical wounds have healed, the scars are still there as a constant reminder of what Ty put me through. But the one good thing, I will never have to worry about him hurting me again. He has ten years behind bars to sit and think about his abusive behavior. And hopefully, during that time, he'll get some help for his anger. And self-hatred. I loved him the best

I knew how, but it wasn't enough. I needed to love me first. And I do now.

Ty knows about my son. But he'll never have an opportunity to know him as his father. I petitioned the courts to have his parental rights terminated, and won. I know it will take me a while to get past what I went through with him. With the help of my therapist, I'm sorting through my baggage, peeling back my past one layer at a time. And I'm stronger than I ever imagined. I still have a long way to go. A part of me misses him. How could I not when every time I look into my son's face I see splashes of him? But I'm okay with it. My son may have Ty's genes, but he will not be anything like him. I will make sure of that. He will know how to treat a woman. Love a woman. Respect a woman. He will know never to raise his hand to any woman. Period.

You know. Despite everything, I have forgiven Ty. And I wish for him to find the peace that I have found. I can't control how another person thinks, acts, or feels, but I can surely control how I respond to it. From this day forward, I control whom I let in my life and to what degree. And the one thing I'm sure of, no man will ever again beat me with his hands or his words. I will not allow another human being to have control over me again. No man will ever again define or re-define me as a woman.

Yes, I lived through it, for whatever reasons. But I have made a conscious choice to move past my circumstance of tragedy. And now I am free to love me. Free to just be.

And it's a beautiful feeling. For the first time in my life, I finally realize that I do not have to ever be a victim of anything, because victory begins with me.

Dywane D. Birch, a graduate of Norfolk State University and Hunter College, is the author of Shattered Souls *and* From My Soul to Yours. *He has a master's degree in psychology and is a clinically certified forensic counselor. He lives in New Jersey where he continues to work with incarcerated young adults while working on his third novel.*

THE STRANGER

TRACY PRICE-THOMPSON

His eyes, hooded and sleeted with rage, slithered around the room in search of prey. Beyond the doorway, Paris stood terrified, tiny chill bumps rippling like Braille on her thin arms. An angry pulse marched up and down William's right temple as he stormed into the kitchen, blotting out the light and forcing the air from the room. Bowing her head, Paris snagged her lip between her teeth as he stabbed two thick fingers into the steaming mug of liquid sitting on the table before them.

"Tea ain't hot."

She snatched the oversized cup, ignoring the scalding liquid that sloshed over her fingers and spilled onto the blue and white speckled tablecloth that was embroidered with tiny angels, harps in hand. Wincing under his glare, Paris placed the mug into the microwave and turned the dial up high. She grabbed a dishrag from a nearby drawer and made busy wiping at the spill as William yanked his high-backed chair away from the head of the table and plopped himself down.

"What in the fuck is this?" He stared at the yellow fluff of his breakfast. "You know goddamn well I can't stand no eggs runnin' all over my plate."

Paris moved automatically, her hourglass figure clad in a thin robe, her long brown hair brushing her shoulders. She took the plate from the table and slid it into the microwave beside the bubbling tea, turning the timer up high again and awaiting his next command.

Wasn't shit wrong with the eggs or the tea, she reassured herself. William was just mad because his horse had come in last again, giving him reason to find fault in anything she did. Especially since what she was going to do today didn't involve him. Thank God he'd be leaving soon on a two-week haul. The last time he'd stayed gone that long he'd brought home a kilo of coke, ten gold bangles, and a bad case of the clap. She turned off the microwave, set his breakfast on the table and waited.

"Yum," William said, but his eyes weren't on his plate. They had crawled over her cleavage and were dropping lower. Paris glanced down and saw that her robe had slipped open revealing her shapely thighs and sister-girl hips. Her fingers fumbled as she redid her buttons, praying they would stay. But it was too late. William was looking at her "that way" again and she swallowed hard, fighting the urge to gag.

He'd already taken her. Taken her roughly and in several different positions; each one more painful and humiliating than the last. Twice around midnight, and then again as she tried to slip out of bed at 6 a.m. Sore between the legs and repulsed by the memory, she tucked a few strands of hair behind her ear and reached for the toaster just as funnels of dark smoke began to shoot from its mouth.

"Dizzy bitch! What in the hell is wrong with you?" William pushed away from the table and stood up. He cast an angry shadow over her. "Can't a working man get a decent meal in his own goddamned house?"

Expecting a blow, Paris ducked and cringed, then grabbed at the charred slices of toast, juggling the hot bread as it seared her fingers. Bitch, Slut, Parrot, Ho. Born in Mississippi and named for the most beautiful city in the world, it was a shame she'd never made it any further than this asshole and the Bronx.

"Dumb ass!" William cursed, then seized the back of her neck and bent her over, shoving her down until her cheek was pressed to the countertop. Paris didn't resist. The jagged scar near the base of her right ear began to tingle and, instinctively, her eyes flew to the wooden knife rack sitting near the window. It was empty. All the knives were under the sink in a shoebox. Taped closed and double wrapped in plastic bags.

And then his hands were on her, lifting her robe and rubbing the thick mounds of her ass. Paris closed her eyes and prayed. Not again. Please, not again. Outside the kitchen window sheets of rain pounded the pavement as he spread her cheeks and entered her, ramming her so hard she slid forward on the counter and felt the toaster's heat on her face.

Just hold on, Paris pleaded with herself as he brutalized her from behind. William liked it raw. She was so torn and sore down there until, no matter where he chose to enter her, it all hurt the same. He moaned in her ear, clutching her hips as he moved in and out of her anus without lubrication. Paris bit her lip as her breasts brushed rhythmically against the countertop. This would make what, three, no, four times? In less than eight hours? How much more could he have in him?

"Turn around," William commanded, withdrawing from her abruptly.

Paris stood shakily. She could smell herself as she turned to face her husband. His erect dick rose from his fly, its shaft wet and angry. William sat down in his chair.

"C'mere."

Hell no, Paris thought, even as she moved toward him. Hell fucking no. He must be crazy. I ain't doing that no more. Fuck him. I ain't doing that shit. But today was Tuesday, and that meant William could mess everything up. Sometimes you just had to do what you had to do.

Seconds later her nose was buried in his pubic hair as she sucked and licked him with long, broad strokes. The stench coming off of him was overpowering and Paris choked as her head bobbed up and down in his lap, his fingers yanking at her hair as he fucked up into her mouth.

"Damn, Girl," William panted, ready to burst. "You ain't...worth much," he managed, moaning between words, "but you can suck a...mean dick!"

Paris wanted to bite him. Just clench her jaws and bite his foul dick off and take whatever punishment came. Instead she squeezed around the base of it and sucked hard enough to collapse her cheeks as his seed spurted from him and filled her mouth. She braced herself. You can do it, Paris, she told herself, panic rising and tears stinging her eyes. You can do it. This was the worst part but she had to fake it or his fists would be flying around her head, blackening her eyes and cracking her jaw. Clenching her hands, she braced herself and swallowed. Deep long gulps, pretending hard to like it.

"Yeah." William sighed above her. "Do that shit, Parrot girl. Get it all. You're the best."

❖ ❖ ❖

Sex was only a diversion.

He used his dick to degrade her. He used it as a prelude to the beatings.

William held the cold slices of charred toast in his hands. "Make me some more toast."

"There isn't any more. We're all out of bread."

"There isn't any more," he mimicked. "We're all out of bread. Bitch still covered in Mississippi mud and trying to sound all proper. Like some damn white girl."

Paris picked up the bread and began scraping the black away with the back of a teaspoon. She fingered the scar near her ear. Even a butter knife could be deadly in William's hands.

"Hur' up, Stupid," he rasped, then leaned forward and shoveled the half-cold eggs into his mouth. Paris placed the scraped slices on a napkin, then offered them meekly.

"Goddammit!" William flicked his wrist, knocking the toast from her hands. "What you tryin' to do? Poison me? You make me sick! Don't know your titties from your toenails and can't cook worth a damn!"

It's Tuesday, Paris thought, and squatted down to scoop up the scorched slices of bread. It's Tuesday. "I'm sorry, William. I'm—"

"You goddamn right, you sorry! If your trifling ass wasn't all the time downstairs finger-painting like some idiot, you could make sure there was food in the house! Listen here." William breathed. "When I get back tonight, I wants something decent to eat, so you best get your ass out there and make some groceries 'cause tonight I wants you to call my mama and invite her and Ralphie and Terri over for dinner. I wants you," he went on, "to fix us a few steaks, some taters, and one of them big ole tossed salads Terri always likes. And then I wants you to bake me and my mama a German chocolate cake."

Forgetting her fear, Paris stood. "William," her words came out in a hot rush. "Today is Tuesday. My paintings are going on sale at Jerel's gallery at noon and I'll be gone all day. How about we take Mama and them out to dinner tomorrow night, huh? We could go to that rib place down on Sutter that Ralphie likes so much. Terri could get her a salad there, too—"

William's fist hit the counter so hard the dishes rattled in the drain. "I didn't say shit about tomorrow, so what fuckin' part of tonight didn't you understand?" He moved in on her. "Know what, Parrot? Make that two chocolate cakes and some nana puddin', too."

What? Paris wanted to scream. Fuck you and your mama! Instead she scampered out of the kitchen without another word. Anything she said at this point would only send him soaring into pisstivity, and that was exactly what William was looking for.

Any excuse to kick her ass.

As she tucked her hair under a clear plastic cap and stepped into the shower, Paris bit down on the insides of her cheeks until it hurt. William ought to bake his own mama a damn cake. She lathered her body and carefully washed her privates with a soft loofah sponge, wincing as the soap swirled between her legs.

Paris was country, but she wasn't stupid or without talent. Thanks to Jerel Morrison, owner of the Village Art Express, she'd finally taken her painting to a new level. After falling in love with samples of her artwork that had been displayed at a local college, Jerel had offered to feature ten of her selections in his Fifth Street gallery, and the public bidding was scheduled to begin today. Paris knew how important it was to make a good impression on her prospective customers, and a fresh manicure, a bumping hairstyle, and the perfect outfit were all mandatory indulgences.

She'd taken the day off from her job as an accountant with Jackson Hewitt to have enough time to prepare herself. Now she'd barely have time to get through her morning facial before hurrying to Mozelle's for her weekly hair treatment. If she had any chance of fitting everything in, she'd have to hit the grocery store last, and then come back home to get dressed for the showing.

Paris replaced the sponge on its hook and frowned. Goddamn nana puddin'. And he wanted the pudding made from scratch, too. Instant from the box just wouldn't do. She stood under the spigot and rinsed her light brown skin. There was no way she could get to Pathmark and still make the showing on time. If there was any hope of getting to the gallery before her customers arrived she'd have to shop at the supermarket right next to the beauty parlor and have the groceries delivered to the house.

She'd have to shop at RICHARD'S.

Stanley Summers zipped the fly of his starched brown uniform, and buttoned his shirt all the way to the top. After pulling on his heavily scuffed dark-brown brogans, he stepped back to admire himself in the splotchy mirror that hung over the back of the employee lounge's door.

Hah! he thought happily, his broad grin revealing twisted stumps of decaying teeth. I done pass my probationary period and dey done gived me my uniform jes lak dey promise!

Stanley carried nearly three hundred pounds of hard-earned muscle and his frame was easily the width of two average-sized men. A thick scar ran along the line of his right jaw; a thinner scar bisected his bottom lip and crawled all the way down to the mound of his Adam's apple.

He rubbed his meaty hands across his chest and felt the embroidered RICHARD'S patch on the left, and his own name stitched in script on the right. Grinning crazily at his reflection, Stanley was pleased. Not only had they given him an extra pair of slacks, they'd even stenciled his name and social security number inside each waistband.

This would be Stanley's first experience working inside of a building instead of outside in the elements. His cocoa-colored uniform made him feel like a security guard—but without the gun. As big as he was, guns scared Stanley shitless but he could get loose with a knife.

Stanley's good friend Eddie Johns had finally talked the manager of the produce department at RICHARD'S Supermarket into giving him a job. For five months, Stanley had wandered the 149th Street subway station begging passersby for spare change. Ruddy complexioned and obviously able-bodied, the pedestrians had little sympathy for him and he scarcely collected enough money to fill his gut.

Prior to falling down on his luck, Stanley had worked for a family-owned scrap metal company. Twelve months a year he hauled and stacked large, heavy pieces of metal, and during the summer, he also kept the yard swept clean. For seven years, Stanley sweated for the Lambert family, lifting and dragging the cumbersome iron and metal sheets to the commercial ovens to be melted down and sold for scrap. He'd been a good worker, too, always polite, never late, and in seven whole years, he had never missed a single day of work.

But did the Lamberts appreciate him? Nooo, Stanley thought, with a hint of residual anger clouding his simple features. Nooo, they were mean and ungrateful. A bunch of hood-wearing crackers who had treated him like so much black shit.

It had taken all five of the Lambert brothers to knock Stanley down. They'd swung two by fours and iron pipes at his face and head, leaving him semi-conscious. Those honkies had even grabbed jagged pieces of metal and pulled down his pants to slash at his privates. The oldest Stanley brother had tried to castrate him. He got three of his teeth kicked out for his trouble.

Ain't that jes' lak a honkie? Stanley thought. Tryin' to take ever'thang away from a black man, even his dick? And they din' even wanna gimme my lass' week's pay!

All because he had a small problem. Not even a really big one. Just a leet-lil' one. Shit. Stanley chuckled. I cain't hep it if I got that smell, the one that makes bitches wanna pull off dey panties and go straight to da' bone! Mistah Lambert shoulda unnerstan' cause he gived off that same odor 'round that twenny-two-year-old stock gal I catched him fuckin' in the storage room!

"I oughtta let them kill your retarded ass!" Tyrone Lambert had hissed as he and his younger brother took turns pulling his five sons off of Stanley.

Retarded? Stanley had thought as hot blood filled his mouth and agony exploded in his busted scrotum. Who da fuck he callin' retarded?

"You better disappear, Pervert! Dis-a-fucking-pear, or I swear they're gonna find one big, black, dead nigger in this alley tonight!"

The memory of the beating threatened to roast Stanley from the inside out. It weren't even my fault! he whined to himself. Mr. Lambert's niece was the pervert, not me! They shoulda' kept her outta my face! All the time flouncing by me in those lil' tiny skirts wit her ass hangin' out ever'whare, fat white titties jigglin' in those halter-tops! I din' bother none wit her; it was she who was riling me! Anyways, she old enuf ta' know what she want. She see a man what's big ever'whare, and likes what she see. Like most wimmens, she go for it! Shit, fo'teen is old enuf to lick and to split!

Slow but not stupid, Stanley had immediately split the scrap metal business. He spent the next six months sleeping at the Y and panhandling on the streets until Eddie was able to hook him up with a job in the produce section at RICHARD'S.

Stanley checked himself in the mirror one last time. He posed with his hands in his pockets, then at his sides, and then again in his pockets.

"Fuck dem redneck Lamberts," he mumbled as he walked from the lounge. "I look bettah in dis here monkey-suit than I did in dem rags they had me wearin'."

Although the physical pain of that day had vanished, Stanley's memory of it was still fresh and clear. And so were the mighty waves of desire that fueled his small, but growing problem. With his hands still in his pockets, Stanley giggled, then whispered out loud, "What's long lak a carrot, but thicker'n a cucumber?" Fingering his rock-hard penis through the material of his pants, Stanley stepped into the crowded store and headed toward the produce department.

Paris pushed through the double doors of RICHARD'S Superstore and entered the shopping area in full stride. Her freshly permed hair bounced around her shoulders and framed her pretty features and heart-shaped face. The digital clock above the doorway read 10:22 a.m. and, if she planned to make it to the gallery by lunchtime, she'd have to get her ass in gear. Damn! She twisted her lips in annoyance, then yanked a metal cart from a tangled jumble near the door and made her way up and down the aisles, tossing items into her cart without much thought.

Pausing in the produce department, Paris squeezed a few lemons and inspected a head of lettuce. Two large tomatoes, a bunch of ripe bananas, a bag of purple onions, a small green pepper, and a bag of croutons completed her selection, and a few minutes later she stood in front of a young Hispanic boy wondering why in the world she was there.

"I said, paper or plastic?" the boy repeated, chewing a wad of gum. Paris blinked several times before answering. She licked her lips and scratched her earlobe. "It doesn't matter," she finally answered. She reached into her pocketbook and found her wallet. "But I want my groceries delivered."

"Not a problem," the cashier replied, and blew a huge bubble. The scent of Bazooka flooded Paris's nose as he handed her some change along with a pencil and a small yellow notepad. "Just write down your address."

The interior of the room swam in slow, crazy circles.

Paris shook her head, desperately trying to make sense of the pounding in her skull and the fluid gushing from her nostrils. The last thing she remembered was coming home after shopping at RICHARD'S , changing her clothes, then going down to the basement to get the complimentary print she planned to donate to the gallery. She pressed a manicured hand to her nose and it came away bright red.

"You gon' stay down, Bitch? Or am I gone hafta fuck you up again?"

Agonized, Paris forced herself into a sitting position with her back against the wall, then gathered her legs beneath her and attempted to rise. Her canary-yellow Donna Karan suit was stained with splotches of blood and a multi-colored array of paint that had splashed down on her when the stranger slammed her into the easel head first, breaking her nose. And now the storage room—thanks to William a.k.a. her art studio—was in shambles. Paints and papers were scattered across the floor like a gale wind had swept through. A male voice grated at her ears.

"Oh, you tryna git up? You's about a hard-headed bitch, huh?"

The stranger raised his fist and threatened to deck her again, even from the other side of the room.

"...W-w-wait a minute, please...what do you want from me? Who are you...?" Her heart pounded and the high-pitched whine in her voice made her feel sick.

"Bitch!" the stranger exploded, jumping over the felled easel and knocking huge stacks of paper to the floor. "Don't you wurry none 'bout who the fuck I am!" He wound her hair around his fist and yanked her head back until she thought he'd pop her spine. "Jes' shet the fuck up," he barked, slapping her first open-handed and then backhanded, "an' take off dem goddamn clothes!"

Take off my clothes? Paris thought through a cloud of hazy pain. Who the hell was he? Some overgrown junkie looking for a hit? No, maybe that gambling son of a bitch had jerked this fool out of some money. Maybe this giant of a man had come looking for William and found her instead.

Did this motherfucker just tell me to take off my clothes?

Her mind raced. How did this fool get in my house? What in the hell does he want? And why is he dressed in a RICHARD'S uniform? Formulating answers was out of the question. Her nose was swollen and throbbing and he had her head crammed back in an agonizing position. The last thing Paris saw was his huge fist as it came crashing down toward her face.

And then her world went dark.

Stanley dragged her limp body across the room like a rag doll. His breathing was heavy, though not from exertion. The basement was cool and dimly lit, and he headed toward an ancient sofa pushed catty-corner against the V in the far wall.

She didn't weigh more than a minute and Stanley hauled her over stacks of paintings, boxes containing old magazines, milk crates filled with Motown favorites, and Maxwell House coffee cans crammed with soiled paintbrushes. All the while, he cursed and swore.

"Shit ever'whare! Bitch come in da store smellin' fine an' lookin' sweet, an' here her house is a pure mess!"

He reached the sofa and sat down heavily, his weighty frame sinking down into the worn foam cushions and his long legs splayed out in front of him. He cradled the lady between his knees and retrieved a switchblade from his back pocket. Placing the knife next to him on the cushion, he unbuttoned and unzipped the starched pants he'd so proudly stepped into that morning. To his delight, they still held a crease, and only a trace of dust was visible on the heavy brown fabric.

He let the lady slide to the cement floor as he stood up and kicked off his heavy boots. Then he stepped out of his pants, freed his erection, and pushed his boxer shorts down to his ankles. Seated once again, Stanley gazed at the unconscious woman on the floor between his legs. He'd seen her in the store many times before, always carefully choosing her vegetables as if they were potential lovers. This bitch was hot. The way she massaged the oranges and kneaded the ripe peaches told him she had passion.

Once he'd masturbated behind a huge stack of crates as she fondled and stroked the dick-sized cucumbers he'd placed on sale that day. He could have sworn she'd licked her lips and looked directly into his eyes as his force gushed into his palm in a warm, sticky flow.

She wanted him.

And he wanted her. And he promised himself he'd have her.

As luck would have it, Kyle, one of the day shift delivery boys, had called out sick with the trots and since Stanley had finally earned the right to wear a RICHARD'S uniform, he was asked to fill in for him. When the lady entered the store, Stanley followed her around with his eyes. He watched her pay for her groceries, and as soon as she began writing down her address, he ran over and volunteered to make the delivery.

She lived on Gunhill Road, an uphill bike ride from RICHARD'S, and the older guys were happy to let him have it. With her forty-seven dollars' worth of groceries filling the basket in front of him, Stanley quickly pedaled the two miles to her two-story brick home. An ivory Mazda 626 was parked in the lady's driveway and, on impulse, Stanley tried the driver's side door.

It opened.

Bitch gots ta' be mo' careful!

Quietly closing the car door, Stanley stepped onto the tidy porch and twisted the shiny brass doorknob.

It turned.

Stealthily, he entered the house. The sounds of Luther Vandross immediately filled his ears, just as they'd muffled his entrance. He let his primitive eyes scan the spacious room. Unframed Black art and African masks hung on nearly every wall. Low-seated oak tables supported sculpted figures of ebony natives, meshed and locked in passionate positions. Soft, buttery leather furniture gave the room a comfortable feel.

When a quick search of the ground floor proved fruitless, Stanley scratched his head. Where could she be? Should he try upstairs, or should he go down? Since the music flowed up from the basement, Stanley headed in that direction. Tiptoeing like a church mouse, he started down the narrow stairwell.

Shadows cloaked the dim, unfinished basement, and a light shone from a room off to his right. With his back against the wall, Stanley sidestepped gracefully until he reached the lit room.

He peered around the corner.

The lady was bent over a large stack of art paper attempting to free a sheet from the bottom of the heap. Why'ont she jes grab one from de top? Stanley pondered before filling the room with his presence. He swung his mallet of a fist in a perfect uppercut, catching the lady flat in the face, the force of his blow lifting her tiny body backwards and into the air.

She hit the floor and before she could open her mouth to scream, Stanley seized her throat and flung the tiny creature across the small room. Her head slammed into an oversized wooden easel and she crumpled to the ground in a silent heap.

There! She lay quiet in a disheveled pile. Tame and cooperative. Just how he liked them.

And now, Stanley's large hands stroked the soft hollow of the lady's throat as he imagined how far he could thrust himself down there. He was willing to bet she could hold a lot more of him than that cock-teasing teenaged niece of Mr. Lambert's did.

He looked at the lady. It was time for her to wake up and get to working on his small problem that was actually quite large indeed. Stanley bent over her still form and proceeded to awaken her.

Pain exploded in Paris's left thumb. From a great distance, her brain managed to register the agony and nudge her body into action. Instinctively her thumb sought refuge in her open mouth, but then an identical fire attacked her right thumb.

Paris shrieked, closing both hands into fists, her blazing thumbs tucked inside. It took her a moment to realize what he'd done. To realize that the stranger had used the jagged tips of his own nails to pierce the tender flesh beneath her thumbnails, digging deep enough to draw blood and restore her to consciousness. This was an old trick someone had once told her would work well, if you needed to rouse a wino.

It worked well for her.

Paris's face felt like a disfigured mask of agony. The slightest movement caused nearly intolerable waves of pain. Stunned, she realized that she'd somehow lost control of her bladder and soaked through her pants.

From the swollen slits of her eyes, her gaze traveled the length of the man sitting before her. He was roughly the size of a well-fed giant.

"You reddy now, Baby?" he asked with a sickening grin. "You gon ack right?"

Act right? Was he crazy?

Using his thick knees as leverage, Paris attempted to push herself away, trying in vain to scoot backwards and away from the half-naked stranger.

"Come back heah, Bitch!" he exploded, snatching his switchblade with one hand and yanking her hair with the other. Paris heard the switchblade click open, its cool metal glinting dangerously in the partial shadows, and she peed again.

Fear paralyzed her. Her breath clawed from her throat in short, harsh pellets as the stranger forced her to kneel between his massive thighs. With the knife blade pressed at her throat, he jammed her face into his foul-smelling groin.

"Pretend lak it's a Popsicle." The stranger giggled, slapping his dripping, monstrous erection against Paris's ear and then guiding it toward her mouth. "A sweet an' juicy red, white, an' blue, Bomb Pop!"

Paris closed her eyes. Her stomach clenched and twisted at the smell coming from him. When was the last time this fool had washed his ass?

Stanley repositioned his weapon. The edge of the knife bit against her windpipe and immediately a small band of blood appeared and white-hot pain encircled her neck.

Her back stiffened and her eyes flew open.

As her face loomed closer to the strange man's dick, waves of acrid bile rose in her throat and threatened to drown her. Paris fought the dizzying sensation, swallowing and gasping around her terror until she feared she'd explode. A fat drop of semen seeped from his dick and Paris found herself engulfed in a boiling rage.

Hell, no! It was Tuesday, goddammit! It was her motherfucking day!

For the first time in her life Paris felt pure hatred.

Hatred that made her much stronger than her ever-present fear.

Her mind began to turn. She stared at the white pearls of pre-cum dripping from the head of his gigantic penis and made herself a vow.

This is gonna be the last motherfucker to ever stick a dick or a knife in my face! Bad enough I have to suck that sorry ass William, but suck this stinking idiot, too?

The lines of distinction between this stranger and her husband grew fuzzy and William's face seemed to float on the stranger's body. Paris had to force herself not to jump on him and beat his ass for old and new. She knew she couldn't whip the stranger in a fistfight, but she could hurt the bastard where it mattered most.

Paris cleared her pounding head and wrapped both hands around the girth of the stranger's penis, sliding them up and down his shaft. Her skin began to crawl but she willed herself to keep the rhythm going.

"Oooh, yeah, thass right, Baby," the stranger chanted. "Gone an git yours. Zoom it, lady...zoom it all da way in! C'mon, Baby, lemme see ya' deep throat it!"

Pumping his hips, the stranger relaxed his grip and propped his knife hand behind his head. Then he lay back and panted, enjoying the feel of her small hands as they pumped around the center of his world. "Yesss," he moaned. "I done finally found me a bitch who want it jes' as much as I do!" The stranger licked his lips. "See how nice you kin ack after you git summa the piss knocked outta ya?"

You nasty motherfucker! Paris swallowed back bile but her hands moved up and down like she was churning butter. She forced herself to lower her right hand and slide her fingers under the soft sac of his scrotum. Immediately, she was repulsed by the texture of his skin and had to will herself not to shrink away. Thick keloid scars felt alien under her fingers, and the smell of his unwashed body was nearly enough to cause her to black out again.

But Paris kept working.

The stranger's hips bucked up and down on the sofa as he pumped up and down with deep strokes. Feeling backward toward his asshole, Paris—her thumbs, nose and lips, and neck still throbbing with red-hot pain—rubbed near his prostrate gland, causing ripples of excitement to shoot through his body.

"Ahhh, yesssss," he groaned as his hips began moving in wide circles. "Take it in ya' mouf, Lady! In ya' fuckin' mouf!"

Deliberately, Paris grasped both of his testicles firmly in each of her hands and lowered her splayed lips toward his throbbing organ. Her teeth suddenly felt like vampire fangs, anxious for blood. As the stranger whimpered his way to an orgasm, Paris slid his huge dick partway into her mouth, and counting to three, simultaneously squeezed his nuts for all she was worth and bit down with all of her might.

A roar tore from the stranger's throat. His powerful muscles locked and froze; trapping him between intense pleasure and intense pain. The switchblade fell from his grasp and clanked heavily to the floor behind the couch.

Balanced on her knees, Paris's jaw trembled and her fists were clenched in a deadly vice grip. The stranger sucked in air and a low moan blew from him. Disgusted, Paris spit out his now deflated dick, which incredibly was at least seven inches long soft, and kept her grip on his balls.

"Oooh, motherfuckah!" she cried. "The tables have turned! Now, who-the-fuck-is-zoomin' who?"

"Lady...please," the stranger whined in a voice too tiny for such a big man. "Please, ya' hurtin' me, Lady."

The stranger quivered and tried to lower his hands, but Paris moved quickly, squeezing even harder, digging her manicured nails deeply into his flesh, piercing his tough scrotal skin and releasing dark red blood.

Sharp grinding noises escaped the stranger's throat.

"If you bring your arms down one fuckin' inch," Paris warned, "just one fuckin' inch, everything inside these two little sacks of shit is gonna spill out on the floor!" She twisted hard again for emphasis, satisfied when the stranger yelped like a little bitch.

Paris rose to a crouched position before commanding him to stand. "Get up slow, motherfucker. Real slow and easy because if you so much as breathe too hard, I'll tear your fucking nuts off and make your stink ass swallow them!"

Gagging and fighting back the urge to hurl, the stranger untangled his feet from his underwear and, with his arms outstretched to the heavens, he came to a shaky, hunch-backed stand.

"Ladeeee, please," he squealed. "Ya' hurtin' me bad, Lady...please, I feel lak I'ma faint—"

"Shut the fuck up and move!" Paris backed toward the basement stairs, forcing the towering man to take one small step forward to each of her full strides backwards. They ascended the stairs in this manner, with Paris twisting his nuts and cursing all the way. At the top of the stairs she paused and touched her tongue to her teeth. At least two in the front felt loose, and fresh blood had begun to seep from her nose.

"You low-down motherfucker!" she spat.

"Please, I-I was jes gonna make you feel good," the stranger stammered. His breath was constricted high in his chest and he'd broken into a cold sweat.

Make me feel good? Paris looked sharply at the stranger and sudden realization hit her like a brick. This fool was retarded!

"Asshole, if you think your donkey dick could ever make me feel good, not only are you a retard—your motherfuckin' bread ain't done!"

She yanked him over to the window by her desk.

"Lady, let me out," he gasped. "Jes let me leave and I swear 'fore God, I'll nevah do nuthin l-l-like dis again. D-d-dis-heah is my firs' time. My onliest time. I ain't nevah done nuttin' so fool as dis befo' an' I swear on my dead mama, I'll nevah do it again!"

"You's a goddamned liar!" Paris crushed his scrotum again. "You've done this shit before because somebody done already poured lye down your drawers!"

"Aaaah! Aaagghhhhhh!" the stranger screamed. "Dammit, Lady! Please lemme go...jes' let me leave outta heah alive!"

"Go, then," said Paris, suddenly calm. "You wanna leave? Then go."

She saw hope surging through his brain but didn't loosen her grip.

"How I'ma go?" he whimpered. "Ya' gotta loose me! Loose me now, lady, fo' the love of God, loose me! Else how I'ma git out?"

"Break out, motherfucker! You broke in, didn't you?"

"Yo' door was settin' wide open, dammit! I din force mahsef in here on you!"

"I didn't invite you in, either," Paris spat, yanking his nuts in opposite directions and wringing them left and right.

"Then call the po-leece, Lady," he whimpered and stomped his feet. "Let's jes call the po-leece an' I turn mahself in!"

Paris thought for a moment. This motherfucker had made every woman's greatest fear her painful reality. He had violated her home and her body. But he'd also done something else. He'd given her something that had been lacking in her life during the last ten years with William. He'd given her courage.

"Okay," she said. "But you're gonna call them. If you can break in my house by yourself, and stick your nasty dick in my face all by yourself, you can call the police by yourself. Now," Paris explained slowly and carefully as if he were a child. "If you think I won't fuck," she jerked his left testicle upward, "you," she yanked the right nut downward, "up..." his balls split east and west, "then you need to call an ambulance before you call the cops!"

"Walk over to the telephone," she commanded, pulling him over to the speakerphone on top of her desk. "Now press that red button that says, 'speaker' and dial 9-1-1."

Following her instructions, the stranger waited until a voice flooded the room from the small speaker.

"9-1-1 emergency, Sergeant Glascow, how may I help you?"

"Sh—sh—she got me by da' balls, Man," the stranger cried. "My name S-s-stanley and she got me by da' balls!"

"Yeah, Man," the dispatcher replied, "that's what happens when you marry 'em and give 'em your checkbook, but this number is for emergencies only."

"Nah, Man, nah, she really hurtin' me bad, she hurtin' my balls, really, really bad!"

"Could you repeat that?" the dispatcher asked, his voice tinged with disbelief. "Is someone there hurting you, Sir?"

"You're goddamn right, I'm hurting him, and I'll kill his black ass, too!" Paris yelled.

Quickly she explained that she'd captured an intruder and gave the policeman her name and address. Then she made Stanley press the red button to end the call. Although her hands were sore and tired and her fingers were sticky with the stranger's blood, Paris felt like she could have held on to him for at least another month.

At least.

"I gotta wee," the stranger moaned.

"What?"

"I gotta take a piss, lady. Real bad."

"Well, hold it till the cops get here, and then you can christen your new jail cell."

"I cain't hol' it, Lady! I swear fo' God, it's comin' out!"

"Dammit! Walk over to that front door and don't try nothing cute because it's your dick and your balls." She yanked him over to the door and instructed Stanley to open the door a small crack and aim his dick toward the porch. For a split second the stranger's body obscured Paris's view. For just an instant her attention wavered.

And that was all it took.

Stanley swung the door toward her with all of his might, catching Paris off balance and off guard. The edge of the door slammed into her face, whipping her around, and Paris howled and grabbed at her broken nose. Stanley moved like white on rice. Leaping onto her front porch he hurled himself over the side rail and, barefooted and bare-assed, took off bounding toward Jerome Avenue.

Paris wanted to rush down the steps and chase him, but she could barely open her left eye, and her right eye was flooded with blood. It would take more than a few stitches to close the gash her teeth had made when the stranger split her lip, and her broken nose made breathing terribly painful.

Instead she slammed the door closed. This time she locked it. Once again she'd been beaten and brutalized and no doubt she looked like a bat out of hell, but this time she felt damned good. She'd finally stood up for herself and somehow she felt stronger. She felt brand-new.

Shit, she told herself. If I can jack that giant motherfucker up, then William better watch his ass. The next somebody to pass a goddamn lick up in here will be me! For years she'd been sexually degraded and physically abused, but now emotionally and mentally, Paris was free. There would be no more rape or torment in the house where she paid the mortgage. Never again would William put his hands around her neck, his knife to her throat, or his dick in her face!

Or anywhere else on her body, for that matter.

There are gonna be some changes around here, she vowed. Some big-time changes! For one thing, she was moving her art studio back upstairs to the spare room. Today. And if William didn't like it he could let the door-knob hit him in the ass on the way out. And as for dinner tonight, his mama could wait on that nana puddin' until the cows came home.

Paris commanded her body to move and limped into the bathroom. She scrubbed the stranger's blood from her hands using some Clorox she found under the sink. In the medicine cabinet she saw the makeup kit she used to camouflage the black eyes, busted lips, and the random assortment of bruises that were always impossible to explain to her friends. Concealer, pressed powder, foundation, rouge, all of it got flung into the trashcan. She was too pretty for makeup anyway. Or at least she used to be. Paris raised her eyes to meet her battered reflection in the mirror but she did not flinch. Blood continued to trickle from her right nostril, and there was a dry film coating her swollen lips. A shudder of revulsion ran down the small of her back.

He stuck his dirty dick in my mouth!

Without hesitation she diluted a half a cap of bleach with a cup of warm water and sloshed it around in her mouth, then rinsed with cold water. She splashed a final handful of water over her face and neck, and dabbed at her wound with a soft pink towel.

Every muscle in her body screamed as Paris crept into her kitchen and opened the freezer. She stood there silently; fighting her emotions as the cold air washed over her. Reaching inside, Paris grabbed a frozen bag of vegetables. Her tears melted the ice crystals as she pressed the frozen peas gingerly to her broken nose. What the hell am I crying about? She admonished herself. For once, I fought back! I even came out on top!

Yeah. There were gonna be some real changes around here.

Paris flung the frozen vegetables back into the freezer and bent down to retrieve the kitchen knives from their hiding place under the sink. Discarding the plastic bags, she tore the tape from the shoebox and, one by one, she stuck the knives into the wooden holder, then slid it over next to the toaster. That done, she shoved her husband's high-backed armchair out of its position and replaced it with her smaller low-backed version, and then she sat down at the head of her kitchen table and smoked one of William's cigarettes as she waited for the police to arrive.

Tracy Price-Thompson is the Essence bestselling author of Black Coffee *(Random House, 2002),* Chocolate Sangria *(Random House, 2003),* A Woman's Worth *(Random House, 2004), and* Knockin' Boots *(Random House, 2005). A Brooklyn, New York native, Tracy holds undergraduate degrees in business administration and social work, and a masters degree in social work. In addition to her novels, Tracy is also the co-editor of the major anthology,* Proverbs for the People *(Kensington, 2003). She can be reached at tracythomp@aol.com.*

The Lonely
Echoes Of
My Youth

D.V. Bernard

It wasn't until about two days after the murder that the police finally found the body—and then, only after a pack of stray dogs was seen outside the building, fighting over the left arm and gorging themselves on the entrails. In the basement of the abandoned building the police found the corpse still tied to the chair—half-eaten, disemboweled and rotting in the late summer heat. Given the fact that the corpse was found in a crack house, the murder was presumed to be a drug killing. Some dazed, hapless crackheads they found on the second floor were rounded up and questioned, but only we kids had known how the body had come to be there.

…We had all been children back then. Even our parents had been childish—in their inability to see and in their determination to remain blind. Now that I think about it, even the wisdom of our old ones had been nothing but a finely tuned acceptance of pain and disappointment. It was only many years later, when I held my newborn daughter in my arms, that the reality of the crime we had committed—and of the crime that had been committed against us—finally began to register in my mind. New life, with all its potential for accomplishment and disappointment, had suddenly terrified me. Having a child compels you to consider all the things you hated about your childhood: all the things you swore you'd do differently when you became a parent. At the same time, this is not a story about the horrors of the ghetto: about a lamentable underclass, with which we all empathize, but for whom we've come to believe that nothing can be done. This is not a story for tears and recriminations—nor is it one of those "feel good" stories about "the triumph of the human will." This is simply the story of our youth—of a time that has passed, but which is always with us, regardless of if we loved it or hated it: regardless of whether we triumphed over it or became its silent victims…

It's strange how a child's mind works. I took the vacant lot a few blocks from our slum for a park. I made an obstacle course out of broken bottles and piles of garbage. I constructed mounds of rubble into pirate forts and jungle gyms. Also, the abandoned buildings beside the lot, within which crackheads bought drugs (and sometimes sold their bodies and souls to low-level drug dealers) became for me Aztec temples to be explored. Drug dealers forging fiefdoms out of America's social blight became for me knights in shining armor—not because I idealized them, but because they were subsumed within my world of fantasy, co-opted by my imagination. Besides, as I was only six, they all left me alone. I would wander through rooms where people were having sex, and where people had guns held to their heads. I passed overdosed crackheads frothing at the mouth; I came upon drug dealers haggling with corrupt police officers, and white crack-heads that had come all the way from the suburbs to share in the black man's misery. All this and more I saw during my daily explorations of the neighborhood.

One of the earliest memories I have is of my mother kissing me good-bye—not forever, but so that she could start her job as a live-in nanny for a family out on Long Island. My mother tried her best, but she was one of those people who grew enraged when she was sad; she lashed out at those around her when her inability to make headway in life—and to make her-self happy—crushed her spirit. I must have been crying at her leaving, because she yelled at me for "being a baby." Then, with a look in her eyes full of bewilderment and shame, she kissed me quickly on the cheek and left. I was six; my mother was 23; my father (who I learned later was one of those unfortunate drug dealers that began to abuse his own product) would have been 25 if he had still been alive.

My mother's little sister was staying with us. Both sisters had been castoffs from their family—disowned by their religious parents. My aunt had a six-month-old daughter whose constant crying seemed to provide the soundtrack of our lives. After my mother closed the door behind her, I joined my aunt in the living room—where she was watching TV. She was in an old bathrobe, breastfeeding her child. The weight she had gained during pregnancy had drooped disconcertingly on her small frame. She hadn't combed her hair for the day; and as she sat there, staring meditatively at the convoluted soap opera, it was as though the child suckling at her breast were draining the life out of her. Her face always seemed drawn. Her movements were slow and deliberate; and because of all this, I was always on my best behavior around her—the way a child was on his best behavior when visiting a sick relative. On some level, I thought that I would break her if I accidentally bumped into her. I found myself whispering when I talked to her, as if fearful that I would shatter her if I spoke too loudly.

It was only when her boyfriend came over, and they disappeared into her room to bring forth the frightful sounds of rattling bed springs and hushed screams, that I would sense any stirrings of life in her; but even then, those stirrings would seem empty somehow—and would always be gone by the time she emerged from the room. I began to think of her room as a magical place; I entered it furtively when she wasn't looking, expecting some new dimension to appear. However, all I would see was the same room, with its bed piled high with soiled linen and dirty clothes, and with its pervasive stench of baby shit and stale urine. Only in retrospect do I understand why her boyfriend's face had always worn a look of bewilderment when he left the room—and why, after a while, he stopped coming entirely.

When summer came and the long, hot vacation days stretched out like a cruel punishment, the neighborhood streets became my refuge. The hotter it got, the deeper my aunt seemed to seep into her strange lassitude. After a while, her sepulchral form began to occupy a place of horror in my imagination, so I stayed out on the streets merely to avoid her—and the sense of panic that rose in me when I watched her. One humid night, when the prickly heat made me toss and turn in bed, I shuffled over to the living room to watch some TV. My aunt had gone to bed by then—it must have been past midnight… *The Exorcist* was on. That must have been the longest two hours of my life. I lay on the couch trembling. I wanted to turn off the

TV, but these were the days before remote controls, and I was too terrified to walk from the couch to the TV. I was convinced that the demon that had possessed the girl in the movie would get me if my feet touched the floor. The demon was hiding beneath the couch, getting ready to pounce on me the moment I ventured from the sanctuary on top of the couch. Also, it occurred to me that if I walked over to the TV and turned it off, then I would have to walk back to the couch in the dark! All of these factors combined to paralyze me. I lay trembling on the couch as the demon girl's head spun around and she threw up green vomit and her body levitated before being "compelled by the body of Christ." Even when I turned my eyes away, I shuddered and cried at the sounds—and the frightful thoughts—that now seemed somehow inescapable. When the movie was over, I lay staring at the TV but seeing only my projected fears. Eventually sleep did seize me, but I had the most fantastical dreams, in which the demon from the movie chased me through dark ghetto streets. Every crevice in the dream seemed to be a hiding place for the demon and every noise seemed to be a prelude to death.

I awoke the next morning with body aches—as though I had been fighting with the demon all night and had barely escaped. I didn't awake screaming or anything like that, but with an awareness—a surety—that somehow my aunt had been possessed by a demon. These thoughts circulated through my mind for days—like a virus infecting my mind, my ability to think and make sense of the world. I watched my aunt from around corners. I remember that since she was breastfeeding, her nipples were chewed up and sore. I doubt she made enough milk, because the baby was always crying and seemed frustrated. However my aunt would hardly seem to notice; she would just sit staring at TV, or whatever the case was, while the child cried or chewed at her nipples until they bled. I remembered my aunt as she used to be. In my mind, I had an image of her as playful and loving—flittering about the world like a butterfly. I couldn't trust these memories, of course, as they came from the deepest recesses of my childhood—where memories didn't come in the form of images, but sensations. I knew only that my aunt, in some earlier incarnation, had been for me a feeling of joy and carefree youth. Even though she was now only 18, she seemed beyond customary classifications of age—or at least beyond my six-year-old understanding of it. My inability to make sense of things, combined with what seemed to be my aunt's obvious unhappiness, left me convinced that something evil had happened to her. Moreover, I figured that whatever sorrows she had, had to have their source in supernatural evil (not only the earthly kind I saw daily on the streets). A life and death battle was going on within my aunt—a struggle for her soul; and while this battle raged I couldn't even sleep, for fear that if the evil won out I would be the next victim.

I had always liked walking through the neighborhood in the early morning, but when my fears for my aunt—and my own soul—began to drive me from the house, I found that early mornings were magical. As night turned into day I connected the banishing of darkness in the outside world to a similar victory within me. Also, the early morning streets were mine. Few people would be on the streets; no loud music or quarrels would invade my thoughts…and I would be free for a few moments.

As many a bewildered parent will tell you, childhood desperation, coupled with an active imagination, can often lead to extremely bizarre choices. There was a voodoo shop in my neighborhood—I don't know what else to call it. People went there to commune with the forces of good and evil—to soothe heartbreak and find guidance for lives that seemed pointless. The shop was in a dusty, roach-infested storefront; the two-story slum that housed it was on a block where most of the other buildings had been demolished—and where these few standing buildings seemed like rotten teeth in a diseased mouth. In a strange way, I thought of this block as the crossroads of our neighborhood, the nexus of all the good and evil potentialities of our community.

Either way, that morning, terrified by the encroachment of evil into my home, I went to see the proprietress of the shop. Rather, I walked up and down the block hoping to catch a glimpse of her. Madame Evangeline was her name, and the faded sign above the shop advertised palm readings and "spiritual consultations." The lights of the store were never on and in the dusty display case there were several exotic statuettes of deities, demigods, saints and demons. Like I said before, it was a two-story building. From what I could tell, Madame Evangeline lived in the shop; on the second floor, there was a wizened old man who continually muttered to himself and scratched the same spot on his chest. The talk in the neighborhood was that Evangeline had cast a spell on him for some transgression that no one could name, but which everyone presumed to involve spurned love and/or cheating ways. I never saw anyone visiting her establishment, and before deciding to seek her out, I had only seen her once. It had been about six months before, when I was on my way to school. I think I was late, because I was rushing along, heedless of the shop that had always triggered an eerie feeling in my gut. Evangeline suddenly emerged from the darkness of the shop to throw out her garbage; at the sight of her, a shudder went though me, so that I almost toppled to the ground. Nobody else was around; I stood there helplessly. Of course, I figured that taking out the garbage was too trivial a task for one whom communed with mystical forces. With the occult forces she had at her command, I figured that she could easily disintegrate her trash in hellfire—or levitate it to the curb. Thus, I figured that her foray to the garbage can had to be a pretext whose ultimate design was my mortal soul. Madame Evangeline was a huge black woman of indefinite age. She came out in a discolored (mostly purple) nightgown. Her stockings were rolled down to the middle of her massive thighs and her pink, fluffy slippers clapped indecorously as she sauntered to the curb. I had frozen about five steps from her. Children always imagine such people to be cannibals; as I looked at her, it occurred to me that nothing but the sweet, tender flesh of six-year-olds could account for Madame Evangeline's huge gut. I watched that gut anxiously, as though paying homage to my unfortunate predecessors. When I looked up, I realized that the occult mistress was smiling at me (and I swear to this day that she licked her lips hungrily!) I turned on my heels and ran!

However, six months later, driven to the brink by the double curse of an active imagination and unnamable terrors, I found myself willing to risk adding girth to Madame Evangeline's gut. That morning, I walked down the blocks with a peculiar single-mindedness—a feeling that only Madame

Evangeline had the power to battle my aunt's demon and restore her soul. I passed the Arab deli that was our neighborhood's version of a supermarket (and which had that shelf of porno magazines in the back that the neighborhood boys were always lurking around). I passed the God's Heavenly Assembly church, whose sign had a missing section and now actually read, "God's Heavenly Ass." I passed Won-Dolla-Fong's fruit stand, where everything cost one dollar and where people would purposely ask him how much something cost, just so that he would scream, in that strange way of his that negated all the consonants, "won dolla!"

Just as I neared Madame Evangeline's shop the door opened and she emerged with another bag of garbage. She saw me and smiled again. I forced myself to continue walking toward her. She was dressed just as she had been the last time I saw her, so that it was as though no time had passed.

"You gonna run away again?" she asked me. She had a heavy accent—Haitian.

When she addressed me, I stopped walking, but nodded my head to answer her question. My eyes were already beginning to tear up; and when I could no longer hold it in, I blurted out that I needed her help.

She looked at me warily for a while. Then, grunting and shrugging her shoulders, she said, "Everyone needs help." She tossed the bag to the curb, so that the few empty cans and other pieces of trash jangled resoundingly in the relative silence of the early morning. "Come with me," she said then, returning to her shop.

I walked stiffly behind her. In the shop there was an unwholesome odor of musk and decaying things, which burned the back of my throat. A few candles gave light to the darkness, and overhead there were spices and herbs and what looked like small reptiles drying. There wasn't a counter in the shop—only a central table, on which tarot cards and other paraphernalia of her craft stood in wait. The actual goods that she sold were scattered everywhere in bags, sacks and pouches. She sat me at the table, then sat down across from me. A candle was burning on the table between us, highlighting her face unsettlingly.

The story of my aunt's demon possession came gushing out—I can hardly remember what I said. I'm sure I was crying by then, sniffling between words and phrases…Madame Evangeline merely nodded to what I said, waiting patiently for my story to unfold—and for the vital facts to reveal themselves. She listened as I presume she had listened to thousands of other clients, people who feared for their lives or the lives of loved ones; people who hated someone and came to her for revenge or guidance in revenge. She sat listening to me; after a while she took out a pen and pad and began to write.

I don't know how long we sat like that—maybe only half an hour, but it seemed like forever. Eventually, when my tears began to subside and the horror of my tale dissipated into the darkness of the shop, she stopped me. "Okay, I think I understand you perfect." She got up then, and went to the darkness of the shop—into one of her sacks. When she returned, her face was grave and I shuddered as I watched her. She sat down before me with a heavy sigh, then held out her hand to me. In her thick palm there was what she said was an amulet.

"Take this," she said. "With this amulet in your hand, you'll be magically shielded from all the forces of evil."

"Really?" I said, amazed, a little terrified, and excited by the prospect of being emancipated from my fears.

"Yes, but listen closely," she continued, looking over her shoulder as though checking for eavesdroppers. She leaned in closely to me then, whispering, "Don't lose this sacred amulet! If you do, the forces of evil will be able to take your soul. Do you understand me?"

I nodded, my mouth dry…

"Do you understand?" she demanded again.

"Yes," I managed to whisper, my eyes wide.

"Good," she said, a wide, unnerving grin coming over her face again. Then, presenting me with what she had written down while I retched out my story, she said, "Now that you're protected from evil, here's a list of things I need."

I took the list eagerly, expecting to see "eye of newt" or some other magical ingredient, but all it said was, "Milk, bread, rice…" She gave me $10 and I left to go to the store.

As I walked to the store, I felt free and alive. Madame Evangeline, and the amulet that I kept clenched in my hand, were tangible objects of magic to protect me from all the demons of my imagination. It wasn't until weeks later that I noticed that the amulet had the inscription, Banque Nationale de la Republique D'Haiti. Even then, as I couldn't read French, and had never seen a Haitian penny before, I thought the writing was a magical incantation. Either way, as I walked to the store I felt as though I had received a reprieve of sorts. In a sense, my observations of my aunt had triggered my first pangs of maturity: a battle between reality and imagination. Madame Evangeline and her amulet had been a temporary loophole out of that.

Also, I suppose that these were the days before I lost my innocence. When I say innocence, I don't mean the rosy-cheeked, oblivious version seen on TV. By now, of course, I had seen too much for that kind of innocence to apply to me. When I say innocence, I mean that inner sense that manifests itself in the belief that the world was fundamentally just; and that behind all human behavior was the wish for justice and the peace of mind it brought. It now occurs to me that everyone I encountered had tried to take my innocence from me. All the people that I knew, in their words and actions, set about trying to convince me that there was no justice—either to spare me from the unjust, or because they themselves, robbed of their innocence, wanted to justify their injustice toward me.

I remember that downstairs from me there was a sententious old man called Mr. Williams, who spent the summer months sitting on the stoop and dispensing advice to whoever came within earshot. Philosophical gems on everything from the correct way to wear one's belt to geopolitical realignments that would ensure world peace came gushing out of his mouth. His dentures were too big and were always slipping out. He had a way of clicking his dentures against his gums that I found amazing for some reason. I almost looked forward to the day when I too would be toothless, so that I could click my dentures around in my mouth. I was excited when I began losing my baby teeth, but grew annoyed when new teeth began to appear under the gums. Mr. Williams had an arthritic mutt that seemed as old as he—and which never moved from the step once it had plopped down next to its master. The dog neither barked nor wagged its tail. Only when prodded by Mr. Williams's heel would it show any signs of life; but even then, it would only meander quietly behind its master with an expression on its face like that of an old convict waiting for death to free him from the farce of life.

Anyway, Williams was always outside during the warm months, and after lecturing me on the correct way to part my hair, or some such nonsense, he would send me to the store to fetch him some snacks. When I returned, his instruction would begin. He would devour the entire bag of potato chips in front of me. Every once in a while he would throw a chip to the dog, and the poor creature would look at him with an expression that seemed to say, "Why don't you let me starve to death, you old bastard, so that I can end this torture!" Half the time the dog didn't eat. However, that didn't concern Williams in the least. His eyes would be on me, twinkling in a strange way as he devoured the snacks. Somehow, I would never deign to ask him for some; and of course, he never offered. Instead, he kept up a constant commentary on how good they tasted; when he devoured the contents of the bag and/or gulped down the last of the soda, he would look at me with a strange new intensity, as if waiting for me to burst into tears. He watched my lips for the telltale trembling that many a neighborhood kid had betrayed during Williams's career of instructive sadism. It was either complete guilelessness on my part or some morbid streak that kept me going on with the farce. Every time he saw me, he would send me to the store, and I would go without complaint. When I returned I would hand him the grocery bag and his change, then sit down and watch him eat, while he made his usual commentary on the snacks' deliciousness. I presume that his goal was to teach me that people were greedy assholes, but I somehow refused to give him the satisfaction of teaching me. I'm not sure I was as brilliant and resolute as I make myself sound. All children, I've discovered since becoming a parent and retracing the motives of my own antics, instinctively know that the quickest and easiest way to drive adults insane is to refuse to learn what they are trying to teach. This is especially so when the child realizes that the lesson in question is idiotic—as I did with Williams.

Day after day he repeated the lesson; day after day I returned from the store with his snacks, and watched while he licked his fingers and belched with forced fanfare. He would watch me for any sign of a plaintive expression. I would only stare. Soon, my morbidity grew so brazen that, when he was finished, I would ask him if he wanted me to put the bags and bottles in the garbage can. After weeks and months of this, Williams' act of relishing the greasy snacks became strained. He would eat them as one ate straw, seeming at first enraged with me for not learning what seemed to be a straightforward lesson, then questioning others to see if I was retarded. Eventually, he stopped asking me to go to the store for him. Resplendent in victory, I asked him, after several weeks of mutual silence, why he no longer asked me to go to the store for him. Here, even the dog looked up, surprised for once; Williams, now thoroughly convinced of my madness, said that he wasn't hungry.

I suppose that I must have had similar experiences with other adults in my neighborhood, because they all seemed to regard me as a madman in the making. "That boy ain't right," I would hear people whisper about me. Conversations between adults would always cease as I walked past. The same was pretty much true for kids. I was too young to be friends with most of the kids on my block and too indifferent to the unimaginative games of kids my age to find their company worthwhile.

Whatever the case, as I walked to the store for Madame Evangeline I was free. Even as the streets began to fill with people going to work (and that segment of people who never worked but instead stood about the streets all day) I went to the aforementioned Arab store (with the porn rack in the back). In front of the store some local youths had gathered, as was usually the case. I don't know what exactly their relationship with the Arabs was, but like I said, the youths were always there; and several times an hour, cars would stop at the curb and one of the youths would go to the car to make a furtive exchange.

I had finished my shopping and taken about three steps away from the store (and the gang of youths) when a car rushed around the corner. I turned at the sound of the screeching tires and saw a man lean out of the window with a machine gun in hand. I stood there, frozen, while bullets and bullet-riddled bodies flew all around me. One of the youths (who had been shot in the chest) tumbled toward me and bumped into me as he dropped lifelessly to the ground. I looked around slowly (or so it seemed in my mind) digesting death, consuming the evil of it—yet from the distance of someone impervious to it. By now, all the youths were either dead or writhing in pain on the ground. Only then did it occur to me that it was a miracle that I hadn't been shot as well. I took out the amulet and stared at it as the car rushed away. I can't remember if I actually did grin, but a feeling of amazement came over me as I held the amulet and looked at the bodies at my feet. I was indeed impervious to evil, just like Madame Evangeline had said!

It was the police that finally chased me away; else I might have stayed there forever, reveling in my triumph over evil. The youths at my feet, broken and bloody, had seemed pathetic then, just like everything else in the adult world. I returned to Madame Evangeline's shop in great spirits. She, on the other hand, was merely annoyed that I had taken so long; then, as my prattle and youthful ebullience began to exhaust the last of her patience, she chased me away.

Unfazed, I rushed home, thinking that maybe there would be some change in my aunt. She seemed the same, settling into her usual place on the couch, but I figured that maybe the magic of the amulet needed time to work. I smiled at her and left. I walked about the neighborhood again, then went to my playground, the vacant lot and, beyond that, the crack houses that served as my Aztec temples. It was while I was making my rounds of the basement (and imagining ancient dungeons) that I first came upon Tisha. She was about 13 and had transformed one of the basement rooms into a dollhouse. She had swept away the accumulated trash and drug vials, and laid a plush area rug on the floor. Pink curtains had been hoisted over the shattered windows, and as the sun's rays shone through them, the room was suffused in a pinkish hue. There was a potpourri scent in the air that made me hungry for some reason—probably because it reminded me of cake. And there were dozens of dolls in the place—big, fluffy ones, stylish, diminutive ones—white ones, black ones. With my amulet in hand, this place seemed to be a direct result of its magic. First I had been spared from obvious death, and now I was meeting an angel in a sheltered paradise. Tisha had been tending to the curtains when I entered, but when I stopped in the open doorway the floor creaked, so that she stopped and turned. She was beautiful—so beautiful that I stared in amazement, and perhaps with that strange terror that people felt when they came upon something that encompassed both their dearest dreams and dreams they hadn't dreamed yet, dreams they perhaps didn't have the courage and foresight to dream.

"Would you like to play?" she asked me, smiling. She was from the South and had a melodious drawl that seemed to melt like butter in the summer heat. That drawl had reminded me of Madame Evangeline. It wasn't that they sounded the same (because they didn't) but that accents suddenly seemed to be a mark of magic.

I nodded shyly and entered.

Tisha was her nickname. She had one of those unpronounceable black names with multiple apostrophes and several capitalized letters inserted in the middle. I learned later that she lived in another neighborhood—in another hamlet where there was a (drug) lord no different from our own. I had seen many girls like Tisha during my explorations of the building, impressionable children taken in by the allure of easy wealth and older men. Even the boys were taken in by the allure, so I'm not entirely convinced that what attracted the kids was entirely sexual. The sexuality of children revolved not around the act of sex, but in finding safety and comfort with those older and stronger than themselves. Anyway, most of the impressionable girls became full-blown crackheads—and were turned out when their usefulness to the lord waned; most of the impressionable boys became low-level drug dealers/enforcers/decoys/messengers and either ended up in jail or dead. Of course, this is my view of it now. Back then, I knew only that Tisha was beautiful. Like I said before, a feeling of joy and panic settled over me—like when you're walking down the street and unexpectedly come upon a treasure. After the joy of finding it, your second impulse is to hide it away lest someone (like the owner or another desperate wanderer) might take it away from you. Even as I stood there I was hiding Tisha away within myself. I actively conjured the fantasy that we were somehow separated from the outside world. In time, I even think I began to imagine that Tisha and this place were byproducts of my imagination—and that I would be able to conjure them at any time, like all the little childish fantasies that I kept to myself.

Tisha and I played all that first afternoon, strange games revolving about her dolls and her imagination. She constructed elaborate scenarios, within which the dolls lived full, healthy lives, and in which we were the impresarios of God's will, righting injustices and bringing happiness to the faithful. We played until it became so dark that the rats began to view us as intruders, and the weird noises of the crack house at night began to terrify us. The building was a couple hundred years old, so we imagined that the noises we heard, and the movements we detected in the shadows, were from the ghosts of countless generations. Now that night had come, these ghosts were arising to continue their eternal vigil through the rooms and passages where they had lost their lives and souls. Over there was that 15-year-old crackhead whose brains had been blown out a few weeks ago; here was that tubercular Russian immigrant from 120 years ago, wasting away in rags and surrounded by the 12 members of his extended family, who had shared the same room, the same disease and, eventually, the same gruesome fate. All these restless souls were wandering the gutted apartments, bemoaning their own wasted lives and the lives of those they had managed to love.

Yet, as Tisha and I fled from the building, onto the ghetto streets where the first feeble street lamps had begun to flicker on, it was all another game to us. We were actually laughing when we reached the curb—perhaps reveling in our victory over the spirit world. However, the flashy BMW of our lord was parked at the curb. As we ran out onto the sidewalk, the darkened windows of the vehicle rolled down; the music that had been muffled within the closed vehicle now blared into the night. We froze; our laughter ceased. I looked to Tisha uncertainly, but it was as if she were already lost to me, as though I no longer existed to her and had only been something dreamed up during her afternoon playtime. She left me standing there and walked over to the car. Our lord poked his head out of the window:

"Yo' mama looking for you, Girl."

"Sorry, Binzo."

His calculating eyes looked her over in the darkness—seemed to navigate complex algorithms in the three seconds it took him to look her over from head to foot…then his eyes rested on me and he regarded me with the same combination of uneasiness and antagonism I got from most adults. "What he doing wit' you?" he demanded of her.

She turned and looked at me confusedly—as though she had forgotten that I was there…as though I wasn't there at all and she was wondering what the hell Binzo was talking about. I stared at her longingly—desperately needing some acknowledgement of my existence…but she seemed to look over my head, toward the abandoned building: "…I was just playing," she said.

She said, "I"—not "we." A shiver went through me. I stood there freezing, perhaps seeping into the spirit world I had just fled, with all its desperate, unrealized hopes…and then Tisha was gone. Binzo told her to get into the car, ostensibly so that he could take her home to her worried mother, and I was left on the curb, standing in the deepening darkness.

When I got home, Williams was at his usual place of honor on the stoop, dispensing advice to children who had long learned to ignore him. They were playing some nebulous game involving hitting a ball with a stick and chasing one another—sometimes with the stick. I walked quietly past and up to my room. Technically, the room belonged to my mother and me, but as she was gone, it was mine by default. In the living room, where my aunt was still on the couch, the baby was crying and the TV was playing full blast, as though to counter those cries. Elsewhere in the building, loud music was blaring. In the apartment one story below me, Mr. Johnson's loud, belligerent voice rang out; his tirade, either on food that should have been prepared by now, or an unclean house—or one of the myriad rants that seemingly marked his deep dissatisfaction with his wife, but which was only a reflection of the emptiness of his life—joined in the chaos of the night. Similarly, Mrs. Johnson's tirades on a stingy husband whose toe jam was so bad it "melted her nose holes" joined with the loud music of the neighborhood, and the intermittent gunshots that echoed through the ghetto streets…and the obligatory police sirens.

I lay in the big empty bed for hours—even though I wasn't sleepy. I lay thinking about Tisha and that magical room in the basement. I took out the amulet, wondering if maybe it only worked one time, and had to be recharged by Madame Evangeline after each miracle. I don't believe I slept much that night. Besides my preoccupations and fantasies, the sounds of the neighborhood, which had at times bewildered me—but which had mostly lain on the periphery of my awareness—had seemed inescapable that night. After a while, the Johnsons' various rants and counter rants ceased and were replaced by sounds of screaming and rattling furniture. Sometimes those sounds denoted a horrible fight and the couple would emerge from their apartment with bruised lips and darkened eyes; sometimes those sounds denoted sex, and after all the tumult my neighbors' various demons would be hushed and they would go to sleep. I lay there trying to figure out which it was. However, before I could come to a conclusion, all the sounds from the Johnsons' apartment ceased. The silence seemed ominous somehow and I found myself scouring the air for any sound from them—something that would assure me that they hadn't disappeared like Tisha. It had been as though those sounds had been meant for me—as though the Johnsons had known that I was alone and desperate for the inadvertent conversation that their brutality provided.

As I often did during the summer—when the nights were hot and muggy and the fetid air outside my window gave the impression of fresh air and a cool breeze—I went out on the fire escape. The fire escape looked out on the back alley; beyond the alley there was a vacant lot, which was growing wild with weeds, and pockmarked with rusting cars and a treasure trove of human refuse. After the lot, the hazy outlines of my neighborhood opened up like a cheap whore. A block away, a boy was yelling below someone's window, like a modern-day Romeo trying to catch Juliet's heart. However, instead of sonnets about the moon and unrequited love, the girl's mother came to the window and launched into a string of expletives; other neighbors went to their windows to see what the fuss was about; and soon, neighbors began yelling at the mother and one another. More expletives were exchanged; and the modern-day Romeo, seeing that he wasn't going to get screwed that night, disappeared and left the unromantic adults to their nonsense.

All night, the realities of my existence kept me up. My mind flashed with images of the murdered youths from that morning—but now I saw those scenes without my feeling of imperviousness. I remembered the demon stirring within my aunt, now figuring that maybe I had celebrated too soon and too boisterously, so that evil was building up its forces in order to put me back in my place. Those thoughts, and thoughts I couldn't even name, filled my mind with a conveyor belt of horrors. After a while, the real joined with the imagined; the imagined joined somehow with things I couldn't possibly know about—couldn't possibly even begin to grasp—but which lurked nonetheless in that shadow world between revelation and delusion. It was within this context that my mind returned to the spirits from the crack house—to all those generations of desperate souls who, like me, had been all too aware of the things that were killing them, yet incapable of formulating the means of overcoming them.

…Have you ever noticed that no horror movie has ever been staged in the ghetto? The classic horror movie takes place in a mansion or castle, in places of luxury and ease. Today's horror movies most commonly take place in the suburbs—where dream houses turn out to be haunted by demons and all the nefarious forces that the bourgeois and well-to-do have to fear. Horror is about losing what one has. It's about thinking that one has something—and is secure—only to discover that one is powerless against the forces of the world. In communities being unraveled by socioeconomic insecurity and desperation, the horror is anticlimactic—mundane. Also, the horror movie is about triumphing over the forces of darkness to keep what one has. In contrast, the story of the ghetto is about struggling to attain that which the forces of darkness, either through their duplicity or their indifference, claim one has no right to have. A horror movie about the ghetto would therefore be, by its very nature, a revolutionary medium.

When the sun began to brighten the horizon, I gave up my quest for sleep and peace of mind, deciding to get out of bed. I was drenched in sweat and thirsty. The Johnsons were "going at it" again. This time, it was definitely sex. Mrs. Johnson had a habit of screaming out, "You cocksucker!" when reaching orgasm; and her husband, spurred on by these declarations of love, would be driven into a frenzy. "You asshole!" the woman screamed next, above the frightful din of the shaking bed and their slapping flesh. Outside, a neighborhood stray, confused (or aroused) by their screams, began to howl. The call was taken up by all the dogs in the neighborhood—and dogs blocks away. In my bed, I hung on for dear life as the cruel rhythms of their lust seemed to be shaking the foundations of the world. I expected cracks to appear in the wall; I expected everything to come crashing down—especially after Mr. Johnson screamed his own string of expletives and cried out. However, there was soon silence and what passed for a peaceful calm.

I went to get washed up. My aunt and her baby were sleeping in their room. My aunt was snoring in her usual way that always made me wonder if she was being strangled in her sleep. It used to terrify me, but in time, it merely became another signpost of my life—a reminder that I was still alive and that the people I had known yesterday were still there today, living their lives. Besides, of course by now my thoughts were only about Tisha and that magical room in the basement of the crack house. I had to see Madame Evangeline about the amulet, but first I had to see Tisha—to make sure that magical room still existed. I left the apartment before my aunt awoke. I practically ran to the crack house. In the basement, I was relieved to find that the room was still there. The dolls were still arrayed on the plush rug; the pink curtains still danced lightly on a gust of air beyond the shattered windows. However, as Tisha wasn't there, the magic was gone. I waited around for a couple hours, by which time it was about 10 o'clock. Unfortunately, in my haste to verify the existence of that magical room, I had neglected to eat. Hunger pangs began to gnaw at me (if you'll forgive the pun). That hunger, combined with the sleeplessness of the night before and my mounting bewilderment with life, left me in a dazed state. The heartbreak of the previous evening, when Tisha had seemed not to see me, returned to me then, and I became suddenly terrified that when she finally did return, I would still be invisible to her. I fled back home—where there was at least food to eat and where my loneliness would be straightforward and non-threatening.

My aunt was again in the living room when I got home. The baby was crying and my aunt sat holding it indifferently on her lap. I looked at them both anxiously. My aunt didn't seem to notice me, so after a while, I went about my business. Rather, I went to eat something while my yearnings for the fantasy of Tisha built themselves into a kind of madness…I guess that, at this point, some of you are probably bogged down in the question of if my aunt was a good mother or not. As I write this I sense my own judgmental inclinations being triggered. It springs out of me like a reflex. I've found myself thinking that most human acts of evil are just an evolutionary reaction to stress—to terror and panic and disillusionment that have reached such a state of refinement that that terrified, panic-stricken, person seems outwardly calm. The frenzied violence which one saw on the streets was only a showy distraction. The worst violence always happens in private—within one's soul. That's where dreams die and the human desire to love and be loved festers in the face of disappointment and hopelessness. It is once this evil had entrenched itself that the showy violence of the streets has a fertile breeding ground, and people like my aunt (and those she loves and can't love) became statistics. I'm not saying that my aunt was a "victim of circumstance" or anything so trite. I'm saying that she was a circumstantial human being, undone quite possibly by her inability to grasp the essential truths of her existence—or, as I've said before, the inability of her imagination to see past the horrors of her predicament.

Anyway, after eating, I returned to the room that was mine by default and fell asleep. I dreamed the kind of formless, disturbing dreams that usually plague those incapable of finding rest during the waking hours. I awoke four or five hours later. I awoke abruptly, disturbed by some fleeting image from my dream. I shuddered and sat up in bed, looking around confusedly. The mid-afternoon sun was shining directly into the window and I squinted as I looked over at it. I needed to move, but I felt too tired. At the same time, while I needed to sleep, the residual images of the dream world—whatever they had been—terrified me to the point that I began to think of sleep as a horror to be avoided at all costs. I went to the bathroom again. My yearning for Tisha was still there. I remembered that I had to see Madame Evangeline again. I missed my mother. When she first went away to work, I would be overcome by the certainty that she had returned. That certainty used to always be there when I was about to open the door to come inside the apartment—or in those dreamy moments immediately following sleep, when all seemed possible. I would rush ahead, expecting her to be there, expecting to find her smiling and opening her arms to me, holding back tears as she told me how she had quit her job to be with me. I, in turn, would be rapt in the joy of angels, because her declarations would verify that nothing else mattered but the peace and love that existed in that moment.

When I checked the apartment, I saw that it was empty. My aunt had made one of her rare forays into the outside world—most likely for food and other household essentials. I didn't want to be alone just then. I wanted someone to talk to and play games with—someone whose presence would be a shield against my budding awareness. In this context, my mind returned to Tisha; and for once, I found myself willing to risk the kind of loneliness that came with rejection, if the prize was another wondrous afternoon with her.

Outside, Mr. Williams mumbled his salutations to me; I grunted and rushed past him to meet the girl who literally seemed to be the woman of my dreams. I ran to the crack house with a desperation I had never felt before, and which I probably haven't felt since. I willed Tisha to be there. As I ran, I conjured scenes where she turned to greet me—just as she had the day before. I was so mad with longing for her—or at least for what she seemed to represent in my childish imagination—that I half thought I was dreaming when I rushed into the room and saw her sitting on the rug, playing with her dolls. We began playing without greetings and without the banter that marked true friendships. We played the same games as the day before—with even more virtuosic flights of fancy. However, we played with an underlying desperation that neither of us had the will to acknowledge. Playing there, in that strange room where the curtains suffused everything in a pink, fairy tale hue, and the realities of the outside world seemed magically banished, we were free—but free in a way that bred madness and delusion, not empowerment.

Still, even then, delusions can sometimes bring peace of mind—at least in the short term. As Tisha and I played—rather, as Tisha allowed me to share in her fantasy world—I looked at her and felt grateful beyond reason. She wasn't merely playing, she was summoning ancient magics and I was her apprentice. Now that I think about it, there was always an ancient quality about her, something anachronistic. I had before joined her and Madame Evangeline because of their accents, but now I joined them explicitly because of their communion with forces that seemed to exceed the limitations of physical space and time. Even now, I can't think about her without my mind going to newly emancipated slaves migrating to the north after the Civil War. Somehow, Tisha carried with her the religion of the slaves, an unshakable faith that God was good and on her side, coupled with the resigned, pragmatic awareness that the only joy and peace she would ever experience would have to be in another world. For us, the basement room became that other world. As she played her games, there was about her, that desperate hopefulness seen among those that had experienced a trauma so deep and all-encompassing that they, themselves, could barely come close to conceptualizing what had happened. The only thing they seemed to have was the hope that something better would eventually come their way. Also, now that I think about it, I was probably drawn to her precisely because something about her terrified me. Something about her kept eating away at me. Yet, perhaps even then, it ate away at me in a manner that left me thinking that I was on the verge of unlocking a portal to heaven and eternal happiness.

...I'm not saying that I realized all this back then, of course. Whatever truths I was able to glean that afternoon were all subverted by the realization that I didn't want the afternoon to end. The games we played were wondrous, precisely because they were mysterious to me—and had been conjured by Tisha's imagination. They gave me a window into her soul and her mysteries. Thus, when she brought out a huge teddy bear, I thought it was only another game. However, it was then that she asked me, "Have you ever been angry with anyone?" That entire afternoon, that was probably the first time she had addressed me directly—addressed me as the boy playing with her, not as a character in whatever fantasy she was conjuring.

I felt enlivened—vindicated somehow. However, her question remained in the air. I looked from her to the huge teddy bear, then back to her again.

"I guess," I said at last.

She smiled, going on, "You can do anything to dolls; dolls can be anything or anyone you want…even people you're angry with."

I nodded when she paused.

"Who are you angry with?" she encouraged me.

I didn't really have any particular person in mind, but as she looked at me imploringly, I said, "My mother."

She took my hand then—I remember that her hand was warm and soft—and made me stand up before the teddy bear. I complied shyly. "Hit it," she told me, gesturing to the teddy bear. I looked at her stupefied. "Hit it if you're angry with your mother." I hit it timidly. "Hit it harder! Is that all you have?" she taunted me. I balled my little fists and hit the teddy bear in the buttons that passed for its eyes. "Hit it!" she screamed again, and a strange rage expanded within me—a self-destructive kind of rage that made me lash out at the teddy bear with a vicious right hook. In the wake of the strange outburst, I stood there panting and terrified…and feeling guilty somehow, because I loved my mother and felt that she would know what I had done. Somehow, she would know, and would never come back to me. There was a tearful expression on my face now and Tisha, thinking that my outburst had been cathartic, laughed and hugged me. She pulled me into her budding breasts; she held me with her maturing body, with its promise of womanhood and adult dreams…but my terror and guilt remained.

She left soon thereafter. Binzo bellowed her name from outside—more likely than not from his car window—and she sprang up from our reconstituted game and dashed out of the door, again without acknowledging me. I looked at the teddy bear guiltily, then, hoping to get a final look at Tisha, I went to the window and, standing on a chair, was able to see her running up to Binzo's car. Still, despite her seeming haste, she slowed down about five paces from the car and walked the last remaining steps cautiously—as though anxious of stepping on a land mine. Binzo was actually outside the car, sitting on the hood with one of his expensive new sneakers resting on the bumper and the other one resting on the curb. These were the days of thick gold chains, jumpsuits and Kangol hats, and Binzo was resplendent as he sat there contemplating Tisha. I suppose that Binzo was in his late 20s. His face was scarred, and gold teeth replaced those that had been knocked out—

"Yo' mama told me to take care of you," he announced equivocally as she strolled up and stood before him. He sat watching her undecidedly as she stood before him. There was an uncomfortable, lingering silence. I guess he had expected her to say something—to thank him for following her mother's dictates perhaps—but she remained silent. I've come to realize that men like Binzo, who are used to having their way—especially when it came to poor, desperate young women—think it beneath them to ask for what they want. There is a certain patience about then, born either of calculating wisdom or cowardice. They see the desperation of others and know that eventually those others will come begging for their help. However, in Tisha's case, even though she exuded a certain kind of desperation, there was something unaccountable about it. It wasn't desperation of the type he had seen and known, which was soothed by sugary words, new outfits and the honor of riding shotgun in an expensive car. Her desperation, I'm convinced, wasn't material—but spiritual. The simple calculations of the ghetto defied it. Also, whereas Binzo had learned to be patient with those he wished to corrupt, when he looked at Tisha, there was an expression of frustration—and impotence—in his eyes. Tisha's mannerisms were out-wardly submissive, yet he still wasn't able to get what he wanted. She did what he ordered, but he didn't want to have to order her. He wanted her to come to him—even though he probably didn't care whether her coming was because of love or suicidal desperation. Both were only pretexts that had as their ultimate design sexual intercourse and his total mastery of her.

After about thirty seconds of the strange silence between Tisha and Binzo, he ordered her to get into the car. She complied and they drove off soon thereafter. Having no reason to remain in the darkening room, I left as well.

Another long, steamy night seemed in store for us. I walked home in that languid way seen among those who had nowhere to go and nothing to do. Guilty thoughts about my mother lingered in my head. I found myself thinking that the next time I saw Tisha I would tell her that I had lied. Tisha was again the good fairy to me, and in telling her the truth, I would be able to undo whatever enchantment my hateful words and actions had cast.

On the block, some ten-year-olds were taunting Williams, while he went on a shrill tirade about how in his day a child would never talk to an adult the way they did. His tirade encompassed the children's horrible parents and the futures of jail, pain and pointless deaths. Williams was right, of course: none of those 10-year-olds made it to 25. Two got AIDS; three were gunned down; one was serving a life sentence when he was stabbed in the prison shower. That afternoon, I stood on the sidewalk watching them objectively. Maybe the spectacle of all the name-calling and Williams's flustered attempts to defend himself (and the honor of old people everywhere) intrigued me for a moment. However, in the end, the realization that none of them had anything to say to me made me walk past them and go inside.

In the apartment, I found my aunt in one of her strange moods where she was trying too hard to be happy—and to be nice to me. For a moment, I thought that the amulet was finally working and that the demon had been banished from the house, but the obvious unnaturalness of my aunt's behavior made me increasingly uneasy. Her boyfriend had called and said that he wanted to work things out. Like I said, she was trying to be happy. There was strain on her face; her smiles took effort and were too short-lived to be genuine. She kept asking me what I thought and I began to realize that it wasn't a confidante she wanted, but a co-conspirator, someone to help her carry on the charade of being happy. Her strange joy terrified me—it was a terrible burden that she was trying to hoist on my shoulders—and all I wanted to do was get away.

Her boyfriend showed up a short while later. He had an annoying habit of calling me, "Chief." He, too, was trying desperately to be happy. They disappeared into my aunt's room to continue Act II and I went to the living room and turned up the volume on the TV. I fell asleep on the couch. I awoke hours later to the sound of my aunt and her boyfriend saying loud, demonstrative goodbyes at the front door. Declarations of love were made; promises to make things work out were renewed. However, in their voices there was a rushed, anxious quality—like when someone was making an emergency long distance call from a payphone at a highway gas station. They were forced to scream over the bad connection, talk quickly before time ran out on the payphone and they were left stranded in the middle of nowhere. As my aunt and her boyfriend rushed ahead with their declarations, it was as though they were even then thousands of miles apart.

Ghosts inhabit the imaginations of all human beings; but for children, ignorance and hopefulness continually give flesh to these ghosts. We are born seeing wonderlands and hell dimensions. However, with age and maturity, the customs and limitations of society begin to crush that innate hopefulness. Similarly, the lessons used by society to banish ignorance often have the side effect of withering the soul. At six years of age, I was in a state of flux. By now, I had consumed most of society's kernels of wisdom, even though I hadn't digested them yet. Whether that indigestion came as a result of my inextinguishable hopefulness or because of the same obstinacy I demonstrated with Williams, I can't say. Either way, I clung to life— the essential goodness within me; and when I say "goodness" I don't mean some moral precept. I merely mean that I was still intact. Most of the little compromises that socialization and maturity demanded of us hadn't yet manifested themselves on my psyche and self-concept. I was still me....

In the morning, my aunt continued her attempt to be happy. I awoke to the sounds and smells of breakfast cooking. Still rubbing the sleep from my eyes, I approached my aunt shyly—and with a lingering sense of suspicion. Her baby seemed suspicious as well. It took her new onslaught of caresses and kisses for pokes and prods, and soon began to wail at her slightest approach. While I wolfed down her cooking, she spoke of the wonderful future that was in store for her, all the things that she and her boyfriend had discussed the night before. She was going to re-enter school; and somewhere down the line, there was a glorious career and marriage...and a house in the suburbs where her children could run in the back yard. I wasn't really listening to her, of course. My aunt's dreams were hers, and I had mine. Even as I sat there, all I could think about was Tisha and that magical basement room.

Compelled by that fantasy, I soon left and returned to the crack house. Nobody was there, but once again the reality of the room was a verification of the hours I had spent with Tisha, and therefore seemed to validate my hopes and my existence. The only drawback was that in the next room, one of Binzo's knights was bartering with a bone-thin crackhead—trading a blow job for the drug she craved. Unfortunately, she was so on-edge from her addiction that her teeth chattered. She began chewing the sensitive tissue of his penis, and when a sudden spasm seized her body, the lamentable result was that she clamped down on his penis. The most blood-curdling scream you can imagine shook the foundations of the building. When I rushed to see what was happening, the crackhead was going into convulsions, her jaw still clamped down on the dealer's penis. I don't remember what the dealer's name was—since those guys didn't last long. However, I remember that from then on he was known as "Stumpy."

With all the commotion (an ambulance was called), I left the crack house and began wandering the neighborhood. I figured that this would be a good time to visit Madame Evangeline. However, when I got there, the door was locked, and when I knocked on the door, the crazy old man that lived upstairs looked out of the window and yelled at me for making too much noise. He was pretty much toothless and, as he yelled at me, huge globs of spittle rained down on me. I left with a queasy feeling—not only from the spit, but because Madame Evangeline's absence seemed to be yet another sign that I was doomed.

With nothing else to give me home, my yearning for Tisha became so acute that it occurred to me that if I headed in the direction that she and Binzo had driven off in, then I would eventually find her. I walked until about midday—past neighborhoods no different from mine, to neighborhoods with elegant brownstones…and all the neighborhoods in between. I didn't find her, of course, and this corroborated my budding suspicion that Tisha only existed in that room and its immediate environs. With this new aware-ness, I rushed back to the room. On the wobbly stairway to the basement, I heard her laughter and leapt down the last four steps in my haste to get to her. And maybe she would hug me as she had the previous afternoon. I was almost wild with these thoughts now...but when I was about three paces from the door, I heard other voices—unfamiliar laughs. I stiffened, and when I turned the corner and looked in, I saw Tisha surrounded by five other little boys. I stared with the shock and heartbreak of a man that came home to find his lover in the arms of another. The boys were all about my age. However, as I didn't recognize any of them from school, I knew that they weren't from the neighborhood. Maybe, I considered, they were from Tisha's imagination, conjured in my absence; maybe even I was only the product of one of those conjurings and had no real substance beyond this room. The little boys were hopping about her; I looked from their stupid antics to Tisha, thinking, Wasn't I good enough for you? When she finally saw me standing there broodingly, she called me over. However, I sat to the side, listening to the shrill laughter that seemed to be a desecration of our magical place. I sat there for hours, thinking that Tisha would eventually see how unimaginative the boys were and banish them forever from our sacred room.

...Only in retrospect do I find it strange that a beautiful 13-year-old would seek out the company of six-year-olds. Yet, even as I stood there, I knew that something was very wrong—and it wasn't my puerile jealousy anymore. Though Tisha was physically maturing into womanhood, she acted as though she were six. Gone from her play was the imaginative virtuosity of previous afternoons—maybe that virtuosity had never been there and I had only imagined it in my desperation. As I looked on, I realized that her play with the boys seemed rushed, yet calculating—as though she were on some kind of deadline. It all seemed bizarre to me; and then, she asked the little boys the question she had asked me the day before—except that now, instead of it being "Who are you angry with?" it was "Who do you hate?" The little boys rushed up to give their responses. They didn't succumb to the hesitancy that had gripped me the day before. The boys were natural born haters—perhaps we all are. They had people in their lives who mistreated them—and even abused them. The constant trickle of resentment was easy to dam into a reservoir of hatred. Growing up in the ghetto, surrounded by poverty and people who hated their lives, it wasn't difficult to bring forth hate. Learning to hate was essentially about learning to hate one's self—about realizing that one was in a situation that one didn't have the wherewithal to change. Hatred isn't so much about what others have done to us; it is about what we cannot do to them. Oppressors may disdain those they oppress, but the oppressed always hate their oppressors. There is a power relationship there: the realization that no matter what one does, one will never be able to correct the inescapable injustice of one's everyday existence.

As the boys rushed up to Tisha, they named mothers and teachers and big brothers—and even cartoon characters. Soon, the huge teddy bear came out; then, at Tisha's behest, the boys leapt at it, their little fists flailing, their legs kicking. Some of them bit the bear and clawed at it. The boys were screaming now. They weren't merely boys anymore, but dispensers of justice and righters of wrongs—all this, under Tisha's celestial gaze. I looked on from the periphery. When Tisha smiled at me encouragingly, I got up and went over to the fray and found an unoccupied piece of the bear to kick. However, I really wasn't into it and Tisha seemed to realize it as well, because she practically ignored me for the rest of the afternoon. While the boys punched the unfortunate doll, I returned to the periphery, still waiting for her to come to her senses and banish the others. Of course, with all the flailing limbs, one of the boys got punched in the face. Being the righter of injustice that he was, he leapt at the offender and the two soon began to fight. The others, more intrigued with others fighting among themselves than with righting wrongs, soon began to cheer. Within moments, one of the boys was bloody and crying, but Tisha stepped up quickly and pulled the little boy to her chest, so that the whimpers faded away and the boy found himself ready to fight again. In fact, now the boys were all ready to fight, because they soon began sparring with one another. The boys didn't even pretend to be motivated by justice anymore; they were now only dispensers of violence. Tisha urged them on from her seat of honor. The boys loved these games—and they loved Tisha more completely than I could have. She sat before them like Caesar directing competitors. She urged them on to the full realization of their bestiality. She quieted their

cries; she dabbed their bloody noses with tissues and kissed their wounds…
but she never curtailed their fights, and the boys loved her for this.

As one might expect, a crude hierarchy developed as a result of all these
gladiator battles—but not in the way one might think. Usually, under such
circumstances, the strong rose to the top. However, as Tisha's kisses only
went to the beaten, bloody boys, in time, the boys began to lose on purpose.
I'm almost certain of it. They put out their faces to be punched. Many a
baby tooth was loosened that afternoon. It became a strange mark of
honor. Also, after a while, the tired boys realized that they could forego the
worst of the battles and go straight to Tisha's affection if they gave up and
cried after a few blows. Both boys in the conflict would run to her begging
for comfort, so that for much of that afternoon the basement constantly
rang out with the cries of little boys.

I left them and walked off in a daze. They didn't notice my leaving. It was
all a bad dream. As I walked away, I was desperate to convince myself that
none of it had actually happened. In stepping away from the basement I was
emerging from a bad dream; and like someone awakening from a nightmare,
all that I could hope was that the next time I closed my eyes and returned to
the dream world, it would be the wonderful fantasy I had had before.

However, when I stepped away from the basement, it was as though I had
entered a time warp. Everything was rushing ahead now, as though speeding toward the inevitable conclusion. Soon, I was entering the basement
again. Tisha and the boys were there, but the boys were listening silently—
intently. The boys were sitting on the floor; Tisha stood before them, holding a mannequin. I have no idea where she got it from, but she was using it
to demonstrate the tenets of her religion. It was a religion based on hate and
dolls, and she was telling them that if their hate was true, then the
people they hated would be replaced by the mannequin. It was a strange off-
shoot of voodoo dolls, I suppose. Instead of the person merely feeling what
you did to the doll, now, in exacting vengeance on the doll, the doll would
become the person. The little boys were mesmerized—I was mesmerized.
Yet, as the boys sat there rapt (as though in Sunday school) I looked on from
the periphery. Tisha saw me but said nothing…and I almost wanted to cry.

It was then, at the climax of her sermon, that Tisha sat the mannequin in a chair and handed out steak knives to the little boys. Here, she probably decided to give me one last chance to redeem myself, because she called me over and gave me a knife as well. Soon, we were all stabbing the mannequin—the effigy of those we hated…And I did feel hate then. I hated the outside world in a way that I can't even begin to explain. As my knife penetrated the hard plastic of the mannequin, I wanted everything to disappear but Tisha and that room. I wanted things to return to the way they were that first time. I wanted to get rid of the other boys, and Binzo, and my aunt, and my guilty thoughts about my mother. I wanted all of that to be effaced from the Earth. And when one of the little boys came too close to me, I punched him in the face and kicked him savagely as he lay on the ground crying. The others looked at me, as if just noticing me. When the boy tried to run to Tisha, I slapped him in the face and threw him in the corner. I still held the knife, so it's a miracle that I didn't eviscerate him in my fury. The others looked at me, cowed. Tisha looked at me as well—but there was a smile there that two decades of obsessive consideration on my part hasn't been able to come to grips with. I don't know what I felt at that moment, but I knew that I had risen to the hierarchy of the boys—that I had reset the natural order by surrendering to my brutality.

Tisha came to me then and hugged me—perhaps for restoring the natural order—and I stood there triumphant. I had succeeded where Binzo and all the others had failed, because she had come to me. Yet, I was only a six-year-old boy, and once we parted for the day (again at Binzo's behest from his car) the madness I had felt in the room ebbed somewhat and I felt like someone struggling with the after effects of a drug binge. Even while I shuddered at what I had done, my body and soul craved the drug—was willing to do almost anything to feel that wondrous high again. I even had a headache—as if I actually did have a hangover. I shuffled home like a drunk struggling to get his bearings…Williams was still at his throne; the neighborhood children were again playing their games; and seeing that the world continued in its usual way, I had a momentary pang of courage when I thought of going cold turkey—of never returning to Tisha and the room in the basement of the crack house. That room still seemed magical to me, but in the face of what had happened that afternoon, it now seemed beset by dark magic of the sort that claimed one's soul. Unfortunately, while all drug addicts had such infinitesimal spurts of courage, the drug's imprint on their souls never allowed those spurts to be long lived.

Williams looked at me uneasily as I ran past him and up the stairs. In the darkness of my mother's room (which was still mine by default) I lay rigidly in bed. Mr. Johnson came home and started up his usual antics. Elsewhere, radios were turned up high—either to counter Johnson or to mask their own quarrels or whatever the case may be. Once again, I grew terrified of the collective noise of my neighborhood. Each seemed to be a new well-spring of madness. Each seemed to be calling me to my doom and there didn't seem to be anything I could do to escape. I missed my mother, suddenly and desperately. As yet, I hadn't taken back the hateful things I said to Tisha. I had to find a way to curtail the spell that had been put in motion—and all the spells that bewitched us. I thought about going to Madame Evangeline again, but as had been the case with Tisha after our first parting, I grew terrified by the prospect that she wouldn't be there, and that this irrefutable evidence of my total isolation would extinguish whatever reason I had to go on living.

I slept in fits and starts; several times I emerged from semi-conscious states with a shudder or a muffled cry. However, about two in the morning, I had a wonderful dream, in which my mother had returned. Upon awakening, I jumped out of bed, looking for her bags—for any sign that the dream had been true. Hearing the TV on in the living room, I rushed out, thinking that maybe she had stayed in the living room in order to avoid awakening me. However, with each step I took toward the living room, the euphoria of the dream faded. Then, when I reached the doorway, I saw my aunt's morose form on the couch, staring at a late movie—but with eyes that seemed to see nothing. She had stopped trying to be happy—had run out of the energy necessary to keep the farce going and was back to her old self. I sneaked back to my room and lay there silently until again possessed by my dreams.

Those dreams were undoubtedly turbulent, because in the morning I woke up on the floor of the bedroom, entangled in the sheets. I woke up in a strange terror, fighting to get free of the sheets—as though they were a monster. When I was free, I lay on the floor panting. There were sirens in the air, but I didn't pay them much attention at first. I merely thought of them as a byproduct of my headache. I shuffled to the bathroom. Next, I went to the kitchen where, looking out of the window, I saw the police cars and ambulances that had blocked off the street. The night before the Johnsons had had a particularly bad fight—which I hadn't heard in my daze. As I looked on from the window, the police dragged Mr. Johnson out of the building in handcuffs. He was screaming something, dressed only in his drawers and a pair of slippers. Mrs. Johnson came out on a stretcher— but she was screaming as well. She was a huge woman. In contrast, Mr. Johnson was as slight as a stick. I remember thinking that he looked like one of those starved stray dogs that I often came upon while wandering through the neighborhood's vacant lots. Johnson's ribs protruded horribly, seeming to want to burst through his skin as his enraged screams echoed through the morning air. He was trying to turn around to yell at his wife. In the meantime, the EMTs were trying to put an oxygen mask on Mrs. Johnson, but she kept brushing it aside to scream aspersions at her husband. Both of them were bloody. It was all a sick joke, of course. Besides the police and the ambulances, dozens of spectators were on the street; people were hanging out of windows to get a better look. I don't know what to say about the Johnsons. A day later, they were back home screwing one another. They, of course, had an abusive relationship, but it was silly to say that Mr. Johnson was Mrs. Johnson's abuser. Their relationship was the abusive thing. Their way of communicating—and maybe even of loving— was the abusive thing.

I went outside about half an hour later. My aunt, who was a heavy sleeper, hadn't awakened yet. Outside, the streets were relatively clear by now—just like a cinema 10 minutes after the movie was over. I rushed to the basement— probably because I knew that nobody would be there and I needed to remember the room as it was—without little boys and their strange games.

However, to my amazement, Tisha and the boys were there. The boys were stabbing the effigy again. When I entered, the boys looked at me diffidently, still acknowledging the hierarchy that had been established the day before. However, Tisha still seemed to be rushing ahead, as though running out of time. Shortly after I entered, she gave us some money and told us to go and get some ice cream while she made "preparations."

She told us to come back in about 45 minutes and kept looking at her watch. Actually, she gave the money to me, since I was still the top dog, but outside the building, beyond the magical confines of the room, I knew that I didn't want to be with the boys. I gave them the money and pointed them toward the store. I had an impulse to go to Tisha and help her in her preparations—or just be with her—but in the end, I walked away by myself. I was halfway down the block when I realized that I had lost my amulet. I retraced my steps to the basement, but when I got there, Tisha screamed at me in a strange rage that was tinged with terror, telling me to come back in 45 minutes. I left her—I ran as though fleeing for my life.

Madame Evangeline's warnings about the amulet—and about the vulnerability of my soul should I lose it—made me tremble. I ran back to my room and was relieved when I finally saw it lying on the ground—entwined in the sheets I had fought with during the night. However, even as I held it in my palm, I wondered if it was already too late. I sensed a difference in myself—maybe the dawning maturity I had alluded to before, or a sudden awareness that the forces of evil had already taken my soul. When I remembered how Tisha had screamed at me, I wanted to cry; and in this disconsolate state, Madame Evangeline again seemed like the last chance for my soul.

I ran to Madame Evangeline's shop. I, like Tisha, was running out of time. As I held the amulet in my hand, I considered that maybe we were all trapped in the same spell. The amulet, which had allowed my miraculous escape from certain death, and which had brought Tisha into my life, conjuring her from the yearnings of my soul, was like all things spawned by evil, wrought with hidden consequences—dire tradeoffs that were even then amassing on the horizon.

I again found Madame Evangeline's door locked; succumbing to the accumulated terror of the previous days and weeks, I banged on the door, screaming out, "Madame, help me! Help me, please!"

The old man who lived on the second floor came to the window angrily. I was crying by then, screaming hysterically for Madame to come and save my soul.

"She went back to Haiti!" the old man screamed, spraying me with spit in the process.

I looked up at him in shock: "What! For good?"

"Do I look like a goddamn information service to you?!"

I turned and ran. I was sure that the 45 minutes Tisha had specified had passed by then—and that I had run out of time. I rushed back to the basement, numb with terror, and yet still hoping beyond hope that I would be able to stop the evil I sensed all around me now. It was in the breeze; I felt it emanating from the ground, and shining down on me like the sun. It was everywhere and in everyone. I saw it in the eyes of the people I passed; I heard it in their voices—even in their laughter. I ran for my life—for all our lives. Even when I cramped up and my lungs felt as though they were on fire, I shuffled along, like some kind of cripple.

On the wobbly steps to the basement I cramped up again and promptly tripped, toppling down the staircase. I lay unconscious on the ground for a while; then, in those strange moments between unconsciousness and full consciousness, I heard the laughter of the little boys. However, now, it sounded like the laughter of angels. I lay on the ground listening to the melody of it. Minutes seemed to pass as I lay there dreaming of angels and peace of mind. Maybe I had died in the fall, I thought. Maybe I was dead now and my life of fear and vulnerability was over. However, just then, an inflection in one of the boy's laughter drew me back into the real world. I looked around in a daze, seeing the dark, dour confines of the basement chamber. The laughter that had once seemed angelic, now seemed cacophonous. It was like a jarring alarm bell. I had the impulse to run away right then, but some morbid streak seemed to seize me, and I stumbled to my feet. My muscles were still cramping up, so I shuffled along toward the magical room that had before seemed like the fulfillment of all my fantasies.

Just as I made it to the doorway Tisha was handing out the knives to the little boys. They had been playing before, but she called them to order before the freshly prepared effigy. It was a mass of rags and tape, covered from head to foot. Yet its proportions were unmistakably that of a man, and when I looked closer, I noticed that it wore Binzo's expensive sneakers....

My mind puttered along; I was so weak from all my running and terrors that I could only lean against the doorway. Tisha was saying something now; she was talking so quickly and anxiously that I could barely understand her. However, as I listened closely, I recognized the tenets of her religion: the precept that if one hated someone strongly enough, then when they took out their revenge on the effigy, the person they hated would take its place. For some reason, I gasped; as the boys and Tisha looked in my direction, I gasped again, because I swore that the effigy moved. However, Tisha was rushing ahead now, telling the boys to take their revenge. I stretched out my hand in a last futile gesture to stop them; but the boys, seeing me falter, rushed ahead to claim my place in the hierarchy—to show that they too had brutality to unleash and deserved to be the sole beneficiaries of Tisha's affections. Her face wore the blank expression of a sleepwalker who, while walking about in this world, was seeing the horrors of another world. When the first knife went into the effigy, the body tensed up and blood spurted out of the wound. I screamed—or at least tried to—but in their madness, none of the other boys seemed to notice. Spurred on by Tisha's religion, the boys were stabbing the effigy savagely now. Tisha, still entranced, only stood staring blankly. The little boys were covered in blood by now—and laughing at their triumph over the supernatural world. I went to take a step backward—to retreat from the room and its madness—but by then my trembling was so extreme that I tripped and fell to the ground. In the closed room, the noise seemed like an explosion. Tisha jumped and looked at me; the little boys, covered with blood and with knives still in mid-air, looked back at me with the madness still shining in their eyes...

God, I ran! I ran like I had never run before. Maybe it wasn't even the reality of what I had seen and been a party to that made me run. I was beyond sight by then—beyond the horror of what had happened in the room. Also, even as I ran, I didn't run toward anything: I didn't go home—

or to any place where I might expect comfort. Of course, there was no one I could go to. I ran to a neighborhood I had never been to before. There, I sat on the curb, crying—terrified and alone. I swore that I could still hear the laughter of the boys and the sick sound of knife blades slicing into flesh—and all the other lonely echoes of my youth….

After a while, an old woman came along; seeing me crying, she asked if I was all right, but I ran off again. Hours later, when I finally made it back to the tenement, Williams was on the stoop. A slight drizzle had started up and he was about to go inside; but seeing me enter the block with that strange expression on my face, he stood watching me curiously. I have no idea what I looked like by then. I doubt my mind had had two cogent thoughts since I ran from the basement.

"You all right, Son?" he asked me when I reached the stoop.

I opened my mouth, but couldn't think of anything to say—and in fact had nothing to say. I remember that his mutt was staring at me, too. I nodded to Williams and headed upstairs. On the top of the staircase, just as I had countless other times, I was overcome by the certainty that my mother had returned to me. It seemed real this time—I had a visceral reaction, a feeling of almost insane euphoria. I rushed into the house, already panting, already wearing a grin…but the loneliness of the house was unmistakable; and in the living room, my aunt was at her usual place, staring blankly at the television. The baby was sleeping beside her on the couch. I entered the living room and stood just behind my aunt. After a while, she looked up at me, surprised to see me—or perhaps surprised by the extent of what was on my face. I went to her then, and hugged her and cried. She still sat on the couch, and was no doubt bewildered by my strange outburst. She held me timidly at first; but then, maybe seized by some internal terror of her own, she hugged me tighter.

D.V. Bernard immigrated from the Caribbean nation of Grenada when he was nine years old, and settled in New York City. He is the author of two novels: God in the Image of Woman *(2004) and* The Last Dream Before Dawn *(2003). He can be reached through his web site: www.dvbernard.com*

BREAKING THE CYCLE
RESOURCES

The National Domestic Violence Hotline is the major source for assistance for victims of abuse. Their web site is located at http://www.ndvh.org. The National Hotline for assistance is 1-800-799-7233 or the TTY number is 1-800-787-3224.

The following are state organizations that offer assistance to victims of domestic violence:

ALABAMA
Alabama Coalition Against Domestic Violence
PO Box 4762
Montgomery, Alabama 36101
Phone: 334-832-4842
Fax: 334-832-4803
Hotline:1-800-650-6522
http://www.acadv.org
acadv@acadv.org

ALASKA
Alaska Network on Domestic Violence and Sexual Assault
130 Seward, Suite 209
Junea, Alaska 99801
Phone 907-586-3650
http://www.andvsa.org

ARIZONA
Arizona Coalition Against Domestic Violence
100 West Camelback Street, Suite 109
Phoenix, Arizona 85013
Phone: 602-279-2900
Fax: 602-279-2980
http://www.azacadu.org

ARKANSAS

Arkansas Coalition Against Domestic Violence
#1 Sheriff Lane, Suite C
North Little Rock, Arkansas 72114
Phone: 501-812-0571
Fax: 501-812-0578
http://www.domesticpeace.com

CALIFORNIA

California Alliance Against Domestic Violence
926 J Street, Suite 1000
Sacramento, California 95814
Phone: 916-444-7163
Fax: 916-444-7165
Toll-Free: 1-800-524-4765
http://www.caadv.org
caadv@cwo.com

Southern Office
8929 South Sepulveda Boulevard, Suite 520
Los Angeles, California 90045-3605
Phone: 310-649-3953
Fax: 310-649-2479

Statewide California Coalition for Battered Women
3711 Long Beach Boulevard, #718
Long Beach, California 90807
Phone: 562-981-1202
Fax: 562-981-3202
Toll-Free: 1-888-722-2952
http://www.sccbw.org
sccbw@sccbw.org

COLORADO
Colorado Coalition Against Domestic Violence
P. O. Box 18902
Denver, Colorado 80218
Phone: 303-831-9632
Fax: 303-832-7067
Toll-Free: 1-888-778-7091
http://www.ccadv.org

CONNECTICUT
Connecticut Coalition Against Domestic Violence
90 Pitkin Street
East Hartford, Connecticut 06108
Phone: 860-282-7899
Toll-Free: 1-888-774-2900
info@ctcadv.org

DELAWARE
Delaware Coalition Against Domestic Violence
100 West 10th Street, Suite 703
Wilmington, Delaware 19801
Phone: 302-658-2958
Fax: 302-658-5049
http://www.dcadv.org
dcadv@dcadv.org

DISTRICT OF COLUMBIA
D.C. Coalition Against Domestic Violence
1718 P Street, NW, Suite T-6
Washington, DC 20036
Phone: 202-299-1181
Fax: 202-299-1193
http://www.dccadv.org
dswartz@dccadv.org

Victim Advocacy Program of the District of Columbia Coalition Against Domestic Violence
  DC Superior Court
  Room 4235
  500 Indiana Avenue, NW
  Washington, DC 20001
  Phone: 202-879-7851
  Fax: 202-879-1191

FLORIDA

Florida Coalition Against Domestic Violence
425 Office Plaza Drive
Tallahassee, Florida 32301
Phone: 850-425-2749
Fax: 850-425-3091
TDD: 850-621-4202
Hotline: 1-800-500-1119
http://www.fcadv.org

GEORGIA

Georgia Coalition Against DomesticViolence
3420 Norman Berry Drive, Suite 280
Atlanta, Georgia 30354
Phone: 404-209-0280
Fax: 404-766-3800
Hotline: 1-800-334-2836
http://www.gcadv.org
gacoalition@gcadv.org

HAWAII

Hawaii State Coalition Against Domestic Violence
716 Umi Street, Suite 210
Honolulu, Hawaii 96819-2337

Phone: 808-832-9316
Fax: 808-841-6028
http://www.hscadv.org
clee@hscadv.org

IDAHO

Idaho Coalition Against Sexual and Domestic Violence
815 Park Boulevard, Suite 140
Boise, Idaho 83712
Phone: 208-384-0419
Fax: 208-331-0687
Toll-Free: 1-888-293-6118
http://www.idvsa.org
ahrensa@idvsa.org

ILLINOIS

Illinois Coalition Against Domestic Violence
801 South 11th Street
Springfield, Illinois 62703
Phone: 217-789-2830
Fax: 217-789-1939
TTY: 217-241-0376
http://www.ilcadv.org

INDIANA

Indiana Coalition Against Domestic Violence
1915 West 18th Street
Indianapolis, Indiana 46202
Phone: 317-917-3685
Fax: 317-917-3695
Toll-Free: 1-800-538-3393
http://www.violenceresource.org
icadv@violenceresource.org

IOWA

Iowa Coalition Against Domestic Violence
2603 Bell Avenue, Suite 100
Des Moines, Iowa 50321
Phone: 515-244-8028
Fax: 515-244-7417
Toll-Free State Hotline: 1-800-942-0333
http://www.icadv.org

KANSAS

Kansas Coalition Against Sexual and Domestic Violence
220 SW 33rd Street, Suite 100
Topeka, Kansas 66611
Phone: 785-232-9784
Fax: 785-266-1874
http://www.kcsdv.org

KENTUCKY

Kentucky Domestic Violence Association
P. O. Box 356
Frankfort, Kentucky 40602
Phone: 502-209-5382
Fax: 502-226-5382
http://www.kdva.org

LOUISIANA

Louisiana Coalition Against Domestic Violence
P. O. Box 77308
Baton Rouge, Louisiana 70879
Phone: 222-752-1296
Fax: 222-751-8927
http://www.lcadv.org
frankalcadv@aol.com

MAINE
Maine Coalition to End Domestic Violence
170 Park Street
Bangor, Maine 04401
Phone: 207-941-1194
Fax: 207-941-2327
http://www.mcedv.org
info@mcedv.org

MARYLAND
Maryland Network Against Domestic Violence
6911 Laurel-Bowie Road, Suite 309
Bowie, Maryland 20715
Phone: 301-352-4574
Fax: 301-809-0422
Toll-Free: 1-800-MD-HELPS
http://www.mnadv.org
info@mnadv.org

MASSACHUSSETTS
Massachusetts Coalition Against Sexual Assault and Domestic Violence
Jane Doe, Inc.
14 Beacon Street, Suite 507
Boston, Massachusetts 02108
Phone: 617-248-0922
Fax: 617-248-0902
http://www.janedoe.org
info@janedoe.org

MICHIGAN
Michigan Coalition Against Domestic and Sexual Violence
3893 Okemos Road, Suite B2
Okemos, Michigan 48864

Phone: 517-347-7000
Fax: 517-347-1377
TTY: 517-381-8470
http://www.mcadsv.org
general@mcadsv.org

MINNESOTA
Minnesota Coalition for Battered Women
590 Park Street, Suite 410
St. Paul, Minnesota 55103
Phone: 651-646-6177
Fax: 651-646-1527
Toll-Free: 1-800-289-6177
Crisis Hotline: 651-646-0994
http://www.mcbw.org
ccook@mcbw.org

MISSISSIPPI
Mississippi State Coalition Against Domestic Violence
P. O. Box 4703
Jackson, Mississippi 39296-4703
Phone: 601-981-9196
Fax: 601-981-2501
Toll-Free: 1-800-898-3234 (Monday-Friday 8 a.m.-5 p.m.)
Toll-Free: 1-800-799-7233 (After Hours)
http://www.mcadv.org

MISSOURI
Missouri Coalition Against Domestic Violence
415 East McCarthy
Jefferson City, Missouri 65101
Phone: 573-634-4161
Fax: 573-636-3728

http://www.mocadv.org
mocadv@socketo.net

MONTANA
Montana Coalition Against Domestic Violence
P. O. Box 818
Helena, Montana 59624
Phone: 406-443-7794
Fax: 406-443-7818
Toll-Free: 1-888-404-7794
http://www.mcadsv.org
mcadsv@mt.net

NEBRASKA
Nebraska Domestic Violence and Sexual Assault Coalition
825 M Street, Suite 404
Lincoln, Nebraska 68508-2253
Phone: 402-476-6256
Fax: 402-476-6806
Toll-Free: 1-800-876-6238
http://www.ndvsac.org

NEVADA
Nevada Network Against Domestic Violence
100 West Grove Street, Suite 315
Reno, Nevada 89509
Phone: 775-828-1115
Fax: 775-828-9911
Toll-Free: 1-800-230-1955
Hotline: 1-800-500-1556
http://www.nnadv.org

NEW HAMPSHIRE
New Hampshire Coalition Against Domestic and Sexual Violence
P. O. Box 353
Concord, New Hampshire 03302-0353
Phone: 603-224-8893
Fax: 603-228-6096
Toll-Free: 1-800-852-3388
Domestic Violence Hotline: 1-866-644-3574
Sexual Assault Hotline: 1-800-277-5570
http://www.nhcadsv.org

NEW JERSEY
New Jersey Coalition for Battered Women
1670 Whitehorse Hamilton Square Road
Trenton, New Jersey 08690
Phone: 609-584-8107
Fax: 609-584-9750
TTY: 609-584-9750
Toll-Free: 1-800-572-7233
Toll-Free for Battered Lesbians: 1-800-224-0211
http://www.njcbw.org
info@njcbw.org

NEW MEXICO
New Mexico State Coalition Against Domestic Violence
200 Oak, NE
Albuquerque, New Mexico 87106
Phone: 505-246-9240
Fax: 505-246-9434
Toll-Free: 1-800-773-3645
http://www.nmcadv.org
agnesm@nmcadv.org

NEW YORK

New York State Coalition Against Domestic Violence
79 Central Avenue
Albany, New York 12206
Phone: 518-432-4864
Fax: 518-463-3155
Toll-Free (English): 1-800-942-6906
Toll-Free (Spanish): 1-800-942-6908
Hotline/TTY (English): 1-800-818-0656
Hotline/TTY (Spanish): 1-800-980-7660
http://www.nyscadv.org
nyscadv@nyscadv.org

NORTH CAROLINA

North Carolina Coalition Against Domestic Violence
115 Market Street, Suite 400
Durham, NC 27701
Phone: 919-956-9124
Fax: 919-682-1449
Toll-Free: 1-888-232-9124
http://www.nccadv.org
marybeth@nccadv.org

NORTH DAKOTA

North Dakota Council on Abused Women's Services
State Networking Office
418 East Rosser Avenue, Suite 320
Bismarck, North Dakota 58501-4046
Phone: 701-255-6240
Fax: 701-255-1904
Toll-Free: 1-800-472-2911
http://www.ndcaws.org
ndcaws@ndcaws.org

OHIO

Ohio Domestic Violence Network
4807 Evanswood Drive, Suite 201
Columbus, Ohio 43229
Phone: 614-781-9651
Fax: 614-781-9652
TTY: 614-781-9654
Toll-Free: 1-800-934-9840
http://www.odvn.org
info@odvn.org

OKLAHOMA

Oklahoma Coalition Against Domestic Violence and Sexual Assault
3815 North Sante Fee Avenue, Suite 124
Oklahoma City, Oklahoma 73118
Phone: 405-524-0700
Fax: 405-524-0711
Toll-Free: 1-800-522-7233
http://www.ocadvsa.org
marcia@ocadvsa.org

OREGON

Oregon Coalition Against Domestic and Sexual Violence
115 Mission Street, SE, Suite 100
Salem, Oregon 97302
Phone: 503-365-9633
Fax: 503-566-7870
http://www.ocadsv.com
ocadsv@teleport.com

PENNSYLVANIA

Pennsylvania Coalition Against Domestic Violence/
National Resource Center on Domestic Violence
6400 Flank Drive, Suite 1300
Harrisburg, Pennsylvania 17112-2778
Phone: 717-545-6400
Fax: 717-671-8149
Toll-Free: 1-800-932-4632
http://www.pcadv.org

RHODE ISLAND

Rhode Island Coalition Against Domestic Violence
422 Post Road, Suite 202
Warwick, Rhode Island 02888
Phone: 401-467-9940
Fax: 401-467-9943
Toll-Free: 1-800-494-8100
http://www.ricadv.org
ricadv@ricadv.org

SOUTH CAROLINA

South Carolina Coalition Against Domestic Violence and Sexual Assault
P. O. Box 7776
Columbia, South Carolina 29202-7776
Phone: 803-256-2900
Fax: 803-256-1030
Toll-Free: 1-800-260-9293
http://www.sccadvasa.org

SOUTH DAKOTA
South Dakota Coalition Against Domestic Violence and Sexual Assault
Pierre Office
P. O. Box 141
Pierre, South Dakota 57501
Phone: 605-945-0869
Fax: 605-945-0870
Toll-Free: 1-800-572-9196
http://www.southdakotacoalition.org
sdcadvsa@rapidnet.com

Eagle Butte Office
P. O. Box 306
Eagle Butte, South Dakota 57625
Phone: 605-964-7103
Fax: 605-964-7104
Toll-Free: 1-888-728-3275
willi@lakota-woman.com

TENNESSEE
Tennessee Coalition Against Domestic Violence and Sexual Violence
P. O. Box 120972
Nashville, Tennessee 37212
Phone: 615-386-9406
Fax: 615-383-2967
Toll-Free Hotline: 1-800-289-9018 (8 a.m.-5 p.m. M-F)
Statewide Domestic Violence and Child Abuse Hotline: 1-800-356-6767
http://www.tcadsv.org
tcadsv@tcadsv.org

TEXAS

Texas Council on Family Violence
8701 P.O. Box 161810
Austin, Texas 78716
Phone: 512-794-1133
Fax: 512-794-1199
http://www.tcfv.org

UTAH

Utah Domestic Violence Advisory Council
320 West 200 South, Suite 270B
Salt Lake City, Utah 84101
Phone: 801-521-5544
Fax: 801-521-5548
Toll-Free in Utah: 1-800-897-LINK
http://www.udvac.org
jkbell@udvac.org

VERMONT

Vermont Network Against Domestic Violence and Sexual Assault
P.O. Box 405
Montpelier, Vermont 05601
Phone: 802-223-1302
Fax: 802-223-6943
Domestic Violence Hotline: 1-800-228-7395
Sexual Violence Hotline: 1-800-489-7273
http://www.vtnetwork.org
vtnetwork@vtnetwork.org

VIRGINIA

Virginians Against Domestic Violence
Williamsburg Office
2850 Sandy Bay Road, Suite 101
Williamsburg, Virginia 23185
Phone: 757-221-0990
Fax: 757-229-1553
Toll-Free: 1-800-838-VADV
http://www.vadv.org
info@vadvalliance.org

Richmond Office
1010 North Thompson Street, Suite 202
Richmond, Virginia 23230
Phone: 804-377-0335
Fax: 804-377-0339
TTY 804-377-7330

WASHINGTON

Washington State Coalition Against Domestic Violence
Seattle Office
1402 3rd Avenue, Suite 406
Seattle, Washington 98101
Phone: 206-389-2515
Fax: 206-289-2520
TTY: 206-289-2900
http://www.wscadv.org
wscadv@wscadv.org

Olympia Office
101 North Capitol Way, Suite 302
Olympia, Washington 98501
Phone: 360-586-1022

Fax: 360-586-1024
TTY: 360-586-1029

WEST VIRGINIA
West Virginia Coalition Against Domestic Violence
Elk Office Center
4710 Chimney Drive, Suite A
Charleston, West Virginia 25302
Phone: 304-965-3552
Fax: 304-965-3572
http://www.wvcadv.org

WISCONSIN
Wisconsin Coalition Against Domestic Violence
600 Williamson Street, Suite N-2
Madison, Wisconsin 53703
Phone/TTY: 608-257-1516
Fax: 608-257-2150
http://www.wcasa.org
wcasa@wcasa.org

WYOMING
Wyoming Coalition Against Domestic Violence and Sexual Assault
409 South 4th Street
P.O. Box 236
Laramie, Wyoming 82073
Phone: 307-755-5481
Fax: 307-755-5482
Toll-Free: 1-800-990-3877
http://www.users.qwest.net/~wyomingcoalition/index.htm
wyomingcoalition@qwest.net

U.S. VIRGIN ISLANDS
U.S. Virgin Islands Women's Coalition
7 East Street
P.O. Box 2734
Christiansted, St. Croix
U.S. Virgin Islands 00822
Phone: 340-773-9272
Fax: 340-773-0962
http://www.wcstx.com
wcscstx@attglobal.net

PUERTO RICO
Coordinadora Paz para la Mujer, Inc.
Proyecto Coalicion Contra la Violencia Domestica
P.O. Box 1007 RMS 108
San Juan, Puerto Rico 00919
Phone: 787-281-7579
Fax: 787-767-6843
Pazparalamujer@yunque.net

Comision Para Los Asuntos De Le Mujer
Box 11382
Fernandez Juancus Station Santurce, Puerto Rico 00910
Phone: 787-722-2907

There are specific organizations for people of color. Below are a few but many more can be found on the National Domestic Violence Hotline web site located at http://www.ndvh.org.

AFRICAN AMERICAN
The Institute on Domestic Violence in the African American Community
http://www.dvinstitute.org

ASIAN AMERICAN
South Asian Domestic Violence Organizations by State are listed on:
http://www.research.att.com/-krishnas/manavi/links.htm'0;o

LATINO
Women's Justice Center/Centro de Justicia Para Mujeres
http://www.justicewomen.com

MUSLIM
Muslim Women's Homepage
http://www.jannah.org/sisters/

NATIVE AMERICAN
The National Tribal Justice Resource Center
http://www.tribalresourcecenter.org

ALSO AVAILABLE FROM
STREBOR BOOKS INTERNATIONAL
All titles are in stores now, unless otherwise noted.

Baptiste, Michael
Cracked Dreams 1-59309-035-8

Bernard, D.V.
The Last Dream Before Dawn
0-9711953-2-3
God in the Image of Woman
1-59309-019-6

Brown, Laurinda D.
Fire & Brimstone 1-59309-015-3
UnderCover 1-59309-030-7

Cheekes, Shonda
Another Man's Wife 1-59309-008-0
Blackgentlemen.com 0-9711953-8-2
In the Midst of it All (May 2005)
1-59309-038-2

Cooper, William Fredrick
Six Days in January 1-59309-017-X
Sistergirls.com 1-59309-004-8

Crockett, Mark
Turkeystuffer 0-9711953-3-1

Daniels, J and Bacon, Shonell
*Luvalwayz: The Opposite Sex and
Relationships* 0-9711953-1-5
Draw Me With Your Love
1-59309-000-5

Darden, J. Marie
Enemy Fields 1-59309-023-4

De Leon, Michelle
Missed Conceptions 1-59309-010-2
Love to the Third 1-59309-016-1
Once Upon a Family Tree
1-59309-028-5

Faye, Cheryl
Be Careful What You Wish For
1-59309-034-X

Halima, Shelley
Azucar Moreno 1-59309-032-3

Handfield, Laurel
My Diet Starts Tomorrow
1-59309-005-6
Mirror Mirror 1-59309-014-5

Hayes, Lee
Passion Marks 1-59309-006-4

Hobbs, Allison
Pandora's Box 1-59309-011-0
Insatiable 1-59309-031-5

Johnson, Keith Lee
Sugar & Spice 1-59309-013-7
Pretenses 1-59309-018-8
Fate's Redemption (May 2005)
1-59309-018-8

Johnson, Rique
Love & Justice 1-59309-002-1
Whispers from a Troubled Heart
1-59309-020-X
Every Woman's Man 1-59309-036-6
Sistergirls.com 1-59309-004-8

Lee, Darrien
All That and a Bag of Chips
0-9711953-0-7
Been There, Done That
1-59309-001-3
What Goes Around Comes Around
1-59309-024-2

Luckett, Jonathan
Jasminium 1-59309-007-2
How Ya Livin' 1-59309-025-0

McKinney, Tina Brooks
All That Drama 1-59309-033-1

Quartay, Nane
Feenin 0-9711953-7-4
The Badness (May 2005)
1-59309-037-4

Rivers, V. Anthony
Daughter by Spirit 0-9674601-4-X
Everybody Got Issues 1-59309-003-X
Sistergirls.com 1-59309-004-8

Roberts, J. Deotis
*Roots of a Black Future: Family
and Church* 0-9674601-6-6
Christian Beliefs 0-9674601-5-8

Stephens, Sylvester
Our Time Has Come 1-59309-026-9

Turley II, Harold L.
Love's Game 1-59309-029-3

Valentine, Michelle
Nyagra's Falls 0-9711953-4-X

White, A.J.
Ballad of a Ghetto Poet
1-59309-009-9

White, Franklin
Money for Good 1-59309-012-9
Potentially Yours 1-59309-027-7